SHERLOCK HOLMES
MYSTERY MAGAZINE

VOLUME 2, NUMBER I   SPRING 2011

FEATURES

I0685933

FICTION

CLASSIC REPRINT

POETRY

CARTOON

"A HOUSE WAS DROPPED ON THIS WOMAN, KILLING HER INSTANTLY. BASED UPON THE EVIDENCE, IT'S CLEAR THAT THE MURDERER IS FROM A SMALL TOWN IN KANSAS, OWNS A TINY BLACK DOG, CARRIES A PICNIC BASKET, AND WEARS VERY SHINY SHOES."

Our cover this issue is by Charles Bernard.

Publisher: John Betancourt
Editor: Marvin Kaye
Managing Editor: Karl Wurf

Sherlock Holmes Mystery Magazine **is published by Wildside Press, LLC. Single copies: $10.00 + postage. Subscriptions: $39.95 for the next 4 issues in the U.S.A., from:**
Wildside Press LLC, Subscription Dept.
9710 Traville Gateway Dr., #234; Rockville MD 20850

Ebook version available from Amazon.com & and other etailers.

FROM WATSON'S SCRAPBOOK

Welcome to the fifth issue of *Sherlock Holmes Mystery Magazine*. When the notion of this magazine was first proposed to Mr Holmes, he agreed to permit four issues to be published, after which he would decide whether he still wished to permit the use of his name in the title of the periodical. I am both pleased and relieved (for I *do* receive royalties for this endeavour) to report that Holmes has graciously granted his ongoing permission to allow SHMM to continue.

In celebration thereof, the publisher has devoted this fifth number entirely to Mr Holmes and myself, leading off with my own account of *The Adventure of the Noble Bachelor*. The choice of this story is in keeping with the policy of my colleague and coeditor Mr Kaye, who elects to follow the approximate dating of our cases as proposed by the late scholar William S Baring-Gould. Now some aficionados regard this chronology as flawed, but so far as I am concerned, it is an acceptable guideline because, in truth, even I cannot always be sure when certain adventures took place. It all happened, after all, quite some time ago.

Why, then, I have been asked, do I not simply consult my own notes? Well, over the years, I have lost track of some of them, and even those still in my possession do not always help, and this for two reasons. Firstly, I was not always scrupulously organized in my record-keeping, and secondly, though I admit this a bit sheepishly, sometimes I cannot decipher my own scrawlings. The cliché you have undoubtedly heard concerning physician's handwriting is certainly applicable to this Holmesian amanuensis.

Now before I turn over this literary podium, so to speak, to Mr Kaye, I have two comments to make concerning the stories and articles in this issue.

The tales all are based on actual incidents from Holmes's and my life. Whenever possible, I made my original notes available to the contributors and, if asked, supplied whatever additional details I was able to recollect. In one instance, however, the business involving the giant rodent, my notes were consulted without my knowledge. (The details may be found in Mr Kaye's collection, *The Resurrected Holmes,* St Martin's Press, 1996). While the events reported in this story are essentially correct, the style of its author differs considerably from my own literary voice. But at least, I judge that by now the world is finally prepared to hear about it.

Two articles in this issue discuss a pair of my writings, *The Adventure of the Illustrious Client* and *The Resident Patient.* I have no cavil with their contents, but my authorial ego wishes to alert you that these pieces reveal plot particulars that might perhaps spoil one's enjoyment of my compositions. I hope, therefore, that if the reader has not yet perused these tales, he or she will avail her- or himself of them before the curtain is twitched aside and all their secrets are revealed.

— John H Watson, MD

IN MEMORIAM

Sad news — Len Moffatt, a prolific science fiction and fantasy writer who has contributed poems and an upcoming article to *Sherlock Holmes Mystery Magazine*, died recently. His wife June writes, "Len went into the hospital on the 19th with severe abdominal pain and was operated upon on his 87th birthday. We hoped that he was recovering, but all came to a halt in the wee hours of November 30th."

In the nonfiction portion of this issue, I am pleased to offer a fascinating treatise about results of the friendship between Arthur Conan Doyle and Bram Stoker — *Sherlock Holmes Meets Dracula.*

Its author, Robert Eighteen-Bisang, is head of Transylvania Press and in my opinion, the world's leading scholar and authority on Bram Stoker and *Dracula.* His engrossing thesis reveals hitherto-unguessed correspondences between *The Adventure of the Illustrious Client* and Stoker's great vampire novel.

Bob Byrne provides interesting biographical details about Watson's agent Conan Doyle as he impacted the tale of *The Resident Patient,* and both M. J. Elliott and Lenny Picker review the new BBC TV series that elects to update Sherlock Holmes. My friend and *SHMM* contributor Carole Buggé has also seen these shows and agrees in every particular with Mr Elliott, so I am looking forward to seeing them myself.

The seven Sherlock Holmes stories in this issue cover a deal of ground, both figuratively and literally, for in addition to Holmes and Watson's traditional London settings and its environs, the Great Detective and his faithful companion and scribe do a deal of traveling: to the south and into Cornwall, to the north into Scotland, specifically Edinburgh and St Andrews, and "across the pond" to Manhattan and the legendary McSorley's Old Ale House. This venerable establishment, which dates back to 1854, is still in business. *SHMM* contributors Carole Buggé, Stan Trybulski and I have hoisted many a light and dark beer there, as well as enjoying their excellent soups and sandwiches with the meanest onions and hottest mustard you're ever likely to encounter. On top of its libational and culinary pleasures, McSorley's is allegedly haunted by no less than Harry Houdini. A pair of handcuffs he escaped from hang in a prominent spot over the bar.

A final note about this issue — *221 C Baker Street,* a delightful short story in the form of a letter to Mrs Hudson, was submitted to SHMM by a new (to us) author, Alan McCright. With his gracious permission, it appears as part of our ongoing feature, *Ask Mrs Hudson.*

Canonically yours,
Marvin Kaye

ASK MRS HUDSON

by (Mrs) Martha Hudson

Hôtel des Deux Mondes
22 Avenue de l'Opera
Paris

27th April 1894

My Dear Mrs Hudson,

It is with deepest regret I must inform you that I can no longer stand as your tenant in the lodgings at 221 C Baker Street and shall not be returning to them when I have concluded my holiday.

Though the modest rent and your good Scotch cooking, Dear Lady, satisfy both pocketbook and palate, there exist, I fear, extenuating circumstances, the nature of which I no longer possess the stamina of character to endure. I am confident you realize I speak of none other than my fellow lodger, Mssr Sherlock Holmes.

I must confess, when first I saw your advert for rooms to let, I recognized the address from Doctor Watson's memoirs in *Strand* magazine. I thrilled at the notion of sharing lodgings with the world-renowned Mssr Holmes, offering an additional half-sovereign to the Hansom driver would he but get me there in all haste; that I might arrive before you had let the rooms to someone else. I sobered of this upon meeting you Mrs Hudson, and was humbled and gratified that no less a discerning and gracious lady as yourself deigned to accept such as me into her personal residence. It is this last thought — which I pray shows I hold you in the highest regard — that prompts me to state herein the reasons which prevent me from enjoying any further stay in your lodgings.

Mssr Holmes, inarguably graced with one of the most astute minds of Her Majesty's era, is nevertheless possessed of certain eccentricities, quirks — dare I say — peculiarities, as well as an often bizarre panoply of visitors, which serve to make occupying the same dwelling as he less than amenable.

Mssr Holmes:

Frequently does not sleep for days on end. He paces audibly about, often playing somber strains on his violin into the wee hours.

Constantly indulges in experimentation with various chemistries, the acrid smells thereof invariably penetrating into my rooms.

Considers the practice of marksmanship an indoor activity. I recall, on one occasion of particular note, an inordinate number of pistol shots which I took to be nothing less than a fierce assault on the person of Mssr Holmes by some of his many enemies. When I dared stir from my apartments the next morning, those shots revealed in their result the initials of our sovereign, Victoria Regina, dotting the corridor walls of Mssr Holmes's apartments and the adjacent, common stairway — obviously the work of Mssr Holmes himself.

I come now to the issue of the myriad visitors Mssr Holmes claims not to encourage. While it is far from secret that some of the most revered nobility of Britain and the Continent have passed despairingly and hopefully across his threshold, there are the others:

A seemingly endless queue of police constables and detectives.

Street Arabs.

Transients.

Beggars.

Drunkards.

Rogues.

Thieves.

Reprehensible brutes.

Men with violently amputated appendages, bandages dripping with blood.

Men with harpoons.

And then there is the noise: the sudden *Aha!* or *Halloa!* shouted in the middle of the night. The sound of bodies dropping to the floor. The violent confrontations and scuffles, taking place invariably at breakfast or dinner and not at all conducive to the enjoyment of one's repast.

In addition, whenever I passed Mssr Holmes on the stairs, in the foyer or surrounding environs, he would glance at me and what guests I may have, quickly appraising us, it seemed, from head to toe. I would then see in his face, an unstated comment — perhaps my imagination, I think not. A subtle smirk, a frown, a grin — of disapproval, insight or amusement, I know not which. I came to feel — and you may find this preposterous — that he knew my every thought, my every move and could perceive my every desire as well as those of my companions. I must tell you, Mrs Hudson, these unnerving encounters are a constant occurrence where Mssr Holmes is concerned.

When the nation heard of Sherlock Holmes's untimely and dastardly end at Reichenbach Falls, I grieved with the rest and chastised myself for my petty differences with the world's greatest detective. I assure you, Madam, my consoling of you and your servants at that time was an act of utmost reverence and grief, as well as humility and self-reproach for the less-than-noble feelings I had acquired for the poor, departed man.

The time that followed was, perhaps, the happiest I can recall; I felt those were, indeed, the Halcyon days which would remain always and fondly in my memory. No longer did I tread lightly upon the staircase, fearing the gaze and unspoken criticisms of Sherlock Holmes. No longer did I lay awake night after night as a consequence of the sounds and odours penetrating my rooms from below. No longer did I fear the sight of one whom I felt could peer into the innermost reaches of my very soul.

Then.

Even before I knew that Mssr Holmes had "returned from the dead," the now notorious Colonel Moran fired a shot at a silhouette in the window one floor below mine. Though the bullet pierced a wax effigy — not, as the fiend intended, the head of Sherlock Holmes — one can imagine, but for the Grace Of God, *my* shadow — by mistake — might have been the target. I well appreciate why Mssr Holmes retains a physician as a constant companion and amanuensis.

I implore you to understand, my Dear, Dear, Mrs Hudson that I can no longer thrive under these maddening circumstances, though my respect and affection for you is unwavering.

Please find enclosed with this missive my cheque for 20 guineas above that which I owe you and representing more than a month's rent extra. I am sure the superfluous shillings will find their way to your servants whom I shall miss as I shall miss you. A man will arrive to return my things to my rooms in Chelsea.

I am, Dear Lady, determined now to seek a lifestyle less nerve-wracking, far more serene and, indeed, free of folly.

I remain, Madam,

Ever Your Obedient Servant,

Oscar Wilde

* * * *

Dear Mr Wilde,

I am in receipt of your letter of the 27th of April. First of all, let me thank you for your more than generous contribution to my establishment; I assure you I will put it to good use. I will share some of it with my small but loyal staff, as you suggest: my new scullery maid Mary could do with a new dress for her sister's confirmation, and young Nicholas has had his eye on a red wool vest. I will surprise them both with rather more lavish than usual Christmas presents this year! Your gesture was unnecessary but gracious, as your conduct was unfailingly kind and gracious during your tenancy at 221 Baker Street. Young Nick was always rather in awe of you, as I'm sure you know. He used to say he wanted to grow up to be "just like Mr Wilde." It was so kind of you to have him to your rooms for tea from time to time — it was the highlight of his week.

I must say, my dear Mr Wilde, I will miss you. I have long considered myself to be the luckiest landlady in London, fortunate to have as tenants not only the greatest living detective but also one of the greatest writers and wits of our time. I hope I do not make you blush when I say that I have felt a pride no less than your own mother must feel when your successes in the literary world heaped upon one another like the delicious layers of a Christmas trifle.

Not that your writing is trifling — far from it, dear Mr Wilde. I have enjoyed both your comedies and your more serious works of fiction. I nearly split my sides laughing at *Lady Windermere's Fan* when it premiered at St James Theatre (thanks once again to you for procuring me a ticket.) And I consider *The Picture of Dorian Gray* to be a classic of our time — truly a story for the ages. I predict that it will seize hold of the imaginations of future generations as it has ours. The theme and scope of the writing is surely as universal as it is brilliant.

I understand that you are working on a new comedy, one involving orphans in handbags left in railway stations, mistaken identity and general merriment. I must say, it does sound jolly, and I only wish that you were writing it under my roof as before. If it will not distress you, please think of me on opening night, as nothing would make me happier than being among the audience applauding your latest work of genius.

As to your reasons for leaving, alas, I must confess I do understand them. I would like to come to the defense of Mr Holmes, and explain that his genius and his eccentricities are different weave patterns in the same cloth; you could not have one without the other. But surely a man of your intellectual capacity understands all of this. I can tell from your letter that your decision was neither hasty nor born of anger, and that it was a long time in coming. I assure you, you are not the first tenant to quite Baker Street after falling afoul of Mr Holmes's peculiarities — though you are most certainly the most renowned.

I am very glad you did not give me forewarning, and present me with the predicament of having to choose between you. Indeed, I would have been hard pressed to find a solution, in that case. I must say that you will have an easier time finding new lodgings than would Mr Holmes. Even with Dr Watson to look after him and perhaps temper his extreme ways, it would be extremely difficult for him to find another landlord who would put up with his odd (and occasionally dangerous) habits — not to mention the parade of unsavoury visitors, as you point out.

So I suppose I feel a bit protective of him, seeing as how I may well be the only landlady in London who could stand to have Mr Holmes as a tenant. But the city needs him, Mr Wilde — the world needs him. Sometimes good things come in unexpected packages. Heroes often appear in odd guises, prickly and unpleasant and difficult — Mr Holmes is certainly odd and difficult; no one knows this better than I do. But he is a hero, Mr Wilde, and though it pains me to lose you, I am still proud to call myself his landlady — and, I hope, his friend.

I wish you the very best wishes in all your endeavours, and good luck with your new play. Is it true you are thinking of calling it *The Importance of Being Earnest*? Perhaps with a little more thought, you can come up with a better title. That one strikes me as unlikely; no doubt it will confuse and confound audiences. A comedy should have a straightforward, sprightly title: perhaps something like *Orphans in Handbags.* I hope you do not think it presumptuous of me to add my thoughts to the matter.

I remain, as always, your most devoted fan,

Mrs Hudson

Well, I could not resist sharing the above venerable missives with my faithful readers, but now let us turn to more immediate concerns. Dear readers, here is one of my favourite recipes for rack of lamb. I remember one rainy night in October Mr Holmes came back late from chasing around London, and I had it ready for him. I was shocked to have him grasp me by the shoulders and plant a kiss on my forehead! An unusual display of emotion for him, to be sure, but often the surest way to a man's stomach … well, dear reader, you know the rest.

Ingredients

1/2 cup fresh bread crumbs
2 tablespoons minced garlic
2 tablespoons chopped fresh rosemary
1 teaspoon salt
1/4 teaspoon black pepper
2 tablespoons olive oil

1 (7 bone) rack of lamb, trimmed and Frenched
1 teaspoon salt
1 teaspoon black pepper
2 tablespoons olive oil
1 tablespoon Dijon style mustard

DIRECTIONS

1. Preheat oven to 230 degrees C (if you live in America, that would be 450 degrees F). Move oven rack to the center position.

2. In a large bowl, combine bread crumbs, garlic, rosemary, 1 teaspoon salt and 1/4 teaspoon pepper. Toss in 2 tablespoons olive oil to moisten mixture. Set aside.

3. Season the rack all over with salt and pepper. Heat 2 tablespoons olive oil in a large heavy oven proof skillet over

high heat. Sear rack of lamb for 1 to 2 minutes on all sides. Set aside for a few minutes. Brush rack of lamb with the mustard. Roll in the bread crumb mixture until evenly coated. Cover the ends of the bones with brown wrapping paper to prevent charring. (Be sure you don't light the paper on fire!)

4. Arrange the rack bone side down in the skillet. Roast the lamb in preheated oven for 12 to 18 minutes, depending on the degree of doneness you want. With a meat thermometer, take a reading in the center of the meat after 10 to 12 minutes and remove the meat, or let it cook longer, to your taste. Let it rest for 5 to 7 minutes, loosely covered, before carving between the ribs.

Editor's note: The letter from Mr Wilde was submitted to SHMM as "221 C Baker Street" and was written by Alan McCright. — MK

SCREEN OF THE CRIME

2.0 BAKER STREET, OR HOW SHERLOCK HOLMES CAME TO BE ALIVE & WELL, AND LIVING IN 21ST CENTURY LONDON

by Lenny Picker

Just a few minutes into *A Study in Pink*, the first episode of the new BBC TV series, *Sherlock*, a throwaway reference that will elude non-Holmesians makes clear that the creative forces behind the latest — and by far —most successful chronological reboot of the world's most famous detective, take their Canon very seriously. After introducing a modern wounded and recuperating ex-military doctor named John Watson, haunted by memories of his service in the current Afghan War and at loose ends upon his return to London, the writer Steven Moffat, draws viewers further into a remarkable and convincing alternate universe, with staccato depictions of a terrifying series of suicides carried out by victims with no apparent reason to take their own lives.

Following the death of an affluent man, seen arriving at the airport, and then swallowing a capsule before collapsing on an empty floor of an office building, we are shown two teenagers caught in a heavy downpour. One of them tells his mate that he needs to go back to fetch his umbrella … before he, too, is shown downing a capsule, and turning up dead.

At the subsequent Scotland Yard press conference led by Detective Inspector Lestrade, that second victim is identified as James Phillimore, a name shared with the subject of one of Sherlock Holmes's most famous unresolved cases, alluded to in the tantalizing opening section of *The Problem of Thor Bridge*. There, Watson (that is, the 19th-century injured Afghan War veteran) refers to the puzzle "of Mr James Phillimore, who, stepping back into his own house to get his umbrella, was never more seen in this world." Moffat's present-day Phillimore was also "never more seen in this world" after his fateful decision to retrieve his umbrella — save, perhaps, by the person who somehow managed to convince him to end his life.

Not one viewer in a hundred will find this choice of name noteworthy, but it's clearly a shout-out to those watchers who read Doyle's original tales devotedly. Moffat's and cocreator Mark Gatiss's love for their source material is evident in every scene of the three episodes that comprised the first of what deserves to be many seasons. By seriously and intelligently dissecting what made Doyle's stories — and their leads — so enduring, and almost-universally appealing, Moffat and Gatiss have already staked a claim at being among the most faithful and creative interpreters of the iconic figures of Holmes and Watson.

It's not that they are the first, not by a long chalk, to place the detective and the doctor in a time period later than that of the original sixty stories. (As Holmes himself quoted from Ecclesiastes in *A Study in Scarlet*, "there is nothing new under the sun.") Almost from the beginning of the depiction of those characters on film, writers and producers transported them from Victorian England to times contemporaneous with the movie's filming. In 1932's *Sherlock Holmes*, based on the Gillette play, screenwriter Bertram Millhauser had Clive Brook's sleuth tooling about in London of the 1930s. Even the well-respected Arthur Wontner series of the same vintage set its adaptations of *The Valley of Fear* and *The Final Problem*, among others, decades after they occurred in the originals. Most famously, when Universal took over the film series that Basil Rathbone and Nigel Bruce had begun at 20th Century Fox with two period pieces, they unapologetically set their plots in the 1940s. In the first, 1942's *Sherlock Holmes and the Voice of Terror* followed the opening credits with this explanation for the shift: "The character of Sherlock Holmes, created by Sir Arthur Conan Doyle, is ageless, invincible, and unchanging. In solving significant problems of the present day, he remains, as ever, the supreme master of deductive reasoning."

The shift, by the way, was done with the explicit approval of Rathbone himself. But while the Universal films occupy a warm place in the hearts of many, with few exceptions (such as *The Scarlet Claw*), they are not viewed as being in the spirit of the originals. They actually feature relatively little by way of deductive reasoning, and their continuation of the Fox films's reduction of Watson to a buffoon still raises hackles.

Starting in the 1970s, versions of Holmes on screen began appearing in modern-day America. In *They Might Be Giants*, George C. Scott portrayed a character who deluded himself into believing that he was Holmes himself. A 1976 TV movie, *The Return of the World's Greatest Detective*, featured Larry Hagman, of all people, as a policeman who comes to think that he's really Holmes after being struck on the head. In 1987, Michael Pennington (who was a brilliant Moriarty in the BBC radio Canon starring Clive Merrison and Michael Williams) was a Holmes revived from a cryogenic chamber into the modern world in the TV movie, *The Return of Sherlock Holmes*. A very similar plotline was at the heart of the 1993 TV film *Sherlock Holmes Returns* with another one-time Napoleon of Crime, Anthony Higgins, as the reanimated Great Detective. These efforts, along with the early graphic novel *Son of Holmes: The Woman In Red* (1977), the 1999-2001 cartoon series, *Sherlock Holmes in the 22nd Century* (in which Watson has become a robot!), and Barry Grant's modern-day pastiches, *The Strange Return of Sherlock Holmes* and *Sherlock Holmes and the Shakespeare Letter*, have not left much of an impression either on Holmesians or the public at large.

Given these failures, and the seemingly-obvious notion that to faithfully present Holmes, one must start by keeping him in his own time, skepticism that BBC's *Sherlock*, planting the character in 2010 England, would have any redeeming value was certainly rational. But with Gatiss and Moffat's passion for the characters, stemming from a life-long fascination with them (and an affection for the dozen much-derided Universal films manifested in the person of one villain modeled after a creepy killer from *The Pearl of Death*), and intelligent tweaking of characteristics of their leads and plot elements from Doyle's sixty tales, they have managed to produce not only television films that are remarkably true to the spirit of the original (in countless ways that the 2009 Guy Ritchie film was not), but ones with broad appeal beyond would-be Baker Street Irregulars everywhere.

In a blog entry on the BBC website, Gatiss has written about the origin of *Sherlock*, which, fittingly, came about during rail journeys he and Moffat shared during their work on *Dr. Who*, when they both discussed their feelings about Doyle's creations.

"It didn't take long, though, for us both to shyly admit that our favourite versions of the oft-told tales were the Basil Rathbone/ Nigel Bruce films of the 1930s and 1940s. Particularly the ones where they brought them up to date. This may sound like heresy but really it isn't. Although Steven and I are second to none in loving the flaring gas-lit atmosphere of a lovely old London, it felt as though Sherlock Holmes had become all about the trappings and not the characters.

Also, the original stories are models of their kind. Incredibly modern, dialogue-driven, fast paced and short! What better way to get back to the roots of these fantastic creations than to make Holmes and Watson living, breathing, modern men just as they had been originally?"

The creators of *Sherlock*'s central conceit is that Doyle never invented the fictional characters of Holmes and Watson, and their rich supporting cast. Instead, when, in *A Study in Pink*, their Watson meets his old medical colleague Stamford by chance, and is introduced to an eccentric searching for a flat-mate, the name Sherlock Holmes is new to him. Their meeting parallels the opening of *A Study In Scarlet* closely; Holmes effortlessly displays his brilliance by rattling off a series of accurate deductions about Watson. Instead of the immortal first words Doyle penned — "How are you? You have been in Afghanistan, I perceive," their Holmes asks their Watson, "Afghanistan or Iraq?," before disclosing, in a segment that combines the verbal explanations for the deductions with tight camera shots of the telling clues, how he knew that the good doctor had recently been in combat. Moffat and Gatiss also borrow freely from *The Sign of the Four* in this episode, but instead of having Holmes announcing remarkably-accurate details about Watson's brother from his examination of a pocket-watch, they have him work his intellectual wizardry on the cell-phone Watson carries. Doyle's Holmes magazine essay. "The Book of Life," which Watson famously dismisses as "ineffable twaddle," is replaced by Sherlock's website, *The Science of Deduction.*

In keeping with the multi-media approach to booming TV series these days, you can actually visit that website, complete with a forum, hidden messages for visitors to decode, and a list of archived case files that play upon Doyle's habit of having Watson refer to cases he has written up but not published, for one reason or another. Those archived cases include ones derived from the original Watson's untold tales, such as that of the Abernetty Family, and titles ("The Killer Cats of Greenwich," "The Man With Four Legs,") that pay homage to the long-running radio series, *The New Adventures of Sherlock Holmes*, that began with Rathbone and Bruce reprising their roles. All three episodes are replete with clever twists on the originals that often undercut the expectations of viewers who remember what certain clues meant when Doyle used them. In today's smoke-free environment, Sherlock dubs a case a three-nicotine patch problem, rather than a three-pipe one. Pointing out more would vitiate the pleasure for those who have not yet seen the series; suffice to say that none of the updates or inversions strike a false chord.

But a well-constructed framework is not in itself enough to explain the success and popularity of the series. The cleverness of the writing extends to character and plot as well. *A Study in Pink*, and the third episode, *The Great Game*, both do a laudable job of playing fair with the viewer, and repeat viewings will reveal how crucial evidence was placed before the viewer early on. Bits and pieces of a number of canonical stories are artfully employed. While *A Study in Pink* primarily derives from *A Study in Scarlet*, the other two episodes, especially *The Great Game*, borrow from a number of original cases, including *The Dancing Men*, and *The Bruce-Partington Plans* (with a missile substituted for the naval submarine of the original). *The Great Game* has Holmes racing deadlines set by a homicidal madman to solve seemingly-unrelated crimes in order to save a hostage's life, and *The Blind Banker*, the least-strong episode of the three, has the detective trying to find out why strange symbols have been painted on the interior wall of a bank. Again, saying more about the plots for those who have not had the pleasure of experiencing them would do a disservice to the careful work of the writers Moffat, Gatiss and Stephen Thompson, but any reader interested in discussing them is welcome to email me at the address at the end of my bio line below.

For many, the convolutions of the puzzles will take a back seat to the dynamic portrayals of Holmes and Watson by Benedict Cumberbatch and Martin Freeman. Both are instantly convincing in their parts. Cumberbatch combines arrogance, brilliance, and quirkiness, without making the concept of a modern-day genius serving as a consulting detective anything less than fully plausible. As in the originals, the humanity of the shows is brought out by Watson, here personified by Freeman as a capable professional in his own right, who needs only a focus for his morality, loyalty and intellect that he finds as Holmes's assistant. Their rapport develops quickly, and the development of their bond of friendship is much more convincing than in other portrayals, such as those that diminish Watson's own strengths to the point of caricature.

When the 2009 Robert Downey Jr./Jude Law movie brought Holmes back to the big screen for the first time in almost thirty years, many hoped that the robust box office sales would translate into a renewed appreciation for the original stories and characters. Surprisingly, that hope is more likely to be realized by *Sherlock*, which just a month or so after appearing on PBS's Masterpiece Theatre has become a surprising big seller on DVD. My efforts, in the fall of 2010 to buy a copy in New York City, at one of a dozen branches of megagiant Barnes & Noble over the course of several weeks were unsuccessful; every store in the metropolitan area was sold out, and the demand for the not-inexpensive 2-disk set was so great that Barnes & Noble's warehouses were also out of stock, meaning that shoppers would need to wait about a month to get a copy. In an experience of buying Sherlockian DVDs that extends over two decades and two continents, I have never encountered such a phenomenon. I look forward to the countless scholarly analyses of the programs that I expect will be forthcoming on both sides of the Atlantic, and to the promise of the second season, which may include an episode that is somehow inspired by

The Hound of the Baskervilles. Devotees of the detective and the doctor owe Moffat and Gatiss a debt of gratitude for reinvigorating them, and keeping their memories green.

Lenny Picker, a freelance writer living in 21ˢᵗ-century New York, has not (yet) been called a high-functioning sociopath. He can be reached at chthompson@jtsa.edu.

THE BBC'S "SHERLOCK" — A REVIEW

by M J Elliott

> "Sherlock Holmes, the immortal character of fiction created by
> Sir Arthur Conan Doyle, is ageless, invincible and unchanging.
> In solving significant problems of the day he remains — as
> ever — the supreme master of deductive reasoning."

These words preceded the early entries in the Universal series
starring Basil Rathbone and Nigel Bruce, by way of explaining
the presence of Holmes and Watson in the then-modern world of
1942. In a way, it's peculiar that the makers felt the need to go to
such trouble, since none of the many earlier films took place in
Victorian England. It's a testament to the effect Rathbone's first
two movies — *The Hound of the Baskervilles* and *The Adventures
of Sherlock Holmes* — must have had on the film-going population
at the time. Since then, the detective's cinematic adventures have
remained firmly in period, with the exception of a couple of TV
movies, both of which see him awakened from cryogenic suspen-
sion in the America of the late '80s/early '90s.

It was not until that other iconic character Doctor Who enjoyed
his recent revival that the notion of updating the stories became a
real possibility. Who scriptwriters Stephen Moffat and Mark Gatiss shared a love of those Universal films, and would often discuss
their mutual enthusiasm. "We thought they were actually rather
more fun," says Moffat, "and in certain ways truer to the originals
than many grander and more important film versions. And what
we kept saying to each other was, 'Someday, someone is going
to do Sherlock Holmes in the modern day, and we'll feel so cross
because we should have done it.'" In fact, a US TV pilot, *Elementary* by Josh Friedman, did just that, but the production never saw
the light of day. Moffat and Gatiss, however, were more fortunate.
A sixty-minute pilot proved so satisfying that the BBC commis-
sioned three film-length episodes, which meant that the pilot had

to be scrapped and remounted (thankfully, the abandoned show can be seen as an extra on the DVD).

Young actor Benedict Cumberbatch was cast as the 21st Century Sherlock Holmes, opposite the rather better known Martin Freeman (Tim in the original series *The Office* and Arthur Dent in the film version of *The Hitch-Hiker's Guide to the Galaxy*) as John Watson. The two share an undeniable chemistry which, along with the superb scripts and high production values, ensured Sherlock's massive success, this despite the fact that the series arrived on British screens with little or no fanfare and with only two of the three episodes really hitting the mark.

The first story, *A Study in Pink*, scripted by Moffat, is of course based quite closely upon Conan Doyle's original novel, *A Study in Scarlet*. Watson arrives back in England after being wounded in Afghanistan (how far we've come in 120 years!), and after a chance meeting with old pal Stamford at the Criterion coffee bar, he's introduced to Sherlock Holmes in the laboratory at St Bartholemew's Hospital. They move into 221b Baker Street and are almost instantly drawn into a poisoning case by Inspector Lestrade (played by the George Clooney-esque Rupert Graves).

Episode Two, *The Blind Banker*, is less successful, regrettably. Steve Thompson's script, which has Holmes and Watson investigating a series of assassinations in London's financial district, has little to do with Conan Doyle, save that a plot element concerning coded graffiti suggests *The Dancing Men*. An original story is no bad thing, of course, but the plot could serve another series — say, Midsomer Murders or Inspector Lewis — just as well. *The Blind Banker* may be a perfectly adequate 90 minutes of television, but it isn't quite Sherlock Holmes.

The final episode, Mark Gatiss' *The Great Game*, not only incorporates elements of *The Five Orange Pips*, *The Naval Treaty*, and *The Bruce-Partington Plans*, it also owes a good deal to the 1939 film *The Adventures of Sherlock Holmes*. As in Rathbone's second movie, Moriarty — whose existence is mentioned in *A Study in Pink* — sets a series of puzzles for Holmes to solve in order to prevent the detective from focusing on his true intent, a crime of international significance. This isn't the first Rathbone reference in the series — episode one features an exchange of dialogue lifted directly from Universal's *Dressed to Kill*. *The Great*

Game ends with a confrontation between the two enemies, and a cliffhanger which, thanks to Sherlock's huge ratings, will be resolved in the second series, once Steven Moffat has concluded his work on Doctor Who and Freeman has dealt with any scheduling conflicts regarding his starring role as Bilbo Baggins in Peter Jackson's forthcoming movie *The Hobbit*.

The modernisation of certain elements in Sherlock is well thought out — Watson keeps a blog rather than writes memoirs; the famous sequence where Holmes deduces the sad history of his friend's brother by the examination of a pocket watch now revolves around a cell-phone, and the detective has been forced to abandon his famous smoking habit for nicotine patches — Holmes refers to their first case together as "a three-patch problem." For some, myself included, it jars when the main characters address one another as "Sherlock" and "John," but there is no escaping the fact that in our informal age that is precisely what they would do, and any attempt to have them do otherwise would come across as phoney. And while it was never even considered in the original tales, some fun is had at Watson's expense as he must constantly convince people that he and Holmes are not romantically involved. "Don't worry, there's all sorts round here," he's assured by Mrs Hudson (Una Stubbs). "Mrs Turner next door's got married ones."

It has been hinted that the next series of three adventures will concern Irene Adler, *The Hound of the Baskervilles* and the encounter at Reichenbach Falls — all, of course, with a 21st-Century twist. "It allows you to see the original stories the way the original reader would have read them," Moffat explains. "As exciting, cutting-edge, contemporary stories, as opposed to these relics that they've become." If the second series matches or even surpasses the quality of the first, the present-day Sherlock definitely has a future.

✗

SHERLOCK HOLMES MEETS DRACULA[1]

by Robert Eighteen-Bisang

People of all ages in every part of the world know that Sherlock Holmes is a brilliant, eccentric detective while Count Dracula is a vampire from Transylvania. Like Frankenstein's Monster, Dr Jekyll and Mr Hyde or H G Wells's Martians, these characters have become parts of popular culture.

There is less awareness that their creators — Arthur Conan Doyle (1859-1930) and Bram Stoker (1847-1912) — were friends who collaborated on a variety of projects. Both authors contributed a chapter to the episodic novel *The Fate of Fenella*, which was serialized in the magazine *The Gentlewoman* in 1891-1892.[2] In 1892, Doyle adapted his story "A Straggler of '15" as a one-act play, which he submitted to the Lyceum. Stoker, who had managed the theatre since 1878, felt that this patriotic melodrama about an old soldier who had been decorated for heroism but fell on hard times when he returned to England was an ideal vehicle for his employer, Henry Irving. He advised the actor, "You must own it — at any price. It is made for you." After minor changes to the opening act, it opened under the title *A Story of Waterloo*[3] at the Prince's Theatre in Bristol. Many years later, Doyle told his friend how he had decided on his detective's name. He recalled, "Finally in 1887 I wrote *A Study in Scarlet*, the first book which featured Sherlock Holmes. I don't know where I got the name from. I was looking the other day at a piece of paper on which I had scribbled 'Sherrington Holmes' and 'Sherrington Hope' and all sorts of other combinations. Finally at the bottom of the paper I had written 'Sherlock Holmes.'"

Doyle's enthusiastic opinion of his friend's only masterpiece is evident in a letter dated 20 August 1897:

---

1   An early version of this paper was published in *The Sherlock Holmes Journal* 29:3 (2009) 94-98 under the title "Dracula by Arthur Conan Doyle."

2   Doyle wrote chapter 4, "Between Two Fires," while Stoker penned chapter 8, "Lord Castleton Explains."

3   Eventually shortened to *Waterloo*.

My Dear Bram Stoker,

I am sure you will not think it impertinent of me if I write to tell you how much I enjoyed reading Dracula. I think it is the very best story of diablerie which I have read in many years. It is really wonderful how with so much exciting interest over so long a book there is never an anticlimax. It holds you from the very start and grows more engrossing until it is quite painfully vivid. The old professor is most excellent and so are the two girls. I congratulate you with all my heart for having written so fine a book.

With kindest remembrances to Mrs. Bram Stoker & yourself.

Yours very truly,

Conan Doyle[4]

References to the novel can be found throughout Doyle's work. Dracula's estate in Purfleet is called "Carfax." The use of this name in "The Disappearance of Lady Frances Carfax" (1911) may be a tribute to the novel. As Donald A. Redmond points out "That Doyle uses the name ['Carfax'] in a case which hinges upon a coffin containing an un-dead body, as well as the withered corpse of Rose Spender, is an obvious reference back to the tale of the thirsty Count." Many years later, Pierre Nordan's biography of Doyle notes that his fantasy about Atlantis, *The Maracot Deep* (1929), ends when the monster is "…destroyed somewhat in the manner of the vampire in Dracula."

"The Adventure of the Sussex Vampire" (1924) has Holmes find references to "Vampires in Hungary" and "Vampires in Transylvania" in his index. After throwing down the book with a snarl of disappointment he exclaims:

> "Rubbish, Watson, rubbish! What have we to do with walking corpses who can only be held in their grave by stakes driven through their hearts? It's pure lunacy."
>
> "But surely," said I, "the vampire is not necessarily a dead man. A living person might have the habit. I have read, for

---

4   Doyle's letter to Stoker — which is in the custodianship of the Harry Ransom Humanities Research Center at the University of Texas in Austin — is reprinted here through the courtesy of Sir Arthur Conan Doyle's estate.

example, of the old sucking the blood of the young in order to retain their youth."

"You are right, Watson. It mentions the legend in one of these references. But are we to give serious attention to such things? This agency stands flat-footed upon the ground, and there it must remain. The world is big enough for us. No ghosts need apply."

To date, most scholars and fans have used this passage as a crucifix to ward off any hint of vampires in Holmes's adventures. For instance, Matthew Bunson's *Encyclopedia Sherlockiana* (1984) avers that "The Sussex Vampire" … "was his only encounter with vampires in the Canon, an investigation that proved to be very unsupernatural indeed."

Doyle's admiration of Edgar Allan Poe and his friendship with Robert Louis Stevenson are well documented. Hence, it is not surprising that many of his science fiction, fantasy and horror stories contain supernatural elements. In fact, he described the protagonists of "The Winning Shot" (1893), "John Barrington Cowles" (1884), and "The Adventure of the Sussex Vampire" (1824) as vampires, while the stories "The Captain of the Polestar" (1883), "The American's Tale" (1888), and "The Parasite" revolve around vampire-like monsters.[5]

Since *Dracula* went out of copyright in 1962, dozens of writers have speculated about what would happen if, in Loren D. Estleman's words, the "Sleuth" met the "Tooth." In 1978, Estleman's novel, *Sherlock Holmes vs. Dracula*, opens with the discovery of the "battered tin dispatch-box" in which Dr Watson stored the records of a number of unpublished cases. Later that year, the second book in Fred Saberhagen's long-running Dracula series, *The Holmes-Dracula File*, told us about the hitherto unacknowledged role Holmes and Watson played in driving Dracula from England. Many years later, David Stuart Davies inserted the Count into his sequel to Holmes's most famous adventure, *The Hound of the Baskervilles*. There have also been light-hearted attempts to prove that Professor Van Helsing was, in fact, Sherlock Holmes or that Moriarty was Dracula.

5   "John Barrington Cowles" and "The Parasite" have been included in a number of vampire anthologies, while Doyle's *Vampire Stories* includes nine of his tales that contain traces of vampirism.

Despite thousands of studies, stories, comic books and movies about Dracula and Sherlock Holmes, one of the most important parodies in popular literature has never received the recognition it deserves.

Numerous similarities between Bram Stoker's novel *Dracula* (1897) and Arthur Conan Doyle's tale "The Adventure of the Illustrious Client" (1924) leave no doubt that the story is a rationalized version of the novel. Both tales have the same plot: A wealthy European nobleman comes to London[6] where he ruins one unfortunate woman and threatens a second woman with a fate worse than death.[7] Her friends try to wrest her from the villain's clutches. When all seems lost, they consult an expert with exceptional intellectual and moral qualities — be it Professor Abraham Van Helsing or Sherlock Holmes — who leads them into battle. Their quest is guided by a woman who was "seduced" by the fiend and, consequently, has special knowledge about him. (In Doyle's rational parody, Kitty Winter's awareness of the Baron's "lust diary" replaces Mina Harker's telepathic link to Count Dracula.) The heroes are forced to plot a new course of action when they learn that the monster has left — or plans to leave — London by ship. After a series of twists and turns that include a confrontation in which one of the protagonists escapes through a window, evil is defeated. The champions halt Mina's transformation into one of Dracula's "Brides" and convince Violet de Merville to call off her engagement to Baron Gruner. Life returns to normal.

All good detective stories offer readers more than one clue. In this case, it is not surprising that there are scattered hints that Baron Gruner is a vampire[8] and the story is a parody of Dracula.[9] Descriptions such as: "The mouth… was fixed and rather cruel-looking, with peculiarly sharp white teeth" (from *Dracula*) and "There was a gleam of teeth from between those cruel lips" (from

---

6   Dracula is commonly associated with Transylvania, but most of the novel takes place in London.

7   Kitty Winter warns Violet de Merville, "I am one of a hundred that he has tempted and used and ruined and thrown into the refuse heap, as he will you also. Your refuse heap is more likely to be a grave, and maybe that's the best."

8   In 1978, Brad A. Keefauver pointed out that Gruner can be seen as a vampire.

9   Bill Mason found eighteen points of similarity between *Dracula* and "The Adventure of the Illustrious Client."

"The Illustrious Client") are interchangeable. When Holmes refers to Gruner as "a real aristocrat of crime with a superficial suggestion of afternoon tea and all the cruelty of the grave behind it," who is he describing? Doyle also describes his foe as a "beast-man" with "paws" who emits a "howl of rage." His Baron does not have supernatural powers but, like the Count, he is a master hypnotist who "collects women." The fact that "He is said to have the whole sex at his mercy and to have made ample use of the fact" parodies Dracula's speech in chapter 23 when the vampire turns on his pursuers and taunts them: "Your girls that you all love are mine already. And through them you and others shall yet be mine... ."

Dracula is an erotic horror novel. In a similar fashion, as Christopher Redmond points out, "The dark side of sex dominates... 'The Illustrious Client.'" It follows that Violet's awareness of "... three passages in my fiancé's life in which he became entangled with designing women" may be an oblique reference to the well-known episode in chapter 3 of the novel where Jonathan Harker is "seduced" by a trio of ghostly vampire women. This scene — which opens with "I was not alone ... In the moonlight opposite me were three young women, ladies by their dress and manner" — is the only part of the novel that appears in every important adaptation of *Dracula*. The story does not contain any vampires per se, but both Violet and the "she-devil" Kitty are "pale" and "white." Kitty's remark "What I am, Adelbert Gruner made me" forces the question of what she is and what the Baron made her.

Sherlock Holmes assumes many of Abraham Van Helsing's duties. His belief that their forthcoming case "may be a matter of life and death" echoes the Professor's realization that Lucy's mysterious, wasting illness "... is no jest, but life and death, perhaps more." Both men lead the other vampire hunters and plan the campaign against the monster, while both of them refer to their adventure as a "game" in which they must respect their opponent's intelligence and cunning.

The names of principal characters provide another layer of evidence:

- "Adelbert Gruner" contains all but one of the letters in the name "Dracula." Adelbert furnishes the D, R, A and L; Gruner the U.

- In the novel, Dracula uses the pseudonym "Count de Ville." In the story, the family name of the damsel in distress is "de Merville." If we drop one "e," de Merville becomes an anagram of "Mr de Ville." A play on one of the Count's names could be attributed to happenstance, but imitations of both names cannot be chalked up to coincidence.

- The Baron is likened to "A purring cat who thinks he sees prospective mice." Like the Count, his association with lower forms of life such as bats, rats and wolves symbolizes a primitive state of consciousness.

- In a similar vein, Kitty Winter's given name serves the same function while branding her as the monster's progeny. Calling her "Miss W." may be a nod to Miss Lucy Westenra, who was also the "vampire's" first victim in England.

Any overt reference to Transylvania, the Carpathian Mountains, the Borgo Pass or, perhaps, even a castle, could have given the game away too easily. However, Gruner resides in a "large house" which, like Dracula's castle, is approached by "... a long winding drive." In conjunction with other clues, Doyle's curious association of the Splûgen Pass (which runs between Switzerland and Italy) with Prague may be a cipher for the Borgo Pass. His "error" reflects Jonathan Harker's remark that he "... was not able to light on any map or work giving the exact locality of the Castle Dracula."

Another set of clues point to Bram Stoker. Like *Dracula*, "The Adventure of the Illustrious Client" is presented by an Irishman. Sir James Damery inaugurates Holmes's and Watson's adventure by pleading for their help. His "Irish eyes" and "... large, bluff, honest personality" could be a description of Bram Stoker, but Doyle took pains to conceal his bearded friend's identity by transforming him into a "cleanshaven" aristocratic dandy. Like Stoker, who travelled extensively, Damery is "...a man of the world." The mention of the "Strand" is another clue in Doyle's game of hide-and-go-seek, for many of his readers would have known that the Lyceum is located on the northwest corner of the Strand and Wellington Street.

The task of converting a novel into a story forces the adapter to omit, abridge or combine important characters and sub-plots. However, Doyle's diligent study of the original work allowed him to drop countless hints about important people, places and events in *Dracula*. For example, five tongue-in-cheek allusions to the first page of the novel are present in the story: Both tales open on the 3rd of the month in an unspecified year in the past.[10] The first paragraph of Dracula mentions "Vienna" while Gruner is introduced as "… the Austrian murderer." "Turkish rule" is lampooned by a "Turkish bath" then "The Hotel Royale" in Klausenburgh is transformed into the "Café Royal" on Regent Street in London. Eventually, Harker's research in the British Museum is reworked as Watson's trip to the London Library in St. James' Square.

In the first chapter of the novel Harker's landlady warns him not to go to Dracula's castle: "Must you go? Oh! Young Herr, must you go?" Twenty-seven years later, Watson begs Holmes: "Must you interfere?" Like all mythic heroes, Harker and Holmes ignore these warnings.

Later, as Harker nears the castle, mysterious "blue flames" alert the Count to the location of buried treasure. In "The Adventure of the Illustrious Client," the Baron is also a treasure hunter who collects egg-shell pottery from the Ming dynasty. Holmes's attempt to distract him with "a delicate little saucer of the most beautiful deep-blue colour" strikes a discordant note. In both tales, the color blue is associated with treasure yet, as the director of the Victoria and Albert Museum, Sir Eric Maclaglan, informs us "… there is no Ming pottery of a 'deep-blue colour.'"

In the novel, Dracula's voyage to England aboard the Demeter re-awakens the primitive fear that the dead may arise from their graves to overthrow the kingdom of the living. During the voyage, the vampire emerges from his coffin in the cargo hold, feeds on hapless members of the crew, then tosses their bodies overboard. After mentioning that Baron Gruner had met Violet de Merville on a Mediterranean yachting voyage, Doyle adds "…the promoters hardly realized the Baron's true character until it was too late." Given the fate of the Demeter's crew, this comment is tinged with irony.

Kitty's "leprous mark" evokes the scar on Mina's forehead that links her to Dracula and attests to her transformation into a creature of the night. Her cry, "Unclean! Unclean! Even the Almighty

---

10   Raymond McNally and Radu Florescu's "discovery" of Bram Stoker's Notes led to the discovery that the novel is set in 1893.

shuns my polluted flesh!" is the nadir of the novel. Like many of his contemporaries, Doyle may have seen the ultimate horror of the novel as the vampire's threat to turn prim, proper Victorian virgins into un-dead whores. In contrast, Mina's compassion for Dracula in chapter 23[11] is voiced by Violet: "If his [Gruner's] noble nature has ever for an instant fallen, it may be that I have been specially sent to raise it to its true and lofty level."

Dracula's final death is initiated by the sentence "But, on the instant, came the sweep and flash of Jonathan's great knife." In "The Adventure of the Illustrious Client," Gruner's downfall is preceded by "And then! It was done in an instant … " as Kitty throws vitriol at the Baron's face. The dissolution of the Baron's once-handsome features can be seen as an ingenious parody of Dracula's final death when: "… the [vampire's] whole body crumbled into dust and passed from our sight."

In a letter to John Gore, Doyle claimed: "If I were to choose the six best Holmes stories I should certainly include 'The Adventure of the Illustrious Client.'" We don't know why he never identified this story as a parody of *Dracula*. "The Illustrious Client" contains the sentence: "There was a curious secretive streak in the man which led to many dramatic effects, but left even his closest friend guessing as to what his exact plans might be." This quote may be a confession that describes the author rather than his immortal detective. The simplest explanation may be that it is a token of his appreciation for his friend's singular masterpiece, but this is not the only possibility. In 1922, Bram's widow, Florence, launched a lawsuit against F. W. Murnau and Prana Pictures for their unauthorized adaptation of *Dracula*. She succeeded in having every known copy of the film *Nosferatu* destroyed and continued to defend her rights to her major source of income for the rest of her life.

We know that Bram Stoker wrote various drafts of *Dracula* from at least 1890 to 1897.[12] While there is no evidence that he ever discussed his creation with Doyle, common sense tells us that writers like to talk about their work. The fact that they had known

11   "That poor soul who has wrought all this misery is the saddest case of all. Just think what will be his joy when he, too, is destroyed in his worser [sic] part that his better part may have spiritual immortality." — Mina Harker.
12   For details about the construction of *Dracula*, see: Robert Eighteen-Bisang and Elizabeth Miller.

each other since at least 1892 makes it difficult to believe that they never discussed their creations. We don't know when Doyle wrote "The Adventure of the Illustrious Client" but it is possible that the seed was planted in an unrecorded discussion between him and Stoker. Their ongoing friendship might explain why one of the vampire hunters in *Dracula* resembles Holmes's faithful companion, Dr John H. Watson. Dr John Seward introduces us to his friend and mentor, Professor Van Helsing, and chronicles his teacher's extraordinary abilities and achievements.

In 1888, Doyle chastised Mary Doyle for her favourable comparison of his psychic novel, *The Mystery of Cloomber*, with Robert Louis Stevenson's story, "The Pavilion on the Links:" "You must not say that Cloomber is as good as the Pavilion... The Pavilion is far better ... because it is strong without preternatural help, which I think is always more to the author's credit ..." [while] "it is more compact and the interest never flags for a moment." This belief may have inspired him to transform Stoker's macabre fairy tale into a rationalized detective story.

Doyle's pastiche is full of puns and in-jokes which he may have shared with James M. Barrie (1860-1937), Hall Caine (1853-1931) or other authors who had been friends with him and Stoker. Many of Doyle's fans are aware of Barrie's marvelous spoof of Holmes and Watson, but it requires a working knowledge of *Dracula* to see the aside that "He [Gruner] played polo at Hurlingham"[13] as an indication of the fictional "Hillingham," Lucy Westenra's ancestral estate in London, or to appreciate the humour in "The villain [Gruner] attached himself to the lady, and with such effect...." At the end of the story, Holmes's appearance beneath Gruner's window as a "terrible ghost, his head girt with bloody bandages, his face drawn and white" takes on new meaning if we see it as a spoof of the scene in chapter 23 where Dracula eludes the vampire hunters by jumping through a window. In this case, Doyle has taken his parody to new heights by transforming Sherlock Holmes himself into Count Dracula.

* * * *

---

13   The image of Dracula playing polo may have given Doyle a chuckle or two.

But the best joke of all may be how Arthur Conan Doyle's adaptation of one of the cornerstones of horror literature has escaped the attention of millions of fans for almost a century.

N. B. — Towards the end of his life, Doyle became fascinated with the occult. Dracula ends with a "Note" which says the adventure took place "seven years ago," while the first paragraph of Doyle's story implies that the adventure occurred ten years ago.

BIBLIOGRAPHY

Baring-Gould, William S. ed. *The Annotated Sherlock Holmes*: Volume II. New York: Clarkson N. Potter, 1976. p. 685. n. 19.

Bunson, Matthew E. *Encyclopedia Sherlockiana: An A-Z Guide to the World of the Great Detective.* New York: Macmillan, 1994.

Doyle, [Sir] Arthur Conan. "The Adventure of the Illustrious Client" New York*: Collier's Weekly Magazine* (8 Nov. 1924) 5-7, 30, 32, 34. Rpt. *Strand Magazine* (1925). Rpt. *The Case-Book of Sherlock Holmes* (1927). Rpt.

—. "The Adventure of the Sussex Vampire" *Strand Magazine* (Jan. 1924) 3-13. Rpt.

—. "The American's Tale" *London Society* (Christmas 1880) 44-48. Rpt.

—. "The Captain of the Pole-Star" *Temple Bar* (Jan. 1883) 33-52. Rpt.

—. "John Barrington Cowles" *Cassell's Saturday Journal* 12:19 (Apr. 1884). 433-435, 461-463. Rpt.

—. Letter to John Gore. Cited in Baring-Gould, p. 690.

—. Letter to Mary Doyle (November 20, 1888). Cited in Lellenberg, p. 256.

—. "The Parasite" *Lloyd's Weekly Newspaper* (11 Nov.–2 Dec. 1894) 4 parts.

—. Vampire Stories. New York: *Skyhorse*, 2009. Ed. by Robert Eighteen-Bisang and Martin H. Greenberg.

—. "The Winning Shot" *Bow Bells* (11 July 1893) 61-67. Rpt.

Eighteen-Bisang, Robert. "Dracula by Arthur Conan Doyle" *The Sherlock Holmes Journal* 29:3 (Winter 2009) 4-98.

Eighteen-Bisang, Robert and Elizabeth Miller, ed. *Bram Stoker's Notes for Dracula.* Jefferson, NC: McFarland, 2008.

Davies, David Stuart. *The Tangled Skein*. Channel Islands, Alderney: Island Publishing, 1992. Rpt.

Estleman, Loren D. *Sherlock Holmes vs. Dracula; or The Adventure of the Sanguinary Count*. New York: Doubleday & Company, 1978. Rpt.

Keefauver, Brad A. "Sherlock Holmes and the Secretly Dead: A Case of Near Fatal Close-Mindedness" in *The Baker Street Chronicle* 4:5 (Sept./Oct. 1984).

Lellenberg, John, Daniel Stashower and Charles Foley, ed. *Arthur Conan Doyle: A Life in Letters*. Penguin Press: New York, 2007.

Mason, Bill. "A Tale from the Crypt: Unearthing Dracula in Sherlock Holmes" *Holmes & Watson Report #42* 7:2 (May 2003) 24-32.

McNally, Raymond T. and Radu Florescu. *In Search of Dracula: A True History of Dracula and Vampire Legends*. Greenwich: New York Graphic Society, 1972.

Maclaglan, Sir Eric. Cited in Baring-Gould, p. 685; n. 19.

Nordan, Pierre. *Conan Doyle: A Biography*. Holt, Rinehart & Winston: New York, 1967.

Redmond, Christopher. *In Bed with Sherlock Holmes: Sexual Elements in Arthur Conan Doyle's Stories of the Great Detective*. Toronto: Simon & Pierre, 1984.

Redmond, Donald A. *Sherlock Holmes: A Study in Sources*. Kingston and Montreal: McGill-Queen's University Press, 1992.

Saberhagen, Fred. *The Holmes-Dracula File*. New York: Ace Books, 1978. Rpt.

Stoker, Bram. *Dracula*. New Westminster: Archibald Constable and Company, 1897. Rpt.

—. *Personal Reminiscences of Henry Irving*. London: William Heinemann, 1907 (revised edition).

—. "Sir Arthur Conan Doyle Tells of His Career and Work, His Sentiments Towards America, and His Approaching Marriage" New York: World (23 July 1907) E1a-f.

BIOGRAPHICAL ASPECTS OF "THE RESIDENT PATIENT"

by Bob Byrne

Biographers and devotees of Sherlock Holmes have written much regarding who the detective was modeled after. Joseph Bell is widely regarded as the primary inspiration, a belief bolstered by Sir Arthur Conan Doyle's own words more than once. In his autobiography, *Memories and Adventures*, Doyle said, "I thought of my old teacher Joe Bell, of his eagle face, of his curious ways, of his eerie trick of spotting details. If he were a detective he would surely reduce this fascinating but unorganized business to something nearer to an exact science." Add another comment, "Sherlock Holmes is the literary embodiment ... of my memory of a professor of medicine at Edinburgh University."

But Holmes was certainly not based on just one person. It has been asserted that one can find bits of Doyle himself in the great detective. His second wife said that her husband had the Sherlock Holmes brain, solving mysteries that puzzled the police. Seemingly more likely is that the stolid, patriotic Doctor Watson drew in great part from his creator.

But can we examine one of the sixty Holmes tales and discover biographical pieces of Conan Doyle? As a matter of fact, we need look no further than *The Adventure of the Resident Patient* and Dr Percy Trevelyan.

Trevelyan is a young doctor with great potential but limited finances. He is struggling along, hoping he can save enough so that in ten years he could open a posh practice in the medical district. Quite unexpectedly, a complete stranger named Blessington arrives at Trevelyan's room and makes an astonishing offer. Blessington will let a house, furnish it, pay for maids and take care of the other expenses. Trevelyan just has to run a successful practice and his benefactor will keep three-quarters of the profit. In addition, Blessington will become the story title's resident patient, his heart condition cared for by Trevelyan.

The young doctor, barely believing his good fortune, agrees to the deal and quickly establishes a thriving practice. Before Blessington's arrival, Trevelyan's future appeared to be one requiring a great deal of hard work before he could harbor any hope of success. But his generous benefactor had given the doctor the capital needed to become almost an overnight sensation. Was there a Blessington in Arthur Conan Doyle's life? Well, sort of.

Doyle's start in practice also featured a benefactor, though it is quite a different, yet still absorbing, story. In early 1882, Doyle had just completed a stint as a ship's doctor on an African route. It was not a particularly enjoyable experience and he did not sign on for another tour at sea. Much like Dr Watson in *A Study in Scarlet*, Doyle was 'free as air' and was back in Edinburgh when he received a telegram from a school friend, George Turnavine Budd. Now a doctor, Budd is a larger than life character in Doyle's story.

Back before Doyle had gone on the aforementioned sea voyage, Budd had urgently summoned him to Bristol, where Budd's practice was located. It turns out that Budd had gone bankrupt and hoped Doyle could bail him out. Budd was frustrated to learn that Doyle was in no financial condition to aid him, but then, apparently laughed the whole matter off. In the end, advised by Doyle, Budd gained extensions from his creditors. However, Doyle had no idea that Budd would then flee the town, leaving said creditors with worthless promises.

Now, with Doyle back on land and wondering what to do, Budd sent him another telegram, this time from his new practice in Plymouth. Budd, an outrageous individual, told Doyle that he was a huge success, with thirty thousand patients in the last year and that he wouldn't even cross the street to see Queen Victoria. He promised to give Doyle all his visiting and surgery patients, as well as midwifery cases, guaranteeing his friend at least three hundred pounds the first year.

Though this sounded too good to be true, Doyle packed quickly and headed off to Portsmouth, much to his mother's displeasure. Called by her son 'The Ma'am,' Mary Foley Doyle had a great deal of influence over her son all his life (Doyle can safely be called a mama's boy). She had never liked Budd and did not trust him now. In retrospect, one has to admire her perceptiveness.

It seems that Budd was a talented doctor, a showman, and a quack all rolled into one. He comes across in writings by Doyle and Doyle's biographers as a sort of medical Barnum and Bailey. Albeit, a very successful one. At the end of each day, he would march down the center of the street from his practice, the day's gold and silver earnings held out in front of him in a bag. The word 'bombastic' echoes through the mind when reading about Budd.

Doyle himself acknowledges that his book, *The Stark Munro Letters*, tells "in very close detail the events of this time," with Budd being identified as one 'Cullingworth.' In fact, it is so accurate (with a few exceptions) that in his autobiography he borrowed from that book, rather than rewriting events using Budd's actual name. Safe to say, Budd/Cullingworth was as intriguing a character as Doyle ever made up himself.

Doyle saw firsthand Budd's flamboyant approach to medicine, which consisted of free consultations inevitably concluded with a prescription that was not free. Patients waited hours to see the dynamic Budd and a few were treated by Doyle as the partnership moved forward. As he did throughout his life, Doyle frequently exchanged letters with his mother. Upon learning from her son that Budd was not going to repay his Bristol creditors she wrote many uncomplimentary things about the man. This was not an isolated incident and it would have repercussions.

After displaying a rather sour attitude towards his partner for a time, Budd told Doyle that the practice was suffering and it was Doyle's fault. Upon hearing this, Doyle marched outside and pried his name plate off the front of the building. Emotions cooled a bit and it was agreed that Doyle would depart to start his own practice, aided by a one pound a week loan from Budd, to be repaid when practical. So, Doyle found himself in Southsea, starting up a practice with the aid of a generous patron. Sort of a long distance Blessington. Except, the true nature of George Budd was about to be displayed and he was anything but generous.

Doyle rented lodgings and a place of business, bought the minimum he needed for both and set up for business, barely getting by financially. Now, Budd sprang his trap. He and his wife had been reading Mary Doyle's unflattering letters, but they had given no indication of it to Doyle. Now, having assisted Doyle in becoming irrecoverably committed in Portsmouth and somewhat dependant upon that promised aid of one pound a week, Budd sent a letter to Doyle. In it, Budd accused his ex-partner of having been disloyal under his own roof and severed all ties with him, including not providing the promised loan.

Considering the circumstances, Doyle, in *The Stark Munro Letters*, is rather charitable in his feelings of Budd. He did send a sharp note to Cullingworth saying that he had always defended the man against his mother's comments, but now he had to admit that his mother had been right. This seems relatively restrained in the gravity of the situation. And he sums up Budd by saying "He was a remarkable man and narrowly escaped being a great one." A reading of *The Stark Munro Letters* does provide a very entertaining look at a major character in Doyle's life.

Percy Trevelyan's nascent medical career receives a significant boost when Blessington sets him up in practice. George Turnavine Budd took an unemployed Arthur Conan Doyle in as a partner and then offered to loan him funds to help his college mate start his own practice (albeit, with an ulterior motive). We can see the root of Blessington's sponsoring of Trevelyan in Doyle's own experiences with Budd.

Doyle's imagination produced Blessington, the criminal turned informer who was judged guilty by his fellow miscreants and murdered in his own rooms while doctor Trevelyan slept under the same roof, unaware of events. Happily, nothing of the like actually happened to Sir Arthur. But he did once have a resident patient and that experience certainly had a major impact on his life.

Having gotten a fledgling medical practice underway in spite of Budd's attempt to sabotage it, one of Doyle's neighbors in Southsea was a fellow practitioner, Dr Pike ('Porter' in *The Stark Munro Letters*). One of Pike's patients was a young man named James Hawkins, who was vacationing in Southsea with his mother and sister, Louise. Dr Pike asked Doyle if he would care to consult on the young man. Unfortunately, it was obvious to both men that Hawkins had cerebral meningitis, a fatal disease at the time. Feeling sympathy for the family, Doyle offered to have James stay with him and receive medical care; an offer which was accepted.

Unfortunately, James died not long after coming under Doyle's care. However, not all was lost. Doyle saw a great deal of the sister, Louise, nicknamed 'Touie.' Love blossomed and the two were wed less than five months after her brother died. Hmm..sounds like a case for Sherlock Holmes.

In fact, Doyle relates in *The Stark Munro Letters* that the police had received an anonymous letter stating that there was something suspicious about the death. So, when Munro returned from the funeral, a detective was waiting to talk to him. Fortunately for Munro, Dr Porter had seen the patient the night before he died and this seemed to satisfy the detective and the matter was dropped. Doyle never gave any indication that this little episode really did occur after his real resident patient died.

Percy Trevelyan began carving out his niche with work on the pathology of catalepsy. The Worthingdon Bank Gang used Trevelyan's interest in catalepsy to help them distract him by having one of the members fake the illness on a visit. It is his specialty that is used to 'get to him.' Trevelyan is no general practitioner, like Watson or Doyle himself.

Well, Doyle was a general practitioner through 1890. Then, on what must have seemed like a whim, he sold his practice and whisked off to Vienna to study. He had decided to become an eye specialist. Doyle stayed barely two months and later wrote that he could have learned as much in London. The whole thing seemed like a working vacation for a man wanting a breath of fresh air from his job and domestic life. But apparently he did learn enough to become a specialist in this emerging field.

Settled back in London in the March of 1891, he was living in Montague Place, just around the corner from the British museum and the street of Sherlock Holmes before the detective took lodgings with Doctor Watson. He established an office near the prestigious Harley Street medical district and was acting as a specialist in matters ocular. Whether he actually ever had any patients is an open matter.

Within a half year of setting up shop he had retired from medicine and was determined to make his living entirely as a writer. So, Doyle was a specialist for a very short time. But a few years later he drew on this experience when fleshing out the character of Percy Trevelyan. Interestingly, in *The Stark Munro Letters* Munro has one last meeting with Cullingworth. His outrageous friend is moving to South America to be, yes, an eye specialist.

A HOUSE GONE MAD

by Sherlock Holmes as edited
by Bruce I. Kilstein

It was near winter in 18__ that a strange case afforded my colleague and friend, Dr. John Watson, yet another opportunity to lend his medical expertise to one of my investigations. We had just finished our breakfast and had drawn near the fire against the chill of the damp November morning. Watson perused the morning papers while I lit my first pipe of the day, and the caseload being light, prepared to finish a monograph on the identification of footprints, when Mrs. Hudson announced a visitor. The poor woman had barely enough time to utter Lestrade's name before the boorish inspector from Scotland Yard burst past her and into our study.

"Lestrade," I said, barely glancing up from the preparation of my meerschaum, "so good of you to visit on such a bitter morning. Mrs. Hudson, be a dear and fix the inspector a strong cup of your Turkish coffee. He has not slept for nearly two days, although he has managed not to miss a meal, however hurried, and he will be in want of a stimulant before returning to his wife, who, by now, will be fretting over his apparent disappearance from his investigation in the East End."

I took a long draw on the pipe and savoured both the sweet aroma of the tobacco and the shocked look on Lestrade's face as he struggled to comprehend the nature of my deduction.

"…but, Mr. Holmes," he stammered, "how could you know the nature of my movements, let alone when I have taken meals or contacted my wife? I have just entered your chamber and you have barely even gazed up from your pipe."

Watson looked up from the *Times* with amusement. "Yes, Holmes," he said, "do tell us how you could know the chap's whereabouts?"

"Elementary, my dear fellow." I used my pipe to point out the salient features on Lestrade's person that led me to my deduction. "First, one will note the rumpled condition of the gentleman's suit.

We see several stains in varying degrees of coagulation which represent several hurried meals: two meat pies and a plate of bangers, I should think, by looking at the marks on his cuffs and sleeve. About eight hours between meals will put us between breakfast and the noon meal yesterday. He had no time for tea or I would expect some other traces of that repast. The fact that he has bits of food on his collar and shirt would indicate hasty dining without a proper serviette. He has traces of mud on his braces of a particular color and stench which would indicate a location near the river on the East End. The partially concealed note in his coat pocket is a telegram meant for his wife, which he neglected to post, to inform her of his delayed return."

Lestrade reached into his pocket and removed the telegram. "The wife will be upset," he admitted. "You are correct in what you say, Mr. Holmes."

"You have been busy, Lestrade. Pray take a seat and tell us how we may be of assistance," I said.

Lestrade sat at a small table, and thankfully accepted the hot coffee that Mrs. Hudson had prepared. "Strangest thing I've seen in a long while, sir. I was called yesterday to investigate the death of a Mr. Joshua Wadsworth of Brick Lane. He was a man of sixty-three years age, retired merchant, widower, living on his savings and a modest inheritance that had been his wife's, and residing with his daughter and a small staff. He was found dead by his servant. There was no sign of violence."

"I should hardly think that cause for alarm," Watson said. "Chap probably died of a coronary."

"Well, that was what the servant thought, doctor, until he went to inform the other members of the household. He found them in the dining room. The son, Ernie, who was at home on holiday, had gone stark raving mad. The daughter, Eunice, was in a catatonic state. The maid was clutching her throat, eyes popping near out of her head, according to the servant."

"Interesting, Lestrade," I said. "And what is it you wish from us?"

Lestrade stared into his coffee. "Naturally, with any suspicious death, Scotland Yard was called in. I have examined the premises, interviewed the servant, a Mr. Warren, as well as the young

Wadsworth's fiancée, Lilly Brevant, and have spoken to the doctor caring for the unfortunate children and maid."

"Small wonder you look so tired," Watson said. I admired and envied my friend's endless capacity for compassion.

"Sirs," Lestrade continued, "I can find no motive for, or concrete signs of foul play, but still I have to admit, without an explanation for the condition of the others in the house, I am at a loss to exclude some type of poisoning. I remember too well the case of E.J. Drebber[14], Mr. Holmes."

"True," I admitted. "But in that case there was a clear motive for the poisoning. You have no doubt concluded that the Wadsworths had no immediate enemies and that the doctors have no explanation for the condition of the others."

"Quite correct, Mr. Holmes. Daresay I could use your medical expertise in this matter as well, Dr. Watson," a tired and deflated Lestrade said.

Watson looked out the window and we followed his gaze to the blowing rain that soaked the few hurried passersby who had ventured out upon Baker Street. "I suppose if you think it necessary, my dear fellow. Haven't been down to the Royal London Hospital since we investigated the case of the Jezail bullet. Fresh air will do us all a bit of good."

"Go home to your wife and have a rest, inspector," I encouraged. "The doctor and I will delve into the situation and see if we can shed a bit of light on your little mystery."

Lestrade took his leave and I jotted the facts of the case and addresses in my notebook. I had Watson pack his medical bag and had Mrs. Hudson fetch a boy to secure a hansom and send a telegram to the hospital.

We soon found ourselves hurtling through the streets across London to the East End. Watson had known my methods well enough by now to have refrained from conversation during the ride, in order to allow me to compose my theories. What must have taken the better part of an hour seemed mere minutes to me, lost in thought as I was, but we arrived in good order at a house off of Brick Lane,

14   See *A Study in Scarlet* wherein Lestrade found poison pills at Halliday's Hotel.

Spitalfields. We instructed the cabbie to wait, and were shown in by Lestrade's man, posted inside the door.

"The inspector told me to expect you, Mr. Holmes," the bobby said. "The butler and fiancée are in there." He gestured to a drawing room off the small entrance hall.

We entered the room and found the two staring at a low fire in the hearth. Neither rose in greeting; the woman, obviously in shock, continued her stare while the man looked at us with suspicion. "You must be Miss Lilly and Warren," I said.

"And who might you be?" asked the butler.

"I am Sherlock Holmes and this is Dr. Watson. We have been asked by Scotland Yard to look into the matter of the death of Mr. Wadsworth. Watson, have a look at the young lady, she seems in need of medical attention." Watson located a small carafe of sherry on a nearby table, but remembering the strange warning of poison by Lestrade, thought better of pouring the young woman a drink. I withdrew a small flask from my coat and handed it to him as a substitute.

While Watson attended the young woman, I began an examination of the room. I knelt on the carpet near the hearth and examined a fine layer of ash with my glass. "This is where you found Mr. Wadsworth, is it not?" I asked Warren.

The man looked surprised. "Yes," he said hesitantly. "But how can you know that? I didn't tell that to the police."

"I am sure there is much you haven't told them," I replied. "Like the fact that you moved the body, and smoked one of your master's cigars before sounding the alarm."

This comment, as well as Watson's ministrations, filled our female companion with new animation. "Is this true, Warren?" she asked. The servant did not reply.

"You see, Miss Lilly," I explained, "there is a faint outline of ash on the carpet near the hearth. Your once future father-in-law had collapsed here, shortly after his meal I should think, while he was smoking his evening cigar. If one looks closely, one sees that there are no less than three separate specimens of ash on the carpet. The first, this dark gray ash, is the residue of the gentleman's cigar. Jamaican, I should think. Covering this first residue is a finer layer, no doubt, from the settling of ash from the hearth. This section of the rug without the residue was covered by the body as the dust settled. But this third specimen is interesting. It is the same colour as the first, indicating that it came from the same brand of cigar, but it has landed, in part, on the area covered by the body. This indicates that a second smoker must have been in the room."

Watson and the woman had now drawn near to the deposit on the carpet, yet Warren remained seated. I continued, "From the account given by Mr. Warren to Inspector Lestrade, Wadsworth was alone in the room when his body was discovered. This last bit of ash is undisturbed, indicating that it was deposited *after* the body had been moved."

"The ash would have been smeared if the body fell on it," Watson clarified, as Lilly was looking puzzled.

"Correct, my man," I said to my friend. I turned to the taciturn Warren. "Seems you were in no hurry to alert the authorities to what must have seemed strange developments in the household, Mr. Warren."

Warren met my glance with the determination of a man who had faced interrogation before, but he could not disguise the shade of red his face had taken. "Nothing you can prove, gov'nor," he said.

"We shall see," I replied. I called for the policeman. "Sergeant, see that this man is not let out of your sight for the next hour or so. Are there any other servants in the Wadsworths' employ?"

"With pleasure, Mr. Holmes," the policeman said with a small salute and a reassuring pat of his truncheon. "An old woman, Mrs. Spline, is the cook. Went to do the marketing."

"Very well. We shall need to talk with her. Dr. Watson and I have business at the hospital, but shall return. Miss Brevant, would you do us the kindness of accompanying us to visit Master Ernie?"

Lilly looked very concerned at the strange developments, but nodded and went to get her things.

In spite of the damp chill, the promise of a gold sovereign at the end of the day's work had kept our driver at-the-ready. We guided our young companion into the cab for the short drive to the hospital. I used the time to gently probe her for information while Watson made a futile attempt in the bouncing, crowded vehicle, to catalogue developments in his notebook. "Miss Brevant," I said, "I know that events must seem shocking, but I must ask you, as I am sure the police already have, if you know of any reason why anyone would wish to do the Wadsworth family harm?"

She was a plain girl, neatly-dressed in a garment of good cut that had seen some wear, suggesting a family of middle-class that had fallen on hard times. She maintained poise and dignity. "No, Mr. Holmes. Mr. Wadsworth was respected in the neighborhood, even by those... immigrants, at least that was what Ernie had told me. And if you knew Ernie...well, I never met a soul who didn't like him the minute he was introduced. He was the kindest man I have ever met. The children adore him, as does my employer, Captain Morrison." She lost her composure and began to cry.

Watson did his best to comfort her and offered his kerchief. When she was again calm, he asked, "What immigrants?"

"Jews, mostly," she said.

"This has long been an area of residence for the Jewish community, Watson," I explained. "Ever since Cromwell encouraged diversity and freedoms for various faiths, this area has been a home to Jews, Methodists, the Lascars. But the neighborhood has changed in recent times. As Jews have been accepted into higher circles, many have moved out of the old neighborhood and assimilated in other parts of London. A new generation of Jews faces persecution under the tsar in Russia. Again, a wave of immigration has swept our shores, but these new arrivals do not share our language, dress, or customs. I fear that we are entering a new era of misunderstanding."

"True, Mr. Holmes," Lilly admitted. "But Mr. Wadsworth had a reputation of dealing fairly with everyone. I cannot believe that they would want to hurt him. What were you saying about Warren moving his body? Is that reason for concern?"

"Yes, what do you make of it, Holmes?" Watson asked. "And the audacity to help himself to his employer's cigars while the body lay before him? What gall."

"Yes, the man irks me, Watson, but we are lacking in evidence to hang him. What can you tell me about him, Miss Brevant?"

"Not much, sir. I have only been engaged to Ernie for five months. I am a governess at Morrison Hall in Kent. Ernie was music tutor to the children there. That's how we met. He hasn't said much about the household. Mrs. Spline has been with the family since Ernie was a boy. I believe Warren is new to the household, but was in Mr. Wadsworth's employ in his business. When Mr. Wadsworth sold his holdings and retired, he offered the household position to Warren. Ernie and I had come to his home to spend the holiday and discuss plans for our wedding. I am sorry I cannot tell you more, gentlemen."

"You have done well, given the trying circumstances," I reassured her. "Ah, we have arrived at a familiar place, Watson. When we were last here, you were submitting to the new science of Roentgenology."[15]

Watson smiled when he recalled how the examination, by means of an X-ray photograph, of the bullet, lodged in his shoulder since the Afghan war, led to the capture of a conspirator in a plot against the government. "Bloody cold examination room," was all he said.

We made our way into the hospital, and the porter, expecting our arrival as the result of our telegram, escorted us to the ward where Ernie Wadsworth was lying-in. We made the acquaintance of Dr. Hemmings; the young, resident physician of the ward looked tired and overworked. "A strange case of lunacy," he confided in Dr. Watson. "We had to sedate him to keep him from hurting himself. He seems comfortable now. I have discussed the case with my professors, but they have yet to formulate an explanation of his condition. I suspect that we may need to arrange for his transfer to Bedlam."

"What of the others?" Watson asked. "The sister and Wadsworth's maid?"

"I am sorry to say that the maid has died, doctor."

"The poor thing!" Lilly exclaimed.

"Eunice Wadsworth remains in stable but an unresponsive condition. She is in the women's ward down the hall."

"Would you have an objection to Dr. Watson's examination of the patients?" I asked.

"Certainly not!" Hemmings beamed, obviously glad for some sort of assistance, having had none from his professors.

Watson approached Ernie Wadsworth who, in spite of some sedative, was moaning incoherently upon the bed. Watson checked the pulse, listened to the heart and lungs and with help from the porter, pried young Wadsworth's lids open to examine the eyes. "Strange how the eyes seem to bulge," Watson commented. We

---

15   See *Watson's Wound,* in this volume.

peered over his shoulder to look more closely. "The pulse is irregular and quite rapid, even after morphia has been administered."

"We noticed a similar appearance to the sister's eyes," Hemmings added.

"I should like to see the young lady as well," Watson said.

We left Miss Brevant to sit with her poor, afflicted fiancée while Hemmings escorted us to a nearby ward populated by female patients in various stages of what seemed to be a mental collapse. The room was filled with terrible noises and smells. It seemed all the nurses on duty could do was to try to maintain order. We found Eunice occupying a bed in the far corner of the ward. She lay on the bed, rocking slowly back and forth, eyes staring yet not seeing. "Miss Wadsworth," Hemmings said as he gently shook the girl, attempting to rouse her. Eunice only stared. Hemmings gestured to Watson with a defeated look.

Watson made an examination of the girl. He again checked her pulse and eyes and listened to the heart by means of the stethoscope. "Still can't get used to the bloody contraption," he commented.[16]

"What do these patients have in common?" I asked the two doctors.

"Rapid, irregular pulse and altered mental state," Hemmings said. "One with catatonia, yet the other with mania."

"Both have a protrusion of the eyes," Watson said, stroking his mustache.

"Some family characteristic?" I ventured.

"No, Holmes. If I didn't know better, I would say the ocular findings are the result of Grave's disease."

"The situation was certainly grave for Joshua Wadsworth," I said.

"Grave's disease, Mr. Holmes, is believed to be a disorder brought about by an overactivity of the thyroid gland," the young doctor offered, obviously pleased by his bit of knowledge. He turned to Watson. "Yet, doctor, there seems to be no sign of goiter or nodularity in the necks of the patients."

16   The stethoscope was discovered by Laennec as a means of examining the chest of a female patient without the physician placing his hands upon her, which was deemed inappropriate. Oddly, he is most remembered for his descriptions of diseases of the liver, rather than the invention that would become a standard medical device.

"It all fits, however," Watson replied. "The mental deterioration, the effects of the pulse, sweating. Possibly the cardiac collapse of the father. What baffles me, Holmes, is how such an affliction could overcome an entire household."

"Not an entire household," I corrected. "The cook, butler, and Miss Brevant would not seem to be afflicted."

There was silence for a moment as we all contemplated the facts before us.

"Some infection, perhaps," Hemmings offered. "I have heard that an inflammation of the thyroid could be brought about by miasma."

"Lestrade suggested a poison," Watson added. "Several poisons could have the cardiac and mental effects, but none would cause the protrusion of the eyes."

"There must be some commonality to the victims," I said. "The facts are incontrovertible. This is not a disorder of heredity, or the maid would not have been afflicted. This has to be some disorder of environment, yet the entire household was not stricken, unless…" I could not control the smile as the thought and possible common link occurred to me.

"What is it, Holmes?" Watson asked.

"Watson, let us take up no more of this young physician's time. We have work to do back at Brick Lane." I addressed Hemmings, "Sir, you have been of great assistance to our investigation. Pray, delay any transfer to a hospital for the insane until you hear from us." With that, we left the baffled resident to his charges and began the return to Spitalfields.

The rain had ebbed but the sun still hid behind a thicket of clouds. The wet gloom of the day prevailed as the light began to fade from the late autumn afternoon. The neighborhood around the Wadsworth home was in a state of flux. An old immigrant community had moved on, and a new one was reshaping the fabric of storefronts and street scenes. Old shops were boarded up; new establishments had makeshift signs nailed over the existing boards temporarily. The pedestrian traffic sported a variety of dress from the most modern of London fashion to the threadbare attire of the exiled Jews from Eastern Europe. The effect was that of a calico quilt, a mixture of texture and fabric.

We soon arrived back at the Wadsworth house and found the policeman enjoying tea and small sandwiches. He looked a trifle embarrassed to be found eating on duty, but we put him at ease and told him he could hardly be expected to stand guard over our prisoner without aid of sustenance. The man reported no change from Warren, who had remained the model detainee, seated by the fire.

The cook had returned from market, which explained the policeman's repast. Watson and Lilly accepted tea from the matronly Mrs. Spline. The woman, we learned, had been in the employ of Mr. Wadsworth for more than twenty years. She was badly shaken by the recent events and was quick to inquire about the health of Ernie and Eunice, whom she had attended since they were very young. Watson attempted to keep the news cheerful, but had to admit that there was no change in their condition. The death of the maid seemed a bad portent.

"Miss Lilly," I asked, "have you been dining with the Wadsworths these last few days?"

"No, Mr. Holmes. Ernie and I went our separate ways upon our return to London. I went home to visit my mother and began plans for the wedding. I only arrived here yesterday as the…present crisis was unfolding." She struggled to hold back tears. Mrs. Spline patted her on the shoulder and poured more tea in an attempt to comfort her.

"Mrs. Spline," I said, "you seem an excellent cook, if these sandwiches are any indication of your abilities. Had you prepared a special meal in honor of Master Wadsworth's return?"

The woman brightened at my compliment. "Why, yes, sir, I did. Yorkshire pudding, glazed plums and tenderloin of beef."

"And who is your purveyor of meats, madam?"

"Cohen and Sons. They are just down the road."

I gazed at Warren, who had suddenly become quite interested in my line of questioning. "Do the servants dine on the same fare as the family?" I asked.

"Would that they did," Warren said. "Think they would share a bit of their happiness." He turned bitterly back to the fire.

"Why so interested in the cookery?" Watson asked, between brushing crumbs from his trousers and sipping tea.

"It just might be the key to our mystery," I said. Both Watson and the sergeant looked down doubtfully at their sandwiches.

"Still think I killed the old man?" muttered Warren.

"I think there is every possibility that the killer was Mrs. Spline," I said. Before giving the company time to react, I headed for the door, "Come, Watson. Let us visit the local butcher."

Down a side street, off the main lane, we found a shop with a faded sign: *Cohen and Sons, Kosher Butchers,* with some Hebrew lettering below the English inscription. We entered to find the proprietor behind a counter, wiping a large cleaver on the bottom of an already blood-spattered apron. "Help you, gentlemen? Joint of mutton, slab of bacon, or perhaps some lamb?" he asked.

"You wouldn't be Mr. Cohen?" I asked, already confident of the reply.

"Why, no, sir. Bradley is the name. Just purchased the business from the Cohens. Place is a bit rundown, but I hope to have the shop looking smart for the clientele shortly. I may retain the name on the sign for some time, though. Old Cohen had a good reputation in the neighborhood."

"You know Mrs. Spline, I should think."

"Cook for Wadsworth. She was here earlier today. Shame about the chap, though. Never had the chance to make his acquaintance."

"Is the tenderloin fresh?" I asked. Watson gave a start but held his tongue.

"Nothing but the best, I assure you, my man," Bradley said. He gestured to the back of the shop, where attendants were in the process of carving up a huge slab of meat. "Sold some to Mrs. Spline, special the other day. She seemed quite pleased."

"And do you perform the slaughter on the premises?"

"No, sir, done by my men at the slaughterhouse."

"From which part of the animal is the tenderloin obtained?"

"Generally, sir, it is from the large muscle of the neck," he replied, gesturing to his own throat with the cleaver. "Any interest in the tenderloin? I can put in any special request you have. Have it here for you next day?"

"Not this moment," I replied. "We will be sure to keep you in mind. Thank you for your time."

"My pleasure, sirs," he mumbled, and sunk the end of his cleaver into his chopping block.

We took leave of the disappointed butcher and made our way back toward the Wadsworth house. "What do you know about kosher food, Watson?" I asked.

"Something about the Jewish diet," he said with a shrug. "Knew a chap at school, Marks, wouldn't dine at the club. Wouldn't eat pork."

"Precisely. The Jews consider the pig to be unclean. Our man Bradley at Cohen and Sons offered us bacon. Clearly he has retained the name but not the standards of the kosher butcher. It is not just the type of meat consumed that is proscribed by the kosher law, but *how* the meat is prepared is also of vast import. The slaughter of the animal is carried out in a humane fashion. The animal's throat is slit and the blood allowed to slowly drain from the body over the course of the day."

"Sounds ghastly," Watson said.

"That is the Jewish law. Now, Watson, if the blood is allowed to drain from the animal *before* it is carved into the various cuts of meat, might not certain organs undergo a change in appearance as compared to those of a freshly slaughtered animal?" I allowed Watson to ponder the question as I continued my line of reasoning. "Is not the thyroid gland of the neck intimately associated with the strap-like muscles of the neck?"

"The strenocleidomastoid muscles," Watson agreed, "run from the base of the skull to the collarbone. The thyroid is suspended between them." Watson stopped walking abruptly. The sudden dawning of recognition on his face seemed a light in the fading gray of the day. "I see, Holmes! You think the kosher butcher would easily be able to recognize the thyroid tissue from the muscles of the neck. The blood, having drained away, would render the gland a dull gray colour, while the meaty muscles of the neck would retain their red hue."

"It would be a simple matter to trim away the glandular tissue for the kosher butcher of experience, but perhaps quite another matter for our friend Bradley who is new to the business."

"I have to admit that all the tissue of the neck would look equally red and bloody in the newly killed animal, just as the various tissue types of the cadaver in the anatomy laboratory are much easier to discern than those of the living tissues in the operating theatre!" Watson cried.

"And so, my good fellow, we must conclude that in Bradley's haste to please his new customer, Mrs. Spline, he incorporated a generous portion of the thyroid in the tenderloin, thus poisoning the household with the various products of gland."

"The result," Watson added, "would vary in each person who ate the meat depending on the quantity of glandular secretion ingested, and the relative constitution of the individual."

"Thus, we have the deaths of the fragile maid and Joshua Wadsworth. His children will fare better as they are no doubt, in more robust health. The maid must have sneaked a bit of the loin for herself when no one was watching. Warren and Mrs. Spline were not offered the meat and Miss Lilly was away visiting her mother, hence they have remained unaffected by the malady."

"You make it sound so obvious, Holmes."

"I could not have come to the conclusion without the aid of your medical expertise," I complimented.

"But what about Warren?" Watson asked. "Surely he must be up to no good; he seems very suspicious. And what of the fact that he moved the body and smoked the cigar over the corpse of his employer?"

"Oh, rest assured he is not innocent. He had some plan in mind but was able to take advantage of a most unusual opportunity. He must have known that his employer kept a safe. With the impending wedding, Wadsworth must have kept or transferred some valuables to the safe for the return of the betrothed couple. I should think there would be money and perhaps the jewelry of his late wife to bestow upon the bride-to-be in honor and preparation of the nuptials. Warren would have needed a way to obtain the key from his master, who would have kept it close to his person. I can only imagine what was in the mind of the criminal who so obviously had disdain for his employer."

"But when he found the whole family to be suddenly incapacitated..." Watson followed my reasoning.

"He helped himself to a cigar while searching the body for the key," I concluded. "I think we will find quite an empty safe when we return to the house."

The sound of the police whistle interrupted our discourse. There was a commotion and several policemen came up Brick Lane at the run.

"Watson, did you bring your service revolver?"

He patted the breast pocket of his coat. "I have learned by now to bring it along on these little forays, Holmes."

We hastened to the house to find that a crowd had gathered on the street by the Wadsworth house. Several policemen were forcing their way through the onlookers in an attempt at gaining access to the door. The policeman inside continued to sound the alarm and the crowd began to shout. I pulled Watson by the sleeve and shouted over the din, "Around the back, man! Quickly."

We raced to the rear of the house and found the tradesman's entrance locked. With no time to force the lock, Watson drew his weapon, fired, and blew the hardware off the latch. We burst into the kitchen and found Warren holding a knife to Miss Brevant's throat. The policeman had the whistle in his mouth and truncheon drawn; Warren was backed against a wall of shelves that stored a large assortment of crockery and cooking implements. Warren's blade, poised to pierce the young woman, kept the officer at bay.

"You'll not pin the murder on me, Holmes!" Warren sneered.

"I have no intention," I said calmly. "But if you so much as put a nick in that young woman's throat, I'll see you swing. I will ask you for the contents of the safe."

For a moment, Warren seemed astonished that we had deduced the nature of his crime. "Never, not after the way that man treated me. I got what was due me. He promised me a share of the business. He never gave it, and I was reduced to a servant."

"That gives you no right to take his son's inheritance."

Warren tightened his grip on Lilly. Watson's second shot was deafening in the confines of the kitchen. For an instant, I thought that a shot at the assailant would be sure to injure the young lady as well, but my friend had aimed at the shelf immediately above Warren's head. The projectile brought an array of heavy crockery, pots, pans, and shelving down on the pair. The blow was not enough to render the man senseless but the diversion was such as to separate hostage from captor.

Warren lunged with his knife toward Lilly but was met with a stout crack to the head by the quick-acting officer's nightstick.

This blow forced Warren to surrender both knife and consciousness.

By the time the police carted Warren away, Watson had attended the bruised Lilly Brevant and Mrs. Spline had begun the cleanup. Lestrade had been summoned from his bed. My second pipe of the day was long since due, and I enjoyed the tobacco and look of amazement on Lestrade's face as I recounted the events of the day. We located Wadsworth's safe and, as expected, found it empty.

I credited Dr. Watson with the key elements in determining the cause of the illness that cost two their lives and saved Ernie and Eunice from committal in the lunatic asylum. The two would make a full recovery. Ernie and Lilly honoured us with invitations to their wedding. Sadly, Warren would never divulge the location of the purloined inheritance and would take this knowledge to his spiteful grave.

✗

THE ADVENTURE OF THE SECOND ROUND

by Mark Wardecker

It is with much reserve that I begin this account of the mystery which awaited my friend Sherlock Holmes and me at Sherrinsthorpe Manor in Kensington. In fact, not since recording the tragedy of the Cushing sisters have I felt such misgivings about publishing one of Holmes' cases, and in that instance, my reticence did finally prevent the story's inclusion in most subsequent anthologies. Still, the masterful way in which Holmes illuminated such an obscure conspiracy demands no less than that a record be published. Only this and the fact that the passage of time has swept away many of this drama's principal actors have moved me to finally set it down.

It was late in the month of November, and though no snow had yet fallen, the frigid blasts of winter rattled every pane and resonated in every chimney in London. During one particularly bitter morning, I arose shortly before dawn and was surprised to find my friend awake and already dressed. What was even more surprising was that, in spite of the early hour and the forbidding, slate-grey frigidity which had permeated the city, Holmes was in remarkably high spirits. He was standing in front of a roaring fire and filling his morning pipe which was comprised of all the plugs and dottles left from his smokes of the day before, all carefully dried and collected on the corner of the mantlepiece. Upon my entrance, he picked up a letter which was also on the mantelpiece and turned to greet me.

"Good morning, Watson. I am so glad you have already dressed."

"Good morning to you, as well, Holmes, but I must say that I am surprised to see you up and dressed so early."

"I was awakened about an hour ago by a messenger," he said, as he handed me the letter. "Do you remember my mentioning an Inspector Nicholson of the Yard?"

"Yes. He has called you in on a couple of cases within the past year, hasn't he?"

"Actually, he has enlisted my help on no less than three occasions. He is very young but has already made quite a name for himself in the press. He was the one who finally managed to apprehend the Spotts gang and that without my help. This time, however, he hasn't wasted an instant in contacting me, which can only mean that he has stumbled upon something unusual."

At a nod toward the letter from Holmes, I unfolded it and, in my customary fashion, read it aloud:

> "Sherrinsthorpe, Kensington
> "3:30 a.m.
> "My dear Mr. Holmes, I should be very glad of your immediate assistance in what promises to be a most remarkable case. It is something quite in your line. So far, I have been able to keep everything as I have found it, but I beg you not to lose an instant, as it is difficult to leave Lord Morris there.
> "Yours faithfully,
> "Geoffrey Nicholson."

"Well, this leaves little doubt as to the result of the crime," I remarked, "but I must confess that the name of the victim is unfamiliar to me."

"It is to me, as well. Since Mrs. Hudson has been kind enough to prepare breakfast, why don't you have something to eat while I look him up."

As I sat down to breakfast at the table, Holmes retrieved a red-covered volume from one of the shelves and slumped down into his armchair. When, after several minutes, he stopped flipping through the pages and re-lit his pipe, I hazarded the question: "Well, what does it say?"

"That the victim was noble … not that I doubted it. No, I am afraid we shall have to begin our investigation at the scene of the crime."

With that, I hurriedly finished Mrs. Hudson's excellent breakfast, and in no time, we had abandoned the comfort of Baker Street for a west-bound cab. Holmes, obviously excited over the prospect of an interesting case, talked animatedly of music and the theatre, but I, uncharacteristically, became withdrawn once our growler entered High Street and the precincts of my old neighbourhood. Even Hyde Park and the Gardens looked lifeless on this relentlessly cold morning, and none but the hardiest tradesmen were out and about. Within an hour, we passed through a wrought iron gate and into a long drive, at the end of which stood Sherrinsthorpe Manor, a massive red-brick mansion of three floors. As we alighted and Holmes paid the driver, a moon-faced and somewhat disheveled young man emerged from the entrance, said a couple of words to a constable posted by the door, and hurriedly walked over to us.

"Mr. Holmes, I'm so glad you decided to accept my invitation!" he said smiling.

"It is good to see you, as well, Nicholson. This is my friend and colleague, Dr. Watson."

"It's good to finally meet you, sir. I hate to rush you both, but we should probably have a look at the scene before the coroner arrives to examine the body."

"That's fine, but let me first congratulate you on the birth of your child," said Holmes, causing Nicholson to suddenly turn around again.

"Thank you. Our son Adam was born a few weeks ago. Did Inspector Lestrade tell you?" asked Nicholson with a hint of expectation in his tone.

"No, there are several other indicators. In fact, when I first noticed the wrinkled condition of your suit and that you looked unusually weary, even for one aroused so early, I began to worry that your domestic fortunes had suffered a decline. However, once you turned, exposing the dried milk stain upon your left shoulder, I was glad to find that quite the opposite was true."

"Let's hope Mr. Holmes can make such short work of this murder, Dr. Watson. Follow me, gentlemen."

And with that, we entered the main hall.

"You will probably want to keep your coats on," warned Nicholson. "As I stated in the letter, nothing has been touched, and the French doors of the study have been open all night."

Indeed, it was absolutely freezing in Lord Morris's study, and I was able to feel a blast of wind the moment Nicholson opened its door, which was on the left-hand side of the hall. The French doors were directly across from the entrance, and the only other window, which was closed, was on our left and looked out upon the grounds in front of the mansion. Despite its rifled appearance, the room was neatly furnished, with some scattered Persian rugs, a few armchairs before the fireplace, and a large mahogany desk interposed between the entrance and the French doors. And it was here that Lord Morris sat with his head resting upon the desk's bloodstained blotter. Also upon the desk lay a small pistol, directly in front of his right hand. The man's hunched but tall form still retained its frock-coat with only a pair of black patent leather slippers indicating that his day's exertions were coming to an end.

"Does that gun belong to Lord Morris, Inspector?"

"Yes, according to the butler, Mr. Holmes. It appears to be unfired."

Holmes leaned over and glanced into the gun's barrel. Then, with a nod from Nicholson, he picked it up and began to examine it.

"It is a .41 rimfire, single-shot, Colt derringer. How closely did you examine it, Nicholson?"

"Again, Mr. Holmes, I refrained from picking it up, knowing that you would want to see the room exactly as it was."

"That and the wind would account for the error, for it has, in fact, been fired recently. It is obviously a second round which is undischarged," he said, handing the gun to Nicholson.

"Yes, you're right. I can smell the powder."

"What do you make of the wound, Watson?"

I looked down upon a middle-aged profile that had once been quite dashing but was now pale and expressionless, and replied, "It is obvious from the burns around its rim that it had to have been inflicted at very close range. In all honesty, Holmes, I would probably have taken this for a suicide, if it weren't for the gun's being loaded. Lord Morris' death would have been instantaneous. The wound seems consistent with this pistol, but until the bullet is retrieved from the skull, it is impossible to say for sure that it is the murder weapon. I assume there is no need to infer the time of death?"

"No," said Nicholson. "Perkins, the butler, heard the shot at approximately 12:45 a.m. and entered the room moments after."

"He saw no intruder?"

"No, Mr. Holmes."

"What about all of these papers lying about? Is there anything of any significance?" asked Holmes, as he stooped to look at them.

"Quite possibly there is something significant which is missing, but those I have seen are nothing but household bills."

"Yes. Here is one for coal, for gas, the green grocer's."

"Holmes! There's an appointment book under this armchair," I cried. "It appears the pages corresponding to the past four days have been torn out."

"Excellent, Watson! Why don't you and Nicholson examine the rest of it, while I have a look around."

"Good luck, Holmes. The ground is as hard as a rock out there," replied Nicholson.

Actually, I had almost been able to forget the cold while we were busy in our investigations, but now, I was grateful when Holmes, crawling around on all fours behind the desk, finally made his way onto the patio and closed the French doors behind him. While Nicholson and I paged through Lord Morris's appointment book, I would glance up occasionally to see how Holmes progressed in his search, crawling upon the frozen ground outside, in ever-widening semi-circles. When he returned, I could have sworn he had found some clue.

"What did you find, Holmes?" I asked.

"Nothing whatever," he replied with an odd note of triumph in his voice. "How does your research progress?"

"I told you that you wouldn't find anything out there," said Nicholson. "There's very little of interest in here — mostly Parliamentary meetings and lunch dates with his Bagatelle Club companions. It's all rather pedestrian."

"With whom was the last appointment?"

"His wife," I answered, "for their anniversary dinner."

"I see. May I have a look at it, please?"

Holmes flipped through the book for some time without expressing an interest in any of the entries and then handed it back to the inspector.

"Thank you. I think I am finished with this room for now. Would it be possible for me to interview the rest of the household, Inspector?"

"Certainly. I have already done some preliminary questioning, and it seems that, since only Lady Morris and the butler were in the central part of the house, only they heard a shot. The other servants were asleep in the wings and have been able to add nothing to the account."

"Then it is to Lady Morris and the butler I would speak. Before we go, however, have you been able to determine who benefits directly from the lord's death?"

"Lady Morris has already been kind enough to show me Lord Morris's will, Holmes. She and their only daughter are the two principal heirs, but I would add that, as things stand, these two ladies are already quite well off."

"Excellent work, Nicholson," commented Holmes, as the inspector led us to the sitting room where Lady Morris was waiting. She was an elegant and stately woman, only just beginning to approach middle-age, and dressed in a rather simple black dress. Though she had obviously been crying, she had regained her composure enough to speak and, at Nicholson's request, dispatched her maid in order to fetch Perkins, the butler. After the introductions, Holmes took a seat in the chair opposite the one in which she sat and assumed his most comforting tone.

"Madam, you do us a great kindness in agreeing to speak with us, and I promise I shall be as brief as possible."

"Mr. Holmes, I shall answer as many questions as you like, if they should aid you in catching my husband's killer."

"Thank you. Lady Morris, could you please recount the events of last night, omitting nothing, no matter how seemingly insignificant."

"Yes. I had retired early, before my husband returned from his club, in fact, and awoke to a loud noise. I heard a door open and close in the hall below and began to hurriedly dress myself. Upon lighting the lamp beside the bed, I noticed that the time was approximately 12:45. Within a few minutes, I descended the stairs and saw Perkins stepping out of the room. I could tell from the expression on his face that something was horribly wrong. Perkins's family has been attached to my husband for three generations, and I know him almost as well as I know anyone. He tried to stop me from entering, but I forced my way over the threshold. I saw my lifeless husband slumped over his desk and immediately fainted. After summoning the maid to take care of me, Perkins called the police from the telephone in the hall."

"Lady Morris, are you positive that you heard only one shot?" asked Holmes.

"A loud noise woke me up, and I heard Perkins enter the study. If there were any sounds before those, I slept through them."

"How long an interval had passed between your waking and your descending the stairs?"

"I did not look at the clock again, but it could have been no more than two minutes."

"Did you notice anything about the state of the room when you entered it?"

"I noticed several papers lying upon the floor and that the French doors behind my husband's desk were wide open."

"The derringer in the study — did it belong to your husband?"

"Yes. My husband was never fond of hunting. It was the only gun in the house."

"Which club did your husband attend that evening?"

"The only club he ever attended: the Bagatelle Club, in Regent Street. He loved both cards and billiards."

"You have a daughter?"

"Yes, she is married to an American railroad owner and lives in San Francisco. She is pregnant with our first grandchild."

"With your permission, Lady Morris, I would like to ask you some more general questions. Can you think of anyone who would want to kill your husband?"

"My husband's affairs were largely his own, but no, I can think of no one. There was, however, someone unknown to me."

"Pray, continue," Holmes said, as he leaned forward, steepling the tips of his fingers.

"Three days ago, on Wednesday evening, I was passing my husband's study on my way to the stairs, and I heard him speaking with another man. I could not make out what was being said, but my husband was definitely talking to someone whose voice I had never heard before. I thought this odd, as no visitor had called upon us, so I entered the dining room beside the study and kept watch at the window, waiting for the stranger to appear. I assumed he had entered the study through the French doors, since he hadn't rung at the front door. I was confirmed in this a few minutes later when a tall man, wearing a black overcoat and a broad-brimmed hat, emerged onto the patio. I had never seen him before, but he was about your height, with a full beard and a slight limp. I am sorry that I cannot tell you more, but it was too dark.

"After that meeting, my husband was a changed man. He did not come to bed that night or any succeeding night, for that matter. I couldn't get more than a few words out of him at a time, and once, when I looked in upon him in his study, he looked as though he had been weeping. The only excuse he would give was that he was concerned over a friend of his at the club, Sampson, I believe, who was gravely ill. This was all he offered, and most of the time, I could barely make eye-contact with him."

"I am sorry," said Holmes. "I have only one more question. Do you remember at what time you came across your husband's meeting with this stranger?"

"Yes, it was almost 9:30 when he left."

"Thank you, Lady Morris. I shall let you know as soon as I have any information."

"Thank you, Mr. Holmes and Dr. Watson," said Lady Morris, as she and her maid left the room. "Please let me know if I can provide you with anything further."

As soon as she departed, the butler entered the sitting-room. He was slim and in his fifties, with long and greying sideburns.

"Hello, Perkins. I am Mr. Sherlock Holmes and this is Dr. Watson. I have just a few questions for you."

"I shall try my best to answer them, sir," replied the butler.

"What were you doing when you heard the shot?"

"I was at the other end of the hall, making sure all of the candles and lamps had been extinguished when I heard it."

"You heard only one shot?"

"Yes, sir, and I hurried to the study as quickly as I could. I was sure the sound had come from there."

"At what time had Lord Morris come home that evening?"

"Around midnight, sir. He went directly to his study without saying a word."

"At what time did you hear the shot?"

"When I passed the grandfather clock in the hall, it was 12:45."

"When you entered the study, you found it just as it is now?"

"Yes, sir."

"You saw no intruder?"

"None, sir, but I was slow to act, on account of the shock. It took me a moment to walk over to the French doors."

"Perkins, why did you close the door behind you when you entered Lord Morris's study?"

"I didn't, Mr. Holmes. The wind blew it shut."

"Thank you, Perkins. That will be all for now."

Perkins opened the door for us, and our trio re-entered the hall. Holmes turned once more to Perkins and asked, "Would it be possible for you to call Dr. Watson and I a cab, please?"

However, Lady Morris immediately appeared at the banister and called down, "Nonsense, our driver shall convey you to your lodgings. Perkins, please get Boggis."

After thanking Lady Morris, Holmes, Inspector Nicholson, and I discussed the case outside, while waiting for the coach.

"What do you make of it, Holmes? Was Lord Morris shot with his own gun?"

"So it would appear, Watson. You will telegraph, Inspector, when you know for certain?"

"Of course."

"Holmes, why would the killer load a second round into the gun?" I asked.

"It is much too soon to speculate. Perhaps the killer didn't," said Holmes, with the faintest trace of a grin forming upon his face.

"Nonsense, who else would have done it?" shot back Nicholson. "It could be that the murderer was trying to make it appear as though a different gun had been used, in order to deflect suspicion from someone within the household. After all, only someone familiar with the house could have found the gun."

"There is a germ of a sound theory in that statement, Inspector. The gun and the room's appearance are definitely meant to deflect suspicion."

"I take it you are referring to the room's being rifled?" I asked.

"Yes, Watson. It is suggestive."

"How so, Holmes?" asked Nicholson.

"An intruder could have had but a minute in which to work, before Perkins entered."

"That affirms my theory that it was an inside job — the killer knew where to find the papers he wanted," Nicholson interjected.

"In any event," I ventured, "I think suspicion rests squarely upon this man in the broad-brimmed hat. Find him, and you'll find your killer."

"Yes, Watson. Once we have this stranger's identity, we shall have solved this case."

"Well Holmes, if you have no objections, after I consult with the coroner, I am going to start questioning some of the people in this address book."

"Very good, Nicholson. Watson and I will visit the Bagatelle Club. I shall contact you, if anything develops."

By this time, Boggis had arrived with the coach. Before Holmes gave him directions, he asked my friend if he was Mr. Sherlock Holmes. Once Holmes had affirmed this, Boggis began to draw closer and speak confidentially.

"Mr. Holmes, sir, there is something that has been troubling me about the master, but I'm not sure if it's something I should mention to the mistress."

"Go on, Boggis."

"You see, sir, I'm the one what always drives his lordship to the club, and sometimes, his lordship asks me to pick up some of his friends, as well. Lately, not Lord Morris, but a couple of these friends have been mentioning something peculiar — a 'Bagatelle Shakespeare Society'. But they always sound real smarmy when they say it, like lechers in a dancehall. Now I'm no better than any other bloke, but it seems to me that these two friends had some kind of corrupting influence on his lordship. Does any of this help you, Mr. Holmes?"

"Yes, Boggis. Tell me, had you ever driven Lord Morris and these friends to any destination other than the Bagatelle Club?"

"No, sir. Just heard 'em talk is all."

"Thank you, Boggis."

Holmes said hardly a word on our drive back to Baker Street. I knew better than to interrupt my friend during such spells of silence, for he would undoubtedly reveal all at the appropriate time. Our trip was, therefore, rather monotonous, except for a quick stop at the post office, so Holmes could send a telegram. When we finally arrived at 221 B, Holmes tipped Boggis most generously, and we ascended to our rooms, Holmes to await a response to his telegram and I to await the lunch which Mrs. Hudson was preparing.

After I had eaten, Holmes having elected to instead consume a heroic amount of shag for lunch, I sat down in my armchair and rested my legs upon an ottoman heaped with cushions, for the cold had been bothering my old wound terribly. It was just after I had finally gotten comfortable when two telegrams arrived for Holmes.

"Ah, the first one is from Inspector Nicholson, confirming that Lord Morris's derringer did, indeed, fire the fatal shot. The second is from the Earl of Maynooth."

"The father of Ronald Adair? Is he back in England?"

"He has been back for some time, Watson, and has agreed to meet with us, at the Bagatelle Club. Perhaps he will be able to shed some light upon the affairs of Lord Morris."

Once again, we hailed a four-wheeler and were soon on our way to Regent Street. It was still quite gloomy and cold, but at least the wind had finally died, making our trip somewhat more comfortable. As we approached our destination, I felt a wave of nostalgia as I gazed upon the white façade of the Criterion Bar, for it was there that I first heard mention of Holmes, an event which changed dramatically the trajectory of my life. There was little time for reminiscing, though, for we had soon reached our destination. Upon entering the club, a small, elderly man in the most neatly pressed suit I had ever seen began leading us past table upon table of cigar chewing nobility, all enjoying their games and their brandy.

"Once again, we are moving in high life, Watson," quipped Holmes with a sly smile.

We then arrived at a comfortable, oak-paneled alcove where sat an ample-framed, florid-faced gentleman whom I took to be the Earl of Maynooth.

"Hello, Mr. Holmes. And Dr. Watson, it is so good to finally meet you. Too bad about Lord Morris; terrible business that. I shall do what I can to help, but I must admit that I did not know the man terribly well. Please, take a seat," he said, indicating two sumptuous leather armchairs. After Holmes and I had accepted and lit the cigars our host offered to us, Holmes addressed the earl.

"I realise, sir, that you were not close to Lord Morris, but was it his custom to stay here until late in the evening?"

"Why Mr. Holmes, I, myself, no longer keep very late hours, so I could not positively answer your question."

"Lady Morris said her husband spent a great deal of his time here, but another source of mine intimated that he may have been here less frequently than she thought. Would you, by any chance, know anything about that?"

"Lord knows I have enough trouble keeping track of my own affairs and could not possibly be expected to keep tabs on a veritable stranger. I do know, however, that the lord and a few of his friends were rather fond of the ladies, Mr. Holmes."

"Yes, that is the very thing about which I need to know more."

"I am afraid I do not know much more than that. Besides, it is not fitting for a man of my position to engage in such cheap gossip."

"I understand, sir, but I am afraid that, to find out what happened to the late lord, I must press the issue. What was the Bagatelle Shakespeare Society?"

"Not so loud, man. And do not think for a moment that I would ever forget the service you and Dr. Watson performed for my family in risking both of your own lives to apprehend my son's murderer. I would not miss any opportunity to help you, but I must be discreet. Lord Morris and two of his friends, whose names I will provide to you should it become absolutely necessary, liked to prowl the theatres of the West End in search of conquests. The practice started when the lord met an actress at the Burbage Theatre by the name of Cecilia Benson. He was quite fond of her and went to see her regularly. She then introduced some of her friends to Lord Morris's companions. Since all of the men are married, they would usually come here first and then depart for the Burbage later in the evening."

"Thank you, sir. You have been a tremendous help. Tell me, before we go, how is Sampson getting on?"

"I am afraid I know of no one by that name. Is he a member?"

"Evidently not. Sorry, my mistake. Come, Watson. We must get to the
theatre before it opens for the evening. Hopefully, we will have time for a word with Miss Benson."

"*Mrs.* Benson, Mr. Holmes," the earl corrected. "Cecilia Benson is married, as well."

A short time later, Holmes and I, after another silent cab ride, found ourselves in the Strand before the Burbage Theatre.

According to the signs out front, Cecilia Benson was appearing as Volumnia in *Coriolanus*. We made our way through the large, richly carpeted lobby, the walls of which were lined with caryatides of gilded plaster, to the manager's office. At our knock, a small, rather high-strung man emerged, and we introduced ourselves.

"It is a pleasure meeting you, Mr. Holmes. To what do I owe the honour?"

"It is imperative that I speak to one of your actresses, a Mrs. Cecilia Benson."

"Indeed, I, too, would like to speak with her, for you see, she's been missing for the last four days."

"Holmes, that corresponds with the missing pages of the appointment book!" I said.

"You wouldn't happen to know who saw her last?" queried Holmes.

"Well, sir, that would probably be me. On Tuesday afternoon, I was gazing out of my window at a strange carriage I had noticed which was parked in front of the theatre. Within moments of my turning to look outside, I saw Cecilia walking towards the carriage with a man. They climbed inside, and off they went. I've been making do with her understudy, ever since."

"Could you describe the man who accompanied her?"

"I didn't get a good look at his face, but he was quite tall and walked with a pronounced limp."

"Was he wearing a broad-brimmed hat?"

"Why yes, Dr. Watson. He was."

"What was it about the carriage that struck you as odd?" Holmes resumed.

"It was the insignia upon the side — a cross, in front of which was something resembling a fluttering sheet of linen. Over this, were the initials 'St. V.'"

"Holmes, there was a man named St. Vincent listed in the appointment book!"

"Thank you, Watson. Sir, would it be possible to see Mrs. Benson's dressing room? It might help me to find her whereabouts."

"Certainly, Mr. Holmes. Follow me."

The dressing room was fairly small, its large dressing table taking up most of the space. Amongst the make-up and brushes littering this was a small notebook which Holmes immediately began to examine.

"Watson, there is a page missing."

Holmes then produced a charcoal stick from his pocket and began lightly rubbing the right-hand page which would have lain beneath the missing one. In this way, he was able to reveal the following faint message:

"My Darling,
     "I am to be admitted this afternoon. Please come."

Holmes then searched the rest of the tiny room but revealed nothing further.

Finally, we took our leave, Holmes promising to contact the theatre manager, if he found the missing actress. Before returning to Baker Street, Holmes dropped into a post office to send two telegrams. In the cab, on our way home, I could remain patient no longer.

"Homes, what can it all mean?"

"Surely, Watson, a man of your background should have no problem finding our fugitive actress's location."

"All I can make of it is that she is to gain admittance somewhere with someone who might possibly be named St. Vincent."

"Come now, Watson. The note says nothing of 'gaining admittance' but of being 'admitted'. Surely, that would suggest something to someone such as yourself."

"Well, in my profession, one is usually 'admitted' to a hospital."

"Precisely. Now, let's assume that 'St. V.' does not stand for the name of an individual."

"I'm sorry, Holmes, but I don't follow."

"The cross, the linen, 'St. V.' — surely that would indicate St. Veronica."

"St. Veronica's Hospital for Women! Of course."

"Yes, Watson. I have just sent a telegram to them, asking if Mrs. Benson is a patient and if we can pay a visit tomorrow morning."

"To whom did you send the second telegram?"

"To our good friend, Nicholson, apprising him of our progress."

It was already dark when we arrived back in Baker Street, and I was relieved when Holmes decided to join me for dinner. That night, I fell asleep to the melancholy strains of Holmes's violin and did not re-awake until some time after dawn. When I entered our sitting room, Mrs. Hudson was already setting our breakfast upon the table, and Holmes was reading the paper.

"Good morning, Watson. Have a seat. There should be ample time for breakfast before we resume our investigation."

"You certainly are in a good mood, Holmes."

"I have just heard from a Dr. Smythe at St. Veronica's. Mrs. Benson is, indeed, a patient there, and we are free to visit her at any time after eleven o'clock. I expect this meeting will go a long way in establishing a motive for our case."

"Does that mean you know who killed Lord Morris?"

"My dear Watson, I have known that since yesterday morning."

"But who?"

"All in good time. I must satisfy myself upon a few more points, before I can be absolutely certain of events. Would you like to have a look at today's paper? It contains an account of what we saw yesterday at Sherrinsthorpe."

After breakfast, we departed for the East End. It was there, in the City, that we found the rather ugly pile of a structure known as St. Veronica's Hospital for Women. It was, in reality, more of a mental asylum than a traditional hospital, and its sterile, white, arched corridors reverberated with the screams and moans of its imprisoned Bedlamites. Dr. Smythe, a rather shabby looking bald man with a flaming orange beard, was leading us through a throng of black and white uniformed nurses to the room of Cecilia Benson.

"Here we are, gentlemen, but I must warn you that my patient may not be of much help to you," he said as he swung open the room's heavy door.

Even with no make-up and dressed in a shabby white hospital gown, Cecilia Benson was a stunningly beautiful woman. Her flawless, milk-white skin was emphasized by her long, black hair, and her movements were still incredibly graceful, reflecting her several years upon the stage. Yet, when I looked at her eyes, I noticed a vacancy in their gaze, and I could also detect a slight slackness about the mouth.

"Oh, Smythe, you have brought me company, and a handsome pair they are," she said, touching Holmes' arm.

He did not attempt to hide his distaste and quickly brushed it away. "Mrs. Benson, I would like to ask you some questions about Lord Morris."

"He is dead and gone; at his head a grass green turf, at his heels a stone," she rambled.

"I take it, then, that you know what has happened. Do you have any idea why?"

"As if he had been loosed out of hell to speak of horrors, he comes before me," she said as she turned to me and placed her hand on my leg. Like Holmes, I deflected it but, admittedly, with a greater reluctance.

"Mrs. Benson," resumed Holmes, "can you tell me anything of your husband?"

"I was the more deceived," she said sadly. "There's fennel for you, and columbine; there's rue for you; and here's some for me."

"O, what a noble mind is here o'erthrown," said Holmes in frustration while turning to leave.

"You are a good chorus, my lord," replied Mrs. Benson, and as we left, she began to sing:

> *"For to see mad Tom of Bedlam*
> *"Ten thousand miles I traveled*
> *"Mad Maudlin goes on dirty toes*
> *"To save her shoes from gravel."*

Once outside the door, I made my diagnosis, "Dr. Smythe, it appears Mrs. Benson is suffering from syphilis."

"That is correct, Dr. Watson. She admitted herself on Tuesday and has very rapidly deteriorated."

"You say she admitted herself? There was no one with her?"

"No, Mr. Holmes. She mentioned that her physician had referred her to us but, upon questioning, could not seem to recall his name."

"Thank you for all of your help, Dr. Smythe."

While we were walking back to our cab, Holmes began to speak.

"Watson, we must have the name of that doctor."

"The one who gave the referral."

"Yes, if you could call it that. Would it be possible for you to find out the identity of Lord Morris's physician?"

"I imagine I could make a quick stop over at Bart's and see if any of my colleagues know anything."

"Excellent, Watson. We shall drop you off there, first. I have some business to attend to back in the West End. Remember, get as much information as possible, and meet me back in Baker Street, before supper."

As we agreed, late that afternoon, I returned triumphantly to Baker Street. Holmes was already seated in his armchair with his feet propped up on the fender before the fireplace.

"Good afternoon, Watson. How did you fare?"

"Holmes, Lord Morris's doctor's name is Edmund Samuels. He has offices in Wimpole Street and was in a riding accident two years ago, causing him to walk with a pronounced limp! Here is his address."

"Brilliant, Watson! You have outdone yourself!"

"It is just as you have said, Holmes: 'When a doctor does go wrong, he is the first of criminals. He has nerve and he has knowledge.' It now looks to me like this is all simply a failed attempt at blackmail. But Holmes, where are you going?"

"I have to send one more telegram, Watson. I expect developments. Go ahead and have supper without me. There is no need to wait on my account."

Indeed, Holmes ate nothing that night and shunned sleep, as well. The next morning, I perceived him dimly through a fog of tobacco smoke. He was smoking impatiently, obviously awaiting a reply to the telegram he had sent the previous evening. It arrived shortly after breakfast.

"Watson, I must leave to notify Nicholson and Lady Morris that we shall meet them at Sherrinsthorpe Manor this afternoon. It is at that time that I will clear up this matter for them. You will accompany me, I presume."

"I wouldn't miss it for the world. But really, Holmes, you must eat something."

My entreaty fell on deaf ears, however, and I was left to finish my breakfast in solitude. Later, that afternoon, Holmes, Inspector Nicholson, Lady Morris, Perkins, and I once again found ourselves in the sitting room of Sherrinsthorpe Manor, and everyone but Holmes took a seat.

"Mr. Holmes, am I to understand that you have, in fact, solved this case?" asked the inspector.

"There are but two points which I need to clarify. The first and most pressing of which is how you managed to procure the second derringer round so soon after discovering the body, Perkins."

The butler practically leaped out of his chair and exclaimed, "Surely, Mr. Holmes, you don't think I killed Lord Morris?"

"Nothing of the sort, Perkins, and please, resume your seat. Why don't I reconstruct the events of the evening, as I believe they occurred, and you can fill in the gaps for me when I have finished.

"After you heard the shot, it could have taken you no more than forty-five seconds to reach the room. This event could not have been totally unexpected by you, and you will also have to explain to me how you knew what had driven Lord Morris to suicide. It is obvious to me, however, that you did know, because you managed to rearrange the room so quickly, obscuring what had really happened. You entered the room and closed the door behind you, for if the wind had been strong enough to blow that door shut, it would have also created a larger mess within than what was there when we examined it. Somehow, you found a second round for the gun, and with that came your idea. You reloaded the weapon and replaced it, wiping the powder marks from the lord's hand. To minimize the chance of anyone's noticing the odour of the discharged weapon, you opened the French doors which also made it look as though an imaginary intruder had used them. From the appointment book, you quickly removed the pages which would have scandalized Lord Morris, and it was this which prompted you to create the illusion of the room's being rifled by the imaginary killer. After scattering a few papers from that cabinet, you reopened the door and waited for Lady Morris to appear, which would have been moments later. Am I correct so far?"

Perkins nodded in bewilderment, while Lady Morris sobbed.

"But, Perkins, why?" she cried.

"Madam, Perkins was acting out of a misguided sense of loyalty. However, I am afraid I must point out that Lord Morris's present behaviour deserved no such fidelity or respect. In truth, Lady Morris, he has used you horribly. Of late, Lord Morris had become romantically involved with an actress. Unfortunately, as I found out yesterday, she, too, had been the victim of a husband with a roving eye, and from him, she had contracted a *morbus venerius*. She, in turn, passed this disease on to your husband who, unable to cope with the shame, decided to take his own life."

"He's right, Lady Morris. I came upon the lord, weeping in his study on Thursday. He tried to compose himself and mentioned an ailing friend, but when I observed the doctor's bill upon his desk, he broke down and confessed everything to me. Essentially, he and I grew up together, and I suppose, at that moment, he had to confide in someone. It was also at that time that I noticed the derringer in a drawer of his desk. I had never seen it before, so naturally I thought the worst. Later that evening, I returned to the study and removed the bullet from the breech of the gun, putting it in a pocket of my frock-coat. I knew it wasn't my place to do so, but I hoped that if Lord Morris knew that I had figured out his intention, somehow, it might deter him. The following night, when I heard the shot, I knew immediately what had happened. As I walked down the hall, I reached into my pocket for a key to the study, in case it should have been necessary, and I found the bullet. The rest is as Mr. Holmes said, though I have no idea how he could have known it. Please, Lady Morris, you must understand that I was simply trying to protect Lord Morris."

"At great risk to the health of Lady Morris," chided Holmes.

"Holmes, how did you know it was a suicide?" asked the inspector.

"As Dr. Watson said, the posture of the body and the wound were all consistent with suicide. Why would a killer want to make a crime scene which looks exactly like a suicide look like that of a murder? Also, there was no sign of an intruder. As I said before, how could the butler come into the room within one minute of the shot's being fired and not have discovered the killer going through the appointment book or the cabinets? There really weren't terribly many papers lying about on the floor, but to a butler it would seem like this degree of dishevelment was consistent with a robbery of some sort. No, Nicholson, only the body seemed to be undisturbed. All else seemed rearranged, and there was only one person we knew of who would have had the opportunity to alter the room's appearance. Given all this, all I had to do was discover the reason for the suicide. This proved more time-consuming than I had anticipated."

"What about the man in the broad-brimmed hat?"

"That, Nicholson, was Lord Morris's physician, Dr. Edmund Samuels. According to this telegram I received today, he had come here on Wednesday to examine Lord Morris. He has promised to contact you, as well, Lady Morris, tomorrow."

"Well, I suppose I must now decide how to proceed in the matter."

"Inspector Nicholson, as you and several of your colleagues have already learned, your career can only benefit from working with me from time to time and by placing the utmost trust in my conclusions. However, just because *I*, who am in no way connected with the official police, have come to this particular conclusion does not mean that you, *Inspector*, are in any way officially obliged to accept or act upon it."

"Thank you, Mr. Holmes. I shall take that under consideration."

Privileging honour over self-advancement, Nicholson never did officially solve the murder of Lord Morris, a momentary setback in a career which would soon be redeemed by many successes. At that moment, however, Holmes and I were still unsure of the outcome. It was already growing dark as we made our way home, and outside our cab, a wind had begun to blow from the east, and the snow had finally begun to fall.

SHERLOCK HOLMES — STYMIED!

by Gary Lovisi

"I see you have been unable to resist the allure of the links once again," my friend Sherlock Holmes said to me one afternoon upon my visit to our old digs at 221B Baker Street. He was running his eyes over my attire with disdain, having obviously surmised that I had come over straight from playing a round of golf.

I nodded my acknowledgement. Since my marriage and the sometimes heavy workload at St. Barts I'd seen Holmes only sparingly during the last year, so these occasional visits were moments of great joy for me to see my old friend again and catch up on his cases. My only spare time of late had been taken up with my new guilty indulgence, that fascinating creation called golf.

"A most stimulating and enjoyable exercise," I told my friend.

"Hah!" Holmes huffed sarcastically, "a gross and unmitigated waste of time. Adult men chasing around a little ball in a game of simple and utter luck. I'm afraid *that* is not for me."

"It is a sport, Holmes, not merely a game," I countered, inexplicably upset by his words, feeling it was somehow my duty to defend the sport. "I have found it an enjoyable pursuit over the last few months and have been invited to play at some of the most prestigious courses in England and Scotland, including the very home of golf, the Royal and Ancient Golf Club at Saint Andrews. I have even become friends with Tom Morris himself, Old Tom Morris as he is called, a legend of the game. I tell you it is not a game of luck, it is fraught with hazards and challenges which require a high level of skill."

Holmes brushed all this aside with a casual wave of his hand. If it was not criminal in nature, nor fell within the narrow scope of his interests, he was rarely engaged.

"You know, Holmes," I told him allowing a hint of annoyance to enter my voice, "We are now four years into the 20th Century, a time for new beginnings and newer things — such as golfing. The game has lately set up strict rules of play affecting every contingency. I would think this is one aspect of it that you would find appealing and even approve of."

"Rubbish! You mentioned rules as in a sport, yet you yourself just called it a game. Checkers would be more stimulating."

"Oh, come now, Holmes!" I retorted peevishly.

"You yourself called it a game," he countered with a wry grin.

"That was merely a figure of speech."

Holmes looked at me shaking his head in mock despair, "Watson, poor, poor Watson, I am saddened to hear that you have succumbed to the frippery of such a game of chance. Far better it would be to spend your time and your meager funds on the roulette wheel. Better odds, eh?"

"I beg to disagree. I have found there is great skill involved in every aspect of golfing, from the opening drive down the fairway, to the chipping, and of course putting on the green. It can be most stimulating and challenging. You of all people should not be so quick to disparage a game — or dare I say sport — which you have never once tried yourself."

Sherlock Holmes looked thoughtful and then gave me a wry grin, "You have me there, old fellow. You may be correct. Perhaps some day we shall have a go at it."

"I would be most delighted to do so, Holmes. Perhaps when you are not so heavily engaged with cases?"

"Well, Watson, you have come at the perfect time. Cases have been few and far between lately. It seems the criminal classes have gone on holiday. Most disappointing."

I laughed at his dilemma. "Well, I am sure something of merit will turn up soon."

"Obviously it shall, but tell me more of this golfing mania you have contracted like a bad London cold. I see that there is something that evidently disturbs you about it."

I looked at Sherlock Holmes closely. The man was remarkable. So far I had been quite careful, through neither word nor gesture, to let on to him the true nature of my visit. "You are as perceptive as ever. How did you guess?"

"Guess! Did you say 'guess'?"

"I meant … What I meant to say …" I fumbled quickly.

"Never mind, old boy," Holmes smiled indulgently at my discomfort. "Put it down to my knowledge of your person through our long association. I can see there is something bothering you, and yet you are loathe to bring it up, but it picks at you nevertheless. It is about this game of yours, is it not?"

I sighed, "Yes, Holmes, it is a most depressing problem, but surely it does not rise to the level where your magnificent talents need to be employed."

"Why not let me be the judge of that? As I told you, interesting cases are scant right now so if you have something of merit I should be happy to hear the details."

I nodded with relief that my friend was concerned, collected my thoughts and then began my narrative as I sat down in my old chair across from his own. "You are correct that it has to do with golfing. I have already mentioned that I have made the acquaintance of Old Tom Morris. He is a most decent and gentlemanly fellow. These days he is the greenskeeper at the R&A, the Royal and Ancient Golf Club at Saint Andrews, in Scotland."

"Yes, where they play the British Open. I believe Old Morris even won the championship four times in the '60s?" Holmes stated.

"Why, yes," I smiled. "So you know something of the game?"

"A niggling bit here and there. I heard about the fellow primarily through the mystery that befell his son, Young Tom Morris."

"Young Tom?" I asked casually, but curious. "I had not heard."

"A most tragic affair, Watson. Old Tom's son, Tommy — these days known as Young Tom — was a golfing prodigy. He was a legend in his own time who followed his father into golfing history by winning four British Opens. He was young, barely 24 years of age when his wife and child died in childbirth. Young Tom died three months later on Christmas Day in 1875 of unknown causes. It was all quite mysterious, but most people at the time blamed it on a broken heart."

"A sad tale," I said softly.

"Sadder still was the loving father's reply when asked if such a death could be possible."

"What did he say, Holmes?"

"It is said Old Tom replied that if it were possible for a person to die from a broken heart, then he would surely have died himself at the time."

I sighed. "That is sad. I had no idea."

"Old Tom has outlived his son by a quarter of a century. By all accounts he is a man of unique and outstanding character and talents. I should very much like to meet him some day." Holmes stated, then he looked directly at me and asked, "So now, Watson, tell me what you came here for."

"Well, Holmes, the Open will be concluded tomorrow evening with the presentation of the Championship Cup to the winner — it is a large silver trophy more commonly known as the Claret Jug. The problem is, the Claret Jug has turned up missing."

"Is this jug valuable?" Holmes asked with more interest now.

"Yes, sterling silver, worth a considerable sum — but it is priceless to the club."

Sherlock Holmes nodded, looked at me from his seat and said calmly, "Tell me, has anyone at the club turned up missing?"

I looked at Holmes, shrugged, "No, not that I know of. However Old Tom mentioned to me that one of his boys, a caddy, has gone sick and not reported to work for the last two days. Old Tom says it is most unlike the lad not to be available for any match, much less a championship."

"And is this boy interested in the game?"

"Well, I assume so, most of the caddies are enthusiastic about golfing. Old Tom told me this boy is well-mannered, but rather more fanatical than most about the game."

"I see," Holmes said thoughtfully. Finally he looked up at me with an inexplicable smile upon his face. "Well, Watson, you must know there is little I can do about this here in London."

"I understand, Holmes," I replied softly, apparently defeated, but grateful he had at least listened to my story. "It's just that Old Tom is very upset over the loss of the trophy. It will be a disaster for the Open, for the club, and for the game of golf itself."

Holmes suddenly stood up from his seat and looked at me sharply, "Well then, there is nothing else to do but set off for Scotland at once and remedy this situation. Come, Watson, the game — of golf this time — is afoot!"

Due to the efficiencies of the British railway system, Holmes and I reached Saint Andrews in no less than eight hours and once at the club I introduced the great detective to Morris. Old Tom had also been a winner of the British Open no less than four times, but these days he was a famous ballmaker, clubmaker and course designer. For many years he had been the head greenskeeper at Saint Andrews.

Old Tom Morris certainly looked every one of his eighty-three years of age, sporting a long, flowing white beard that rested on the center of his broad chest. He was dressed in golfing attire, a sporting jacket and plaid cap on his grey head. His left hand often rested in his trouser pocket where he kept an ever-present pipe and he used an upside-down hickory-shafted mashie niblick as a cane. While he never seemed to smile, his piercing blue eyes exuded intense energy and gentle kindness.

I introduced the golfing legend to the detective legend.

"Ach, as I live and breathe, can it be none other than Mr. Sherlock Holmes come hither to Scotland to visit our lovely club?" Morris asked with a thick Scottish brogue and a joyful face that lit up with mirth. He proved a most hearty and cheerful fellow. While it appeared he never cracked a smile and was the epitome of the dour Scot, Old Tom was truly a kind and warm-hearted man. His eyes fairly twinkled as he spoke. "I am so honoured to meet you, sir, and I welcome you to Saint Andrews. I assume Doctor Watson has told you about our little problem?"

"Yes, he has, that is why I am here, Mr. Morris."

"Well, I thank you, but please, just call me Old Tom, good sir."

Holmes allowed a warm smile, "Well, Old Tom, you have a missing trophy and I hear the presentation is later this evening?"

"Aye, the championship is just finishing up and we find ourselves in dire difficulty," Old Tom said sadly. "The Claret Jug, as it is called, has permanently resided at the R&A, as we call the Royal and Ancient Golf Club at Saint Andrews, since 1873. The trophy is presented to the winner of the British Open each year. The winner gets to keep it for a year before returning it to the R&A, thence to be passed on to the next champion. It has lately been returned to the club by last year's winner. Now the trophy has gone missing. I fear it may even have been stolen."

"The good doctor has told me that one of your boys has gone ill and not turned up for work."

"Why yes, that is true. Young Daniel Roberts, a caddy, a good boy."

"And where may we find young Mr. Roberts?" Holmes asked.

"In the village. He lives with his mum over her dressmaker shop."

Holmes nodded, "Then let us repair there immediately, for we have no time to lose."

When we reached the home of the boy we found young Daniel Roberts upstairs in his room in bed with an apparent and dire illness of unknown origin. With the consent of his mother and under Holmes's instructions, I quickly attended to the boy, giving him a thorough medical examination. Finally I walked outside the room to confer privately with my friend.

"Well, Doctor, what is your diagnosis?" Holmes asked me.

"There's nothing physically wrong with the boy at all. But he is terrified of something that he is desperately trying to hide. His heart is pounding fearfully from it."

Holmes just nodded, then walked back into the room with me. There we saw Old Tom and Mrs. Roberts looking sadly upon the boy laying so sickly in the bed. The boy saw us enter and coughed lightly.

Holmes grew grimly serious, "This will not do, Daniel. Doctor Watson has given you a full examination. There is nothing wrong with you. I know you are feigning illness. Time is wasting. You must tell me what you did with the Saint Andrews trophy."

The boy's face fell into despair, he was trapped and looked over to his mother.

"Daniel Roberts, now you tell these men the truth!" the boy's mother commanded.

Daniel looked shocked, fearful with despair, but he did not reply.

"I know you stole the trophy, young man," Holmes declared. "The game is up, so you might as well make a clean breast of it now."

"Come on, lad, 'tis time to speak up," Old Tom prompted, looking dour and disappointed that one of his boys had actually stolen the famed trophy.

The boy began to cry.

"Come now, Danny," Old Tom added gently, "tell me what happened. Why did you steal the trophy? Who did you sell it to?"

"Oh no, that's not the way it was at all, Mr. Tom," the boy blurted through tears. "I took it when the previous winner retuned it to the club a few days ago. I just wanted to see me name on that trophy like all the great golfers of years before, because one day me name could be etched there, too. So I used some ink to write me name there, right below Young Mr. Tom's last win from '72, I did."

"Danny Roberts, you didn't!" his mother shouted angrily.

Holmes motioned her to silence, "Go on, Danny. Where is the trophy now? Did you sell it?"

"Sell it? Of course not, sir! I would never think of such a thing," the boy stammered, obviously upset at the very thought.

"Then what did you do with it?" Old Tom prompted.

Danny looked grim, wide eyes pleading with Old Tom, "I'm so sorry. I was scared, sir. I know I did wrong by putting me name there and was trying to remove it, but it just would not come off. I was terrified! Then I got the idea to take the trophy down to the stream to use the water to wash off the ink. To my relief my name came off, but then I dropped the trophy down into the stream. It went in deep."

"So why didn't you dive in after it?" I asked the boy.

Danny looked up sheepishly, "I can not swim."

"I see," Holmes said, hiding a wry grin.

Danny went on to explain, "I was fearful of disappointing Mr. Tom. He been so good to me and all. He always told me how golf teaches responsibility and good sportsmanship, then I failed him. So I pretended to be ill so I would not have to face him. I am sorry, Mr. Tom."

Old Tom smiled gently, "Think no more of it, lad."

"Will I be going off to prison?" the boy asked nervously.

Old Tom laughed with gentle warmth, "Of course not, Danny."

"So where's the trophy now?" Holmes asked.

"Why, still at the bottom of the stream, where I left it," Danny replied.

Holmes nodded, "Very well then. Now Danny, get yourself out of that bed and let us go and fetch it immediately."

It was early the next morning when Sherlock Holmes and I played our first round of golf. The problem of the day before had been solved satisfactorily; the trophy had been retrieved and then presented in time to the championship winner with nary a hitch. Young Danny had been suitably chastised by Old Tom but was allowed to keep his position as a caddy at the club. Once again all was right and well at the R&A.

Still and all that next day offered us a lovely, brisk, Scottish morning, perfect for a round of golf at the Royal and Ancient Saint Andrews. Old Tom had made a gift of a favorable tee time to Holmes and I, in gratitude for our deed. So my companion reluctantly agreed to play a round. We decided to play a singles match, just him and me, stroke play. Old Tom and Danny even volunteered to act as our caddies, each giving us much needed and helpful instruction and information before we began play.

The course at the R&A was sandy in nature, with small hills that played havoc with even the most well-struck drive, frequently knocking the ball devilishly off-line and into an insidiously placed pot bunker that only the most diabolically warped mind could have created. It was a challenging course to play.

The first hole, known as the "Burn" hole, was a par four. With a good deal of luck, Holmes and I both bogied it with five. We were lucky to shoot only one stroke over par. I did better on the second hole actually making par, while Holmes did better than I on the third. By the fourth hole I began to realize that Holmes seemed to know a lot more about playing golf than he'd ever let on to me. We played a few more holes and we did well enough, mostly through the good advice of our caddies, both of us going over par, of course, but not terribly so.

"Where did you learn to play so well?" I finally asked Holmes, astounded by his quality of play. I was no master of the game, nor was he, but I was surprised by the rapidity with which he had picked up the essentials.

Holmes only smiled, adjusted his deerstalker cap, and replied, "On the train to Saint Andrews, of course. While you slept the hours away, I studied up on the game, reading the golfing books in your pack. I found Horace E. Hutchinson's volume most useful, while *The Art of Golf* by Simpson was highly informative. Did you know it even includes photographic plates of our friend Old Tom demonstrating the value of the swing? His advice is priceless. You may be correct in stating that once you understand this game it opens up a true appreciation of it."

"Posh, Holmes! Golf from books!" I snorted derisively, but I could not help but laud his improved attitude. "Okay, then, we'll see where this leads, we're off to the Tenth. So far we are even, so let's see what you can do on the back nine."

We moved on to the Tenth hole and played through. I went ahead by a stroke, but by the next hole Holmes had drawn even with me. He went ahead on the Thirteenth, but I caught up to him by the Fifteenth. At this point it was anyone's game. Holmes played with grim determination, scowling at bad shots but seemingly elated when he made a good one — in that way he proved no different from any other golfer.

It was on the approach to the last hole that Old Tom announced, "Gentlemen, the Eighteenth Hole. It is a par 4, at 360 yards in length, and you both be even up to this point."

"A close contest, Watson," Holmes said ruefully. "You are quite right, this pursuit can be most challenging. I think I shall win this hole and then put to bed once and for all your obsessive dreams concerning this game."

"I shall give you a good fight, Holmes," I warned.

Sherlock Holmes smiled. "I would expect nothing less, old man."

It had taken us each two strokes to get onto the green of the Eighteenth. Holmes had a difficult 20 foot putt to make the hole. My putt was shorter, being almost 12 feet in distance. Being farthest from the hole, Holmes played first.

Holmes's putt went straight and true right towards the hole. It looked like it just might go in. My face grew grim with the bitter taste of impending doom. Surely his ball was heading straight for the hole and would fall in right away. I looked over at my friend and he appeared elated. Then I saw his ball suddenly stop dead, less than a foot from the cup. Holmes stared at the ball in utter shock and disbelief as if willing it to move on its own accord and go into the cup. But it did not.

Now it was my turn. A grim smile came to my face as I prepared for my putt. Danny, acting as my caddy took out one of his favorite hickory-shafted putting cleeks and handed it to me. "Here, Doctor, try this one. You have a level shot, play it straight and it should go true."

I nodded, my face serious with the competitive spirit as I got into position and made my putt. It was a less forceful stroke than my opponent's. I intended a simple and straight stroke, but my ball immediately veered off, curving in a wide arc. I shook my head with dark trepidation and took a deep breath. I saw that Holmes held his breath also.

All four of us watched intently as my ball rolled in a wide arc, slowly moving closer and closer to the cup with what appeared to be the sureness of inevitability. I let out a tense breath. It looked like I just might make the hole. Then the ball suddenly encountered a rough patch on the green and by some devilish action hooked in front of Holmes's ball and rolled to a dead stop. I tried to figure out what had just happened. My ball now lay between Holmes's ball and the cup by barely over six inches — effectively blocking him from the cup.

"That's the way, Doctor!" Danny, shouted with glee.

Old Tom Morris just laughed with uproarious mirth, "Aye, well played, Doctor Watson, it appears you've stymied Mr. Holmes quite nicely!"

"Stymied?" Holmes blurted. He was obviously not aware of this particular rule.

I was surprised myself by the turn of events but quickly realized it could be a potential game changer for me.

Old Tom explained, "Watson's ball blocks your own from the cup, Mr. Holmes. It's an old and valued rule of golf, called the Stymie. In golf you must hit your ball true to the hole. Hence, when another ball blocks your own, you are stymied. It's your play, Mr. Holmes."

"How can it be played, if Watson's ball blocks mine?" Holmes asked.

"Indeed," Old Tom said most sympathetically, "the balls be just over six inches apart — so Watson's ball canna' be lifted as per the rules. Your only option is to concede the hole, or negotiate the stymie. When a player be stymied he obviously can not putt straight for the hole, but if he strikes his ball so as to miss his opponent's ball and yet go into the hole, he is said to negotiate the stymie. Well, Mr. Holmes?"

The Great Detective carefully regarded his options. They were woefully limited. "You have placed me in quite the pickle, Watson. I shall not concede the hole to you, so you leave me no alternative but to attempt, as Old Tom says, to negotiate this … stymie."

"Bravo, Mr. Holmes!" Old Tom enthused warmly at my friend's obvious pluck. "Here now, use this Jigger, it will give you the loft you need to play your ball."

Holmes took the hickory-shafted Jigger and prepared to make his play. He took his time and hit the ball with a sudden and sharp lifting motion that lofted his ball into the air. I was shocked to see his ball ride over my own — a bare two inches in height and straight towards the hole. Then his ball kicked right *into* the hole — *and bounced right back out!*

Holmes's ball slowly rolled away to rest a few inches from the cup.

It was heartbreaking. Danny grimaced while Old Tom shook his head good-naturedly at the mystical vagaries of the game. I stood there amazed by what I had just seen. Holmes for his part said not one word, his face had become a solid mask of stone. I decided it was not the right time for me to make any comment about what had happened.

It was my turn now. I took my time. With the utmost care I took my putt, lightly tapping my ball so it fell squarely into the cup with a soft plop. I sighed with relief and looked over at my friend.

Sherlock Holmes seemed to hardly believe what had happened. A moment later he mechanically tapped his ball into the hole, officially ending the game, and then he walked away in a rather sullen funk.

I had beat Holmes by one stroke, but my victory was bittersweet.

I thought I could hear my friend murmuring to himself as he walked off the green, something about how he had been right all along, that golf was a stupid game, a horrendous waste of time, and based solely upon luck rather than any true skill.

"You know, Watson, some day that damnable stymie rule will have to go," he commented to me sharply as the four of us walked off towards the clubhouse.

Old Tom Morris cut in before I could reply, "Never, Mr. Holmes! Not while I live! Aye, golfing tradition, it surely be. One of the most sacred rules of the game."

"Hah!" Holmes snorted derisively, dismissing the entire affair. Then he looked at me and suddenly smiled with renewed good humour. "Well played, Watson. I must say, well played, indeed."

"Why thank you, Holmes, that is very gracious of you. It was a close contest. I am sure you will do better on our next outing," I said in an upbeat tone, trying to offer him some measure of support, but I knew the truth. I knew my friend. This was the first and *last* game of golf I or anyone else would ever play with Sherlock Holmes.

I shook my head in consternation as Holmes and I accompanied Old Tom towards his clubmaking shop off the 18th green. We had sent young Danny off, and now the three of us sat down enjoying a few pints, sharing stories about golf and life, and never once did we ever mention the stymie again.

✗

HISTORICAL NOTE

Much of the background of this story is based on historical facts that deal with the Royal and Ancient Golf Club at Saint Andrews, in Scotland, the British Open trophy, better know as the Claret Jug, and the lives of Young Tom and Old Tom Morris. I also want to thank the real Dan Roberts, as well as the Gerritsen Beach Golf Museum Library for their assistance. The Stymie rule was finally taken out of golf in 1952. Before then, players could not lift their ball, but after 1952 they would use a marker on the green and then lift their ball so as not to obstruct an opponent's ball. There are many who wish the Stymie was still in effect.

THE GIANT RAT OF SUMATRA[17]

by "Paula Volsky"

ASCRIBED TO H. P. LOVECRAFT

The chill March fog shrouded London, choking the labyrinth of ancient streets, smothering forgotten courts and squares, lending solid masonry an aspect of vaporous insubstantiality. Baker Street was wreathed in detestable yellow haze, through which the gaslights glowed faintly, like the malignant Cyclopean eyes of moribund nightmares. The scene fille me with a cold, nameless apprehension, amounting to horror; a fleeting sense, perhaps, of frightful cosmic vastness pressing its gigantic weight upon the feeble protective barriers of human understanding. Man's vision, scarcely encompassing the tiny sphere of his own existence, serves to shield rather than inform, and that is as it should be, as it *must* be. For a single clear glimpse of ghastly reality would doubtless shake complacent human sanity to its very foundation.

My spirits hardly improved as I approached 221B, for I dreaded what I should find there. The recent, successful resolution of the problem involving the archbishop's indiscretion had deprived Sherlock Holmes of that intellectual stimulation so essential to his well-being. For some days past, my friend had lain silent and apathetic, sunk in the deepest of black depressions, scarcely stirring from the sofa. He had not, so far as I knew, resorted to the solace of the hypodermic syringe and cocaine bottle, and I could only pray for his continuing abstinence, for it grieves me beyond measure to witness the deliberate degradation of the marvelous mental faculties with which Nature has endowed him.

---

17   Editor's Note: In my anthology, *The Resurrected Holmes*, a considerable number of Dr. Watson's original case notes were reported to have been found by a famous Philadelphia book collector. Because the notes had never been written up by the Good Doctor, the collector paid various famous scribes to ghost-write these long untold cases. Below is one of the best-known of these stories. For legal purposes, the author's name rendered in quotation marks stands in for the ascribed actual (?) writer. —MK

I let myself into our rooms, and a chemical reek at once assailed my nostrils. The sofa was unoccupied. Sherlock Holmes sat at the deal-topped table, its surface cluttered with motley paraphernalia. I could not guess at the nature of his experimentation, but saw at a glance that his countenance had regained its characteristic keenness of expression. He greeted my entrance with a carelessly affable wave of the hand, then turned his full attention once again upon the flasks and retorts before him. Delighted though I was by my friend's return to his own version of normality, I did not venture to question him at such a time, for he would not have relished the distraction. Repairing to the tenantless sofa, I soon lost myself in frowning cogitation. I do not know how long I sat there, before the sound of Holmes's voice roused me from my brown study.

"Come, Watson, twenty-five guineas is not an impossible sum."

I turned to stare at him, for twenty-five guineas was indeed the figure upon which my thoughts anchored.

"The price is not unreasonable, in view of the rarity of the work, and the potential value of the contents." Holmes spoke with his customary detachment, yet could not perfectly conceal his gratification at my look of transparent astonishment. Though he fancies himself pure intellect, a flawlessly balanced calculating machine devoid of emotion, my friend is by no means free of human vanity.

"To what work do you allude?" I inquired, in the vain hope of confounding him.

"To Ludvig Prinn's hellish masterpiece, *De Vermis Mysteriis*," he replied, without hesitation. "You have striven long and hard to beat down Charnwood's price, but the old man holds to twenty-five guineas."

My astonishment increased. "Really, Holmes, in a more credulous age, these displays of apparent clairvoyance might have brought you to the stake."

"Nonsense, my dear doctor. A very simple matter of observation. When you entered, several minutes ago, you were carrying a parcel, whose size and shape proclaimed the recent purchase of a book. The fresh mud upon your shoes, and the moisture clinging to your overcoat revealed that you had walked home. Two bookstores stand within walking distance of our lodgings, and of those two, only Charnwood's, in Marylebone Road, remains open at this hour. The shop specializes in antique literary rarities. It was not long ago, Watson, that you voiced your theory that certain ancient works of occultism, rich repositories of forgotten or forbidden lore, hold formulae of potent restoratives unknown to modern medicine. Amongst the bizarre obscenities polluting the pages of Abdul Alhazred's *Necronomicon,* the Comte d'Erlette's infamous *Cultes des Goules, or* the abominable *Liber Ivonis,* may lie a remedy for the brain-fever, or so you postulate. Alhazred knows no remedy, however, for your incurable optimism."

"There is reason to believe —" I commenced, somewhat nettled.

"I am prepared to concede an improbable possibility," he cut me off imperturbably, and resumed his interrupted analysis. "Of the works I have mentioned, two of them — the *Necronomicon,* and *Liber Ivonis* — are virtually unobtainable. *Cultes des Goules,* in the unlikely event of its availability, would surely prove prohibitive in cost. Thus I conclude *De Vermis Mysteriis* to be the work in question."

"Quite right, but that does not explain —"

"You have failed to secure the prize, however," Holmes continued, with an air of apathy. "Your scowl, your preoccupation, your general aspect of dissatisfaction suggest an unsuccessful attempt to content yourself with a lesser acquisition. Twice within the last quarter hour, you have removed your wallet from your pocket, weighed it in your hand, sighed deeply, and put it away again. Clearly, the root of your indecision is financial. You have, upon occasion, paid as much as twenty guineas for works you deem professionally useful — but never more. The cost of Prinn's grotesquerie must exceed twenty guineas, but not by much, else you would instantly have dismissed all thought of purchase. Charnwood habitually prices his first editions in multiples of five guineas. It is more than probable that the volume in question is offered at twenty-five."

"Correct, in every particular," I confessed. "Bravo, Holmes. As always, when you explain your reasoning, it all seems very clear, very obvious."

"Tiresomely so. I should fear complete stagnation, were no better mental exercise available. Fortunately, a matter of potentially greater interest has presented itself." From the welter atop the table, he plucked a sheet of paper. "This note arrived some hours ago. What do you make of it, Watson?"

Here, I suspected, was the cause of my friend's abrupt recovery of spirits.

Accepting the paper, I read:

> Dear Mr. Holmes,
>
> I am anxious to consult you upon a matter of gravest urgency. It is not an exaggeration to observe that innocent lives will be lost if the missing party is not soon located. My own efforts in that regard have failed, my actions have been noted, and I fear that time is running short. The luster of your fame is such that I must place my trust in your abilities. Therefore, I shall call at half-past seven this evening, in the hope that you will favor me with a reception.
>
> Sincerely yours,
> A. B.

"Singular." I returned the note to its owner.

"Quite. But what does it reveal to you?"

"Very little," I confessed. "The writer, be it man or woman, communicates considerable agitation —"

"Make no mistake, it is a man," Holmes assured me.

"How do you know?"

"Notice the decisive quality of the downstrokes, the vigour of the characters, the authority of the punctuation. A man's hand, unmistakably."

"Of some education —" I essayed.

"Excellent, Watson. At times I almost suspect you less barren of deductive power than you so often contrive to appear. Now, justify my faith. Where was he educated?"

"I cannot begin to guess," I replied, mystified.

"Good. One should never guess, it is an atrocious habit. Note the spelling. 'Luster.' And worse, 'favor.' Note the tone of extravagant, uncurbed emotion. The correspondent is clearly an American. Despite the orthographic crudities, his literacy marks him as a denizen of the comparatively civilized eastern coastal region of that nation."

"We shall see soon enough. It is half past seven."

There was a knock at our door, and our landlady entered. "A lady to see you, sir," she informed my companion. I repressed a smile.

"Show her in." Sherlock Holmes displayed no sign of discomfiture.

Mrs. Hudson withdrew. Moments later, a woman walked into the room.

"A. B." was unusually tall, lanky and large-boned, her height evident despite a curiously stoop-shouldered posture. Her garb was darkly simple, her shoes nondescript, her gloved hands empty. Of her features, little could be discerned. A wide hat draped in heavy veiling completely obscured her face and hair. I thought her age to be around forty years, but that was an estimate based largely upon instinct, as there was little visible evidence by which to judge.

Seating herself in the chair that Holmes placed, she spoke in a low, slightly hoarse tone, unrevealing as her costume. "It is good of you, Mr. Holmes, to receive me upon such short notice, and at such an hour. I am sensible of the courtesy."

"Your note piqued my interest," Holmes returned briskly. "As you have been at pains to stress the urgent nature of the situation, I would advise you to state your name and case without delay." His visitor's veiled face turned to me for an instant, and he added, "You may speak freely before Dr. Watson."

"It is better for all concerned," A. B. returned, "if I keep my name to myself. That is for your own protection as well as mine. Briefly, the facts are these. I am an associate of Professor Sefton Talliard, chairman of the Department of Anthropology at Brown University, in Providence, Rhode Island. Professor Talliard has been missing for some months. His enemies are diabolical, his life is greatly endangered, and it is certain that he had no choice but to flee the United States. There is reason to believe that he has hidden himself in London. It is imperative that I locate this man, as I possess certain intelligence that may preserve his life, and the lives of his surviving colleagues. I am a stranger to this city, however, and ill-equipped to conduct a search. Mr. Holmes, the matter is vital. Will you lend your assistance?"

"By no means," Holmes replied, to my surprise, for I had expected the peculiarity of the entire affair to excite his curiosity.

"I entreat you —"

"Do not trouble yourself. It is useless to suppose me willing to accept a client disinclined to disclose the true facts of his case. In any event, what confidence might you reasonably place in the powers of a consulting detective hoodwinked by so amateurish a charade?"

My friend's acerbic observation quite bewildered me, but the visitor appeared prey to no such confusion.

"I am justly rebuked. Mr. Holmes, pray accept my apologies for an attempted deception motivated less by inclination than apprehension." So saying, A. B. doffed wide hat, veiling, and wig, to reveal a man's face; angular, long of jaw and tall of brow, dominated by a pair of great, feverishly brilliant eyes. There was about that face, with its pallour and its monklike asceticism, a suggestion of ancient lineage, inbred and distilled to the very essence of neurasthenia. When he spoke again, his voice was undisguised, its masculine character and American accent evident. "Nothing I have related has been false, yet I have hardly dared divulge all. Now I will tell you the truth, and I will hold nothing back. Be warned, however — the tale is lurid in nature, and may at times strain your credulity."

Holmes inclined his head, an expression of extraordinary concentration transforming his hawklike features.

"My name," commenced the visitor, "is August Belknap. I am — I was — a professor of anthropology at Brown University. Last year, a small group of my colleagues — five of us, including Professor Talliard — elected to devote our long summer vacation to study and research in some foreign clime. Though the academic specialties of its members varied, a common interest in the religious observances of divers primitive peoples united our group. Material worthy of attention might have been found in countless remote locales. However, we were unanimous in our conviction that certain prehistoric mysteries of extraordinary character persisted yet upon the island of Sumatra.

"Our vacation coincided with the dry season in the East Indies," Belknap continued. "We arrived in June to discover what seemed at first a nearly unspoiled tropical fairyland, where the equatorial forests rise almost at the water's edge, bamboo grows in dense thickets, huge ferns and brilliant flowers flaunt their luxuriance everywhere. Understand that this was a first impression. Presently, the overpowering profusion of vegetation, the steaminess of the perfumed atmosphere, the unremitting intensity of light and shade — the extremity in all things — began to wax oppressive, even repellent. But this sense did not develop at once.

"Our time was limited. Having established ourselves in an airy thatched house on piles that we were obliged to purchase outright from the owner, (for the natives possessed no concept of rental) we set to work.

"Our initial efforts met with little success. The lowland islanders, of the short, brown-skinned Malay stock, were peaceable and accommodating enough, voicing no objection to the foreign presence in their midst. Their habits were frugal, their lives industrious, their practices modest and agreeable enough, if unexceptional. Most of them were Mohammedans, and as such, unlikely to furnish the sort of anthropological arcana we had travelled so far to find.

"It was not long, however, before information of a more promising nature reached our ears. The pacific lowland farmers took a certain childlike delight in relating gruesome tales of the Dyaks, or hill Malays, who reputedly practiced magic, believed in ghosts, and preserved the heads of their enemies. Initially, I dismissed these accounts as fantastic exaggerations or fabrications, designed to awe gullible strangers. Sefton Talliard, however — whose knowledge of these people and their customs greatly exceeded my own — assured me otherwise. A number of the Dyak tribes, he maintained, cherished the belief that preservation of an enemy's head enslaved the spirit of the dead man. The Dutch authorities have prohibited headhunting, yet the practice continues, and, to this day, the magic tribal ceremonies often witness ritual decapitations.

"None of our party, I fancy, harboured any great desire to witness a beheading, yet all of us burned to behold the secret rites that our hosts described. The desire sharpened when we learned of a certain peculiarly degenerate tribe, some of whose members reputedly possessed blue eyes, legacy of European forebears. These mongrelized Dyaks, whose tribal title translates as 'the Faithful,' were little more than savages, inhabiting caves in the upland forests, subsisting solely upon the game they hunted, the edibles their women gathered, and anything they could steal. Held in extreme terror and loathing by all neighboring tribes, by reason of their rapacity, their magical prowess, and their unbridled ferocity, the Faithful were said to worship the ghastly deity known as Ur-Allazoth, the Relentless, a demon-lord of bestial aspect and limitless appetite.

"I shall not weary you, Mr. Holmes, with an account of our investigative efforts. Suffice it to say, in the end we managed to engage the services of a Dyak guide, who, tempted by the prospect of munificent reward, undertook to lead us through the forests to the very site of the Faithful mysteries. This task he performed in greatest secrecy, upon a clear but moonless night — the dark of the moon coinciding, as it happened, with a tribal ceremony of considerable moment. Neither blandishments nor threats, however, induced our guide to conduct us beyond a point some quarter-mile distant from our goal, and thus we were obliged to cover the last several hundred yards of the trek unassisted. This furtive feat proved relatively undemanding, for the crimson glow of the ceremonial bonfires, and the swelling murmur of native voices drew us infallibly to our destination.

"Presently, the sound of music reached us — a thin, uncanny shrilling of daemonic flutes — notes so indefinably alien, so inexpressibly obscene, that my soul shrinks at the recollection. Then and there, in the red-litten forests of Sumatra, my heart misgave me, and I paused, trembling in every limb. Similarly hesitant and shaken was the young assistant professor, Zebulon Loftus. Such effeminacy awoke the ire of our leader, a man of assured and dauntlessly ambitious character. Talliard's silent communications were eloquent, and presently, Loftus and I resumed progress.

"Minutes later, we reached the edge of a great clearing, and there we halted, cloaking our presence in the blackest of tropical shadows.

"How shall I describe the scene that we witnessed there, in that place?" Belknap's hand tightened almost convulsively upon the dark plush of his pelisse. "Words may perhaps convey some inkling of the material reality, but never capture the sense of pervasive evil, the intimation of nameless horror informing the sultry atmosphere, the overpowering pressure of invisible, incalculably vast malignity impinging upon our fragile sphere. I will therefore confine myself to an unadorned statement of the facts."

Holmes nodded gravely.

"The clearing before us," the visitor continued, "was roughly circular in shape, its circumference edged with a pale of bamboo stakes, each stake topped with a human head, each head wreathed in clouds of long, black hair, that stirred and drifted with every passing breeze. The facial features, frozen in expressions of the ghastliest terror, were perfectly preserved. The jumping, flickering firelight lent those distorted visages a lifelike aspect dreadful to behold, and a host of staring eyes seemed almost to follow the leaping gyrations of the Faithful assembled there. Some several score had gathered, and it was obvious at a glance that we confronted a debased mongrel people, combining the worst attributes of the Malay and Negrito races, rendered all the more repugnant by the clear evidence of an unspeakably degraded European infusion. Never in my life have I beheld human beings whose repulsive external aspect spoke more clearly of the depravity festering within.

"The savages, wholly unclothed, shambled and capered to the wailing, unearthly music of those damnable flutes. As they danced, they sang, or chanted, in a tongue bearing no resemblance to the local Malay dialect, a tongue that I sensed had been old when the world was still young. The meaning entirely eluded me, yet often I caught the name Ur-Allazoth, and knew that they called upon their monstrous god. This deity, I had no doubt, found representation in the great statue looming at the center of the glade. Whose hand had fashioned so mind-searing an abomination I cannot pretend to guess, but surely the work lay far beyond the skill of the primitive Faithful, for the artistry was unimaginably hideous, yet masterly, bespeaking the twisted genius of a perverted Leonardo. The being darkly depicted in polished stone was alien beyond conception, beyond endurance. To gaze upon that impossible nightmare form was to experience some intimation of eternal diableries lurking without the realm of our perceptions, of eldritch foulness poisoning all the cosmos. The idol was squat, bloated, abhorrently misshapen, every contour an assault upon human vision. The four limbs were sinuous, attenuated, edged with spikes and tipped with suckers. The head was thoroughly beastlike, sharp-snouted, and razor-tusked, with protuberant eyes of some highly polished crystalline substance that reflected the firelight in shifting gleams of deepest crimson. A long, squamous tail wrapped itself thrice about the entire body of this execrable entity that was, though never of our world, oddly reminiscent in shape and character of an enormous *rat*.

"The image of Ur-Allazoth crouched atop a pedestal of black stone, incised with bands of curious glyphs, and inset with small plaques of wondrously carven, glinting matter. A broad ledge of great stone blocks encircled the pedestal, and this ledge supported a chopping block.

"I will not relate the sickening particulars of the ceremony that followed. The sacrifice of a dozen drugged and stuporous victims, the rolling heads and spurting blood, the abandoned gyrations of the Faithful, the wild ululation, the relentless shrilling of those infernal flutes, (a sound that will haunt me to my grave) and above all, the inexplicable sense of a huge, malign sentience pervading the atmosphere — I will leave it to your imagination to furnish the details. Imagination is apt to fall short of the dreadful reality, and perhaps that is all to the good. I will only note that I myself was faint and queasy before the rite was half completed. Abe Engle was swaying upon his feet, Tertius Crawley had turned his back on the scene, and poor young Loftus had collapsed in a swoon. Of the five of us, only Talliard remained composed, resolute, and fully attentive. The intermittent gleams of firelight, stabbing fitfully through the shadows, revealed our leader, jotting copious notes into the journal that he never traveled without. I must confess, Talliard's utter coolness in the face of the horror we confronted at once impressed and revolted me.

"The ceremony concluded at last. The savages withdrew, bearing the bloodstained remnants of their revel. The fires burned on, their ruddy light bathing empty glade, incarnadined block, staring heads, and unspeakable idol. Loftus recovered his senses and sat up slowly, gazing about with a stunned and vacant air. Engle drooped, Crawley fidgeted, while I stood dully longing to depart the accursed spot. Sefton Talliard, however, was unready to go. Casting a brief, searching glance right and left, our leader strode forward with an air of fearless resolution, never faltering before he reached the base of Ur-Allazoth's image. There he halted, and, to my amazement, proceeded to sketch the statue in pen and ink, reproducing the murine lineaments with commendable accuracy.

"Pride forbade me to display cowardice. Mastering my own reluctance, I advanced to join Professor Talliard. Drawing paper and crayon from my pocket, I quickly took rubbings of several bands of glyphs. While I was thus engaged, Engle approached to record measurements, while Crawley occupied himself with a survey of preserved heads. Only poor Loftus remained inert, huddled on the ground at the edge of the clearing.

"Our respective tasks were soon completed. I could scarcely contain my eagerness to go, but Talliard would not budge before prying one of the small, carven plaques from the pedestal of the statue. His temerity shocked me, but there was no arguing with our autocrat, and I did not attempt it. He slipped the thin plaque between the pages of his journal, returned the book to his pocket, and then, to my unutterable relief, signalled a command to withdraw.

"We hastened from that spot, stumbling our way through the dark, back to the point where we had left our guide. The fellow was not there, and inwardly I cursed him for a deserter. Perhaps he had indeed fled, without collecting his recompense, or perhaps some darker fate befell him there. I cannot say, for we never looked upon his face again.

"I scarcely know how we found our way through that stygian forest to a friendly Dyak settlement. There we spent the night, a night of broken slumbers, filled with delirious dreams. In the morning, we commenced the three-day trek back to our lowland village, and our thatched dwelling perched on piles. This transition was accomplished without incident, yet throughout its entirety, I was unable to rid myself of a profound perturbation — a keen, nerve-racking sense that our progress was continually *observed.* There is no overemphasizing the power of this sensation — it was instinctual, elemental, and shared by us all.

"The feeling intensified throughout the ensuing days. Strive though I might to absorb myself in the task of deciphering the message of the glyphs, I could neither evade nor ignore that psychic oppression. Only the imminence of our withdrawal from the island of Sumatra lightened my mood.

"We had booked passage to Java aboard the cargo vessel *Matilda Briggs.* Two days prior to departure, tragedy befell us. Tertius Crawley was murdered. Our colleague's headless corpse was discovered at dusk by young Loftus, whose own nervous reaction to the sight was immediate and intense.

"Mr. Holmes, Dr. Watson, the isolated villages of Sumatra possess nothing corresponding to an American or British system of justice. Legal administration resides largely in the hands of local elders, and rarely are matters referred to the distant Dutch authorities. In this case, the village chieftain merely expressed his regret that the devilish magic of the Faithful had prevailed once again, together with his recommendation that the body be interred without delay, lest evil spirits seek the site of violent death. Crawley was buried at dawn. His head was never located.

"You may well imagine my sense of overwhelming relief, as I watched the coast of Sumatra recede, from the deck of the *Matilda Briggs*. The vessel was bound for Batavia, by way of the Strait of Malacca. I had hoped the sea voyage might serve to calm my unstrung nerves. On the second day, however, one of the crew discovered Abe Engle's headless remains, crammed into a barrel deep in the hold. A thorough search of the ship revealed the presence of a stowaway, easily identifiable by his blue eyes as a member of the mongrel tribe of the Faithful. Interrogation proved useless, as the prisoner displayed comprehension of no tongue other than his own debased dialect, which poured from his lips in a venomous, continuous stream. He seemed entirely fearless, and the expression of malignity glaring from his pale eyes was shocking to behold.

"Presently tiring of incessant, unintelligible abuse, the captain ordered the suspect locked in a storage closet belowdecks. Confinement failed to quell the Dyak's defiant spirit, and from that closet issued the sound of his voice, upraised in an unholy chanting audible throughout the ship.

"Engle was buried at sea. His head was never located. Throughout the obsequies, the malignant chants rising from below counterpointed the captain's readings from the Psalms, and the blasphemous juxtaposition chilled the hearts of all listeners. The verbal outpouring had now assumed a character all too recognizable to the surviving members of our group — it was that same invocation to Ur-Allazoth we had heard in the upland forests upon the night of the Faithful's vile ceremony. The passage of time could not damp the prisoner's loquacity, and throughout the hours that followed, the chanting never ceased. More than one of the *Matilda Briggs* deck hands spoke of gagging the noisy Dyak, or even of slitting his throat, but no one attempted to act upon these threats. It is my belief that the sailors feared their captive, and understandably so.

"The ship sped southeast, toward Java. The voice of the prisoner never abated, and the sound cast a black and smothering pall over all on board, with the possible exception of Sefton Talliard, whose nerves seemed proof against any assault. On the night that we neared Batavia Bay, I retired early, and the last recollection I carried with me into slumber was the sound of the prisoner's voice, infused with a certain new and curious note of exultation.

"I awakened at dawn to a clamorous uproar. Footsteps thundered overhead, an alarm clanged, men shouted wildly, shrieks of mortal terror tore the air, and through it all, I could still distinguish the hoarsened, malevolently triumphant voice of the captive Dyak, calling upon Ur-Allazoth.

"Rising from my berth, I made for the deck. Before I reached it, a violent impact rocked the *Matilda Briggs*. The shock threw me from the ladder, and I fell, striking my head violently upon the cabin floor. For a time, I knew nothing more.

"When I regained my senses, around mid-morning, it was to find myself lying, sick and sore, in the boat of the *Matilda Briggs*, together with Talliard, Loftus, and some half dozen sailors. Of the ship, and the rest of her crew, nothing was to be seen. That she had gone to the bottom of Batavia Bay was clear, but the circumstances of the wreck were impossible to ascertain. Talliard claimed ignorance, the sailors offered the most incoherently fantastic tales, and Zebulon Loftus, when pressed for an account, vented peal upon piercing peal of maniacal laughter. To my surprise, I found that the valise containing my personal belongings had been preserved, by Talliard, of all people. In response to my thanks, our leader merely responded that the rubbings I had taken from the pedestal of Ur-Allazoth's image were worth saving.

"Batavia Bay is heavily travelled, and we were rescued in a matter of hours. The inquest that followed is a great blur in my mind. The official verdict was that the *Matilda Briggs* had struck a rock and sunk; a falsehood I made no attempt to challenge.

"We returned to Providence, where young Loftus, whose sanity was shattered, entered a mental hospital. The academic year at Brown commenced, and I returned to work, in every hope of resuming my former tranquil existence. For a while, it seemed I had done so. I so far regained my equilibrium that I dared confront the challenge of deciphering the message of Ur-Allazoth's glyphs; while Talliard disclosed our findings to the world in lectures of dazzling brilliancy. Apparent normality reigned for some months, until December, when we received news that Zebulon Loftus had escaped incarceration. Two days later, his frozen, decapitated body was found in a meadow not half a mile from the hospital. His head was never located.

"Around this time," Belknap could not repress a shudder, "I began once more to experience the peculiar sensation of being watched, that I thought I had left behind me in the East Indies. Often I thought to glimpse dark forms haunting the shadows as I made my way through the tortuous streets of Providence, and once I caught the baleful gleam of uncanny blue eyes tracking my progress. Confiding in Talliard, one icy winter night, I learned that he harboured fears identical to my own; and painfully acute those fears must have been, for that self contained, overweening individual to acknowledge them. Upon that occasion, he even spoke of flight, and suggested the possibility of finding refuge in London. At the time, I hardly expected him to resort to such measures. But two nights later, both Talliard's office and my own were ransacked. The next day, Sefton Talliard disappeared.

"He was either dead, or fled to London. In the absence of a corpse, I suspected the latter. Within the fortnight, I'd powerful incentive to follow him. For some weeks past, my work with the glyphs had scarcely progressed. Many of the pictographs, though commonplace symbols in that backward area of the world, were arranged in sequences that seemed senseless and random as the ravings of a lunatic. At length it dawned upon me that the symbols composed a rebus, phonetically representing words in the Dutch language of the seventeenth century. Inexplicable that a solution so obvious should have eluded me for so long, but thereafter, as you may well imagine, my task was greatly simplified, and translation proceeded apace. Eventually, the following message resolved itself. Closing his eyes, Belknap repeated, from memory, *The hold of divine Ur-Allazoth looses not, and loses naught. Whosoever profanes His image, dividing or diminishing the sacred substance thereof, shall be pursued to the ends of the earth and beyond, even unto the shrieking, formless reaches beyond the stars. Nor shall pursuit abate, before the worldly waters ruled by the Relentless have closed upon that which is His.*

"You see the significance, Mr. Holmes?" Belknap opened his eyes.

"Indeed. I had, inevitably, anticipated the rebus," Holmes replied. "As for the rest, the urgency of the matter is apparent. These devotees of a being whose nature demands further investigation have followed the despoilers of their deity's image all the way from Sumatra. Clearly, they will not rest until they have recovered the plaque stolen by Sefton Talliard. In order to preserve your own life, as well as Professor Talliard's, the immediate return of the stolen item to its self-proclaimed owners is essential."

"That is my conclusion. But my own efforts have failed to locate Talliard here in London, and lately, I have noted the presence of silent blue-eyed hounds upon my trail. Within the last forty-eight hours, they have drawn near, and I fear that my time is all but gone. Can you assist me, Mr. Holmes?"

"Beyond doubt. There is one point, however, that must be noted, at the outset; which is, that your colleague appears to withhold information of some vital significance. In view of the character-portrait you've limned, that is hardly surprising. Presumably the nature of the missing piece will reveal itself when I have located Professor Talliard, which I fully expect to do in a matter of hours, if not less."

"But that is astonishing, Mr. Holmes!" the visitor exclaimed. "I have scoured London for weeks, without gleaning the slightest clue."

"I've certain local resources, to which a stranger in the city is unlikely to enjoy access," Holmes replied, not unkindly. "Now, Professor Belknap, here is a question of some import. Were you followed to Baker Street, this evening?"

"I believe so." Belknap shivered. "Yes, I am quite certain of it."

"Excellent," Holmes replied, to my amazement.

I could not fathom my friend's clear satisfaction, and the visitor was equally confounded.

"I must leave you, for a little while," Holmes abruptly informed his client. "I shall return within the half hour." He departed without further explanation, leaving me alone with August Belknap, who, unaccustomed to the eccentric character of my friend's genius, appeared thunderstruck.

It was perhaps the slowest half hour I have ever endured. Poor Belknap, distracted and raw-nerved, could not even pretend interest in the tales of the Afghan campaign with which I endeavored to entertain him, but started and flinched at every unexpected sound. Presently, all conversation died, and we sat in comfortless silence, until the clock struck nine, and, to my unutterable relief, Sherlock Holmes reappeared.

"The apparatus has been readied," Holmes declared. "It remains only to set the machine in motion. For that, Professor, I must request use of your amusing disguise. We are much of a build. My own clothes should fit you well enough to serve on a foggy night. Take them, return to your own lodgings, and do not stir forth until you have heard from me. Where are you staying?"

The visitor named an address in Fleet Street.

"I assume you frequently change location?"

"Every few days," Belknap admitted. "But I never succeed in throwing them off the track for long."

"After tonight, that should not signify." So saying, Holmes ushered the visitor into his own room.

When they emerged, minutes later, I could not forbear staring, so startled was I by the transformation. August Belknap, clad in borrowed Inverness and deerstalker, might at a glance have been mistaken for Sherlock Holmes. Holmes himself, in feminine array, complete with wig, wide hat, and veiling, was altogether unrecognizable.

"Now, Professor," Holmes instructed his client, "Wait for half an hour after Dr. Watson and I have departed —"

"Eh!" I exclaimed.

"Then return to Fleet Street, and stay inside tomorrow. You are the lesser target, and probably not in immediate danger, but do not open the door to anyone other than myself or Watson."

"Mr. Holmes, I will follow your instructions without fail."

"Capital. And now, my dear Watson, I trust you will not suffer a lady to venture forth unescorted?" Holmes's amused smile was dimly visible through the veiling.

"Venture forth where?" I inquired.

"Not far. A half-hour's stroll should suffice."

I remained unenlightened, but acquiescent. Pausing only long enough to don an overcoat, I accompanied Sherlock Holmes out into the fog-blinded March night. Together we set off at a leisurely pace along Baker Street.

To the end of my days, I will always remember that walk, and I will never recall it without a pang of profound uneasiness. For that sense of *being watched,* so graphically described by Professor August Belknap, was present, powerful, and impossible to ignore. I could have taken my oath that the shadows seethed with silent, sliding shapes, and I could literally feel the pressure of invisible regard. It was all I could do to refrain from glancing continually back over my shoulder, and the flesh between my shoulderblades positively tingled in anticipation of a blow. I considered Belknap's account of the Faithful's headless victims, and my own head momentarily swam.

If Sherlock Holmes shared my misgivings, he showed no sign of it. His step was unhurried, his manner unconcerned, as he launched into an impressively knowledgeable discussion of the evolution of the kabuki dance drama. My friend spoke brilliantly, yet I scarcely heard a word of his discourse, for my ears were attuned to nothing beyond the tap of footsteps in the fog behind us. And my disquiet, already intense, increased a hundredfold when Holmes led us from the relatively well-lit, populous public thoroughfares, into the silent pathways of Regent's Park. We were nearing the Zoo, before he finally paused, in a region of impenetrable shadow.

"That should be enough," Holmes opined.

I did not waste breath begging for an explanation, but waited in silence as he divested himself of hat, wig, pelisse, and skirts, to reveal ordinary masculine attire beneath.

"Now, Watson, we separate," he decreed. "You may take the direct route back to Baker Street, and I shall go roundabout. And by this time tomorrow night, we shall beyond doubt have located the missing Professor Talliard."

With that, he vanished silently into the dark, leaving me alone, bewildered, filled with resentment, and more than a little apprehension. I made my way home without hindrance. Belknap had left, and Holmes had not yet returned, which was just as well. If I had encountered my friend at that moment, I should hardly have found myself capable of civility. I retired early, and slept soundly, my dreams somehow flavoured with the sound of Sherlock Holmes's violin.

Holmes had resumed his chemical experimentation by the time I awoke. His violin lay on the sofa — evidently he had been playing it during the night. His pallour and shadowed eyes suggested sleeplessness. Still somewhat piqued by last night's events, I refused to question him, but rather, occupied myself with a series of errands that kept me out and about for the entire day. Around twilight, I returned to Baker Street, to discover Holmes still occupied with his test tubes, beakers, and burners. Nor was his attention to be diverted from these items, until a dubious Mrs. Hudson entered to announce the arrival of "Master Wiggins, and associates."

"Ah, show them in," Holmes instructed, his face alight with eagerness. Noting my puzzlement, he explained, "The Baker Street Irregulars. They have been at work since I put them on the case last night."

Here, then, was the explanation of Holmes's half-hour absence of the previous evening. He had withdrawn to confer with his juvenile surveillance squad.

Moments later, a sextet of ragged and remarkably filthy little street Arabs burst into the room. Their chief Wiggins, tallest and oldest among them, swaggered forward to announce with an air of victory, "Plunker 'ere cops the prize."

The Plunker in question, a superlatively disreputable urchin, flashed a snaggle-toothed grin.

"State your findings," Holmes commanded.

"Shadowed yer last night, Guv'nor, as per orders." Master Wiggins appeared to act as official spokesman of the party. "Soon spied the others on yer trail, just like yer said, and rummy little apes they was, too. Not 'arf ugly. Arfter yer gives 'em the slip in the Park, they splits up, so *we* splits up. Plunker follows one of'em as far as Notting 'ill Gate, and finds more of the same, 'angling about a lodging 'ouse. Plunker keeps an eye peeled, twigs their game, and knows 'e's nailed yer man. And there you 'ave it."

"Well done, gentlemen. Can you furnish an address?"

Wiggins obliged.

"Second storey, front room," Plunker offered.

"Well done," Holmes repeated. He produced a guinea. "Plunker, your reward."

"Cor!" Plunker's crooked grin widened.

"For the rest of you — the usual scale of pay, for two days work." Holmes distributed silver. "Gentlemen, until next time."

The delighted irregulars withdrew, no doubt to our landlady's relief.

"Phew!" I observed.

"There is no time to be lost, Watson," Holmes declared. "Sefton Talliard's hours are numbered."

A hansom carried us to the house noted by the youthful intelligencer. The place was respectable-looking, well-maintained, and unremarkable. We alighted from our vehicle, and I gazed searchingly about, but caught no glimpse of lurking figures. The sense of being watched, so unnervingly acute last night in Regent's Park, was absent now. And yet, I knew not why, I found that my hands were icy, and my heart was cold with a formless dread.

A couple of taps of the polished brass knocker drew the landlady. Holmes introduced himself as a friend of the American gentleman on the second floor, and she admitted us without demur. We hurried upstairs, and rapped on Sefton Talliard's door. There was no response, and my sense of dread deepened.

The room was locked. Our combined strength easily sufficed to force it open, and we burst in to confront a scene I shudder to recall. I am a surgeon, fully accustomed to sights that many would consider ghastly, yet all my experience could not fully prepare me for the spectacle of Sefton Talliard's headless corpse, sprawled on a blood-drenched bed. I think an exclamation escaped me, and I recoiled a pace or two. Sherlock Holmes was guilty of no such weakness. Casting a keen, penetrating eye about the death chamber, he stepped first to the locked window, then to the fireplace, which he knelt to examine briefly. Thereafter, he turned his attention upon the clothing, books, papers, and personal articles that lay wildly scattered everywhere. That Talliard's room had been thoroughly rifled was altogether apparent. The object of my friend's search was less evident, however. Initially, I assumed that he sought the plaque sacrilegiously pried from the pedestal of Ur-Allazoth's image, but that could scarcely be; for surely the murderers, here before us and purposeful beyond civilized ken, would already have reclaimed that article. It then occurred to me that Holmes sought Talliard's missing head, but such proved not to be the case. At length, a muted grunt of satisfaction announced his success, and, from that dreadful bloodstained tangle, he plucked a small volume bound in red morocco.

I was not so dull that I failed to recognize Professor Talliard's prized journal, as described by August Belknap.

Settling himself back upon his haunches with the utmost deliberation, Holmes proceeded to read, indifferent to the presence of the mutilated body on the bed, not two yards behind him. I could scarcely endure it.

"Holmes —" I entreated.

"One moment — ah!" Holmes's expression altered remarkably, and he sprang to his feet. "There — yes — I had suspected something, but this I did not foresee."

"Foresee what?" I demanded.

"Come, we must find Belknap at once."

"We cannot leave this place, Holmes!" I expostulated. "We have happened upon a murder. There are authorities — appropriate channels — proper procedure —"

"They will wait," Holmes informed me. With some effort, he tore his eyes from the journal. "My client stands in mortal peril. Should he perish, it is through my own failure of intellect."

Such a prospect was not to be contemplated.

"No delay, Watson! Belknap's life hangs by a thread." Thrusting Talliard's journal into his pocket, Holmes rose and rushed from the room, without a glance to spare for the dead man. After a moment, I followed. What Talliard's landlady must have made of our sudden departure, and her subsequent discovery in the American lodger's room, I did not care to ponder at that time.

Before I reached the street, Holmes had already secured a hansom. I jumped in, just as the vehicle sped off east. The ride was endless, and conversation one-sided, for Holmes declined to answer my queries, or indeed, to speak at all. Eventually, I gave over interrogation. Traffic was heavy upon the London streets at that hour, the fog was opaque, our progress was slow, and apprehension twisted my vitals.

At length, we reached the Fleet Street address of August Belknap; a surprisingly mean haunt, for it seemed that Holmes's client, desirous of self-submersion in London's maelstrom, had sought concealment in cheap lodgings above some barber's shop.

The shop was still open. We rushed in, and, without pausing to consult a proprietor of remarkably demonic aspect, sprinted to the back, and up the stairs, to pound the door of August Belknap's room.

We called him by name, and he admitted us at once. Before the first question escaped the fugitive academic's lips, Sherlock Holmes demanded, "The photograph of your late wife, Belknap — where is it?"

Belknap stared, his feverish, astonished eyes widening. Impatiently, Holmes repeated the query, and his client's wordless gesture encompassed the plain oak bureau in the corner. Pulling the top drawer open, my friend swiftly located and drew forth the silver-framed portrait of a round-faced young woman, irregular of feature, but sweet and grave of expression. I confess the professor was no more mystified than I. All confusion vanished, however, when Sherlock Holmes pried the backing from the frame, to reveal the flat, marvelously carven plaque secreted behind the photograph.

"Good God!" Belknap ejaculated.

His reaction was surely unfeigned. It would have required the talents of an Irving or a Forbes-Robertson to counterfeit such perfect amazement.

"You must rid yourself of this object," Holmes informed his client. "That is your sole chance of survival."

"Mr. Holmes, 1 knew nothing of this. I will gladly dispose of the thing. I will bury it — pulverize it — donate it to a museum — carry it back to Sumatra, if need be —"

"Useless," Holmes returned. "Quite useless. There is but one solution to your dilemma. Your own translation of the Sumatran glyphs, Professor, should instruct you."

"'Nor shall pursuit abate,'" Belknap recited, "'before the worldly waters ruled by the Relentless have closed upon that which is His.'"

"Just so. Come, there is not a moment to lose."

Holmes exited, and we followed him down the stairs, past the flame-eyed proprietor, and out into mist-shrouded Fleet Street. He led us east, and as we went, the cold chills knifing along my spine, and the intolerable pressure of invisible regard, warned me of unseen stalkers, near at hand. August Belknap's face was white and set; he, too, sensed the hostile presence.

We reached Ludgate Circus, and now, for the first time, I actually glimpsed the short, impossibly agile human shadows gliding through the fog, and I caught the glint of luminously malignant blue eyes. Even Sherlock Holmes could not feign total indifference. We quickened our pace, and our pursuers did likewise, drawing perceptibly nearer as we turned south toward the Thames.

I could not fathom my friend's purpose. Neither he nor I carried a weapon. I assumed that August Belknap was similarly unarmed. Rather than seeking the comparative safety of well-peopled streets, however, Sherlock Holmes was leading us straight on toward empty Blackfriars Bridge.

We were running now, unabashedly in flight, our footsteps echoing through the fog. Hearing no clatter of pursuit, I chanced a glance behind, to descry no less than six of them, swift and seemingly tireless, noiseless and uncanny as predatory wraiths.

Reaching the bridge, we started to cross. Halfway to the Southwark side, however, Holmes halted abruptly, one hand raised on high. Clasped in that hand was the plaque pried from the image of the Faithful's god. I've no idea at all what substance composed that small tablet. Whatever it was, it seemed to glow with some pulsing internal light of its own, and never in all my days have I seen the like. Even in the midst of the darkness, and the swirling fog, the plaque was clearly visible.

"Ur-Allazoth!" Holmes called out, in a clear, strong voice that pierced the night like a dagger.

So sharp and sudden was that utterance, and so unexpected, that I started violently at the sound of it, and beside me, I heard Belknap gasp.

"Ur-Allazoth!" Holmes repeated the call, and then sang out a string of indescribably outlandish syllables.

"Ia fhurtgn iea tlu jiadhri cthuthoth zhug'Isht ftehia. Iea tlu."

That is the best I can do to reproduce that fantastically incomprehensible burst of gibberish.

It seemed to me then that the inexplicable, infernal light of the stolen plaque in Holmes's grasp responsively intensified. As a man of science, I can scarcely account for such a phenomenon, but I did *not* imagine it. Blinking and confused, I looked away, glancing back to behold our six pursuers, grouped at the end of the bridge, motionless and preternaturally intent. My confusion deepened as their voices rose, to wail thinly through the fog:

"Ia fhurtgn ieat tlu jiadhri cthuthoth zhugg'lsht ftehia. Iea tlu."

There was something in the sound that roused my deepest, most elemental terror and detestation.

As the final loathsome syllable faded, Sherlock Holmes flung the plaque from Blackfriars Bridge. The lucent object fell like a shooting star. Before it struck the river below, the mists roiled, and a violent upheaval convulsed the water. The Thames shuddered, black waves smashed themselves against the piers of the bridge, and a funnel-shaped whirlpool spun into existence. Astounded, I gazed down, and thought for one mad moment to glimpse a vast and almost inconceivable shape. There was solidity there, I imagined; a slithering of boneless attenuated limbs, a flash of spikes and suckers. The moment passed. The plaque vanished into the whirlpool, the waters closed upon it, then swiftly calmed themselves. The Thames flowed on, untroubled.

Slowly, doubting my own senses, I turned to look back upon our Faithful pursuers. For an instant I beheld them — six anonymous, attentive figures, ghostlike in the mists. Then they vanished, fading into the fog, and I saw them no more.

Two nights later, we sat in our lodgings, the ever-present London fog still testing its weight against the window panes. Most of the previous day had been spent in conference with the police, who, swayed by the hysterics of Sefton Talliard's landlady, had initially evinced some disposition to suspect our complicity in that unhappy academic's decapitation. The information, however, regarding the nature of Talliard's shadowy enemies — provided by August Belknap, and substantiated by the testimony of Wiggins and Plunker of the Baker Street irregulars — had much allayed such suspicion. And Holmes's own masterly analysis of the murder-site had demonstrated beyond all question that a brace of small, acrobatic killers had entered the locked room by way of the chimney, dispatched the sleeping Talliard, ransacked the room, and exited the way they had come, bearing their victim's head — which will, I strongly suspect, never be located.

The constabulary, their doubts satisfied, had dismissed us, and we came away with Holmes miraculously retaining possession of Sefton Talliard's journal. The book now lay open before him, and my friend was frowning over it.

"I am scarcely satisfied," he complained.

"What, Holmes!" I returned. "Against all odds, you succeeded in preserving your client's life — assuming that his enemies are now mollified."

"August Belknap has nothing more to fear from the Faithful," Holmes said, shrugging. "But that is not the point. The information placed at my disposal regarding Professor Sefton Talliard's ruthless, cool, and unscrupulous character should have alerted me to the fellow's intentions, early enough to forestall another ritual beheading. It should not have been necessary for me to read his very words in his own journal."

"What did he say?" I inquired.

"See for yourself." Holmes extended the morocco-bound volume. "And do not neglect the account of the destruction of the *Matilda Briggs.*"

Sefton Talliard's hand was decisive and legible. It was with disapproving interest, but no great surprise, that I read of his plan, motivated by self-serving fear, to transfer the stolen plaque, object of alarming Faithful attention, from his own possession to that of the unwitting August Belknap. The photograph of Belknap's late wife, a memento of immense sentimental value, prized and carried everywhere by its owner, offered the perfect place of concealment. This transfer, accomplished hours prior to the embarkation of the *Matilda Briggs,* clearly accounted for Talliard's unwonted generosity in preserving the valise, containing the personal property of his colleague.

There followed a brief passage, written on shipboard, and phonetically rendering the invocation to Ur-Allazoth ceaselessly howled by the Dyak prisoner locked in the hold of the vessel:

Ia fhurtgn iea tlu jiadhri cthuthoth zhugg'lsht ftehia. Iea tlu.

And finally, the following passage, penned in the immediate aftermath of the disaster, caught my eye:

. . . cannot begin to convey the horror of the Being that rose from the sea to confront the Matilda Briggs. *There are no words — there are no sane human concepts fit to encompass the immensity of that primeval terror — that overwhelming, insupportable foulness — that gibbering, slavering, slobbering, quivering, towering, tittering obscenity — that burst from the sea like a corporeal nightmare, shattering the boundaries of time, space, and reason. God help me! My mind quakes at the recollection, my sanity trembles. How shall I speak of a creature, gigantic and jigglingly gelatinous beyond description, ancient beyond earthly reckoning, hideous beyond the tolerance of human vision, combining in one abominable form, all the worst aspects of plague-bearing rat, giant kraken, squid, serpent, and leveret? How shall I speak of the stench that killed courage, the howling aural assault that blasted intelligence? How shall I limn an incarnation of the immemorial, destroying lunacy that humanity calls Chaos? Oh, I cannot — I simply cannot! All about me, men were going mad. The Thing was closing fast upon us, and I knew at a glance that the Matilda Briggs was lost ...*

"Gad." I looked up from the page. "What do you make of it, Holmes?"

"I would not necessarily discount the professor's veracity," my friend returned languidly. "For when you have eliminated the impossible, whatever remains, however improbable, must be the truth. Nevertheless, we should do well to keep the matter to ourselves, Watson, as it is a story for which the world is not yet prepared."

THE ADVENTURE OF THE NOBLE BACHELOR

by Sir Arthur Conan Doyle

The Lord St. Simon marriage, and its curious termination, have long ceased to be a subject of interest in those exalted circles in which the unfortunate bridegroom moves. Fresh scandals have eclipsed it, and their more piquant details have drawn the gossips away from this four-year-old drama. As I have reason to believe, however, that the full facts have never been revealed to the general public, and as my friend Sherlock Holmes had a considerable share in clearing the matter up, I feel that no memoir of him would be complete without some little sketch of this remarkable episode.

It was a few weeks before my own marriage, during the days when I was still sharing rooms with Holmes in Baker Street, that he came home from an afternoon stroll to find a letter on the table waiting for him. I had remained indoors all day, for the weather had taken a sudden turn to rain, with high autumnal winds, and the Jezail bullet which I had brought back in one of my limbs as a relic of my Afghan campaign throbbed with dull persistence. With my body in one easy-chair and my legs upon another, I had surrounded myself with a cloud of newspapers until at last, saturated with the news of the day, I tossed them all aside and lay listless, watching the huge crest and monogram upon the envelope upon the table and wondering lazily who my friend's noble correspondent could be.

"Here is a very fashionable epistle," I remarked as he entered. "Your morning letters, if I remember right, were from a fish-monger and a tide-waiter."

"Yes, my correspondence has certainly the charm of variety," he answered, smiling, "and the humbler are usually the more interesting. This looks like one of those unwelcome social summonses which call upon a man either to be bored or to lie."

He broke the seal and glanced over the contents.

"Oh, come, it may prove to be something of interest, after all."

"Not social, then?"

"No, distinctly professional."

"And from a noble client?"

"One of the highest in England."

"My dear fellow. I congratulate you."

"I assure you, Watson, without affectation, that the status of my client is a matter of less moment to me than the interest of his case. It is just possible, however, that that also may not be wanting in this new investigation. You have been reading the papers diligently of late, have you not?"

"It looks like it," said I ruefully, pointing to a huge bundle in the corner. "I have had nothing else to do."

"It is fortunate, for you will perhaps be able to post me up. I read nothing except the criminal news and the agony column. The latter is always instructive. But if you have followed recent events so closely you must have read about Lord St. Simon and his wedding?"

"Oh, yes, with the deepest interest."

"That is well. The letter which I hold in my hand is from Lord St. Simon. I will read it to you, and in return you must turn over these papers and let me have whatever bears upon the matter. This is what he says:

> MY DEAR MR. SHERLOCK HOLMES: Lord Backwater tells me that I may place implicit reliance upon your judgment and discretion. I have determined, therefore, to call upon you and to consult you in reference to the very painful event which has occurred in connection with my wedding. Mr. Lestrade, of Scotland Yard, is acting already in the matter, but he assures me that he sees no objection to your cooperation, and that he even thinks that it might be of some assistance. I will call at four o'clock in the afternoon, and, should you have any other engagement at that time, I hope that you will postpone it, as this matter is of paramount importance.
> —Yours faithfully,
> ROBERT ST. SIMON.

"It is dated from Grosvenor Mansions, written with a quill pen, and the noble lord has had the misfortune to get a smear of ink upon the outer side of his right little finger," remarked Holmes as he folded up the epistle.

"He says four o'clock. It is three now. He will be here in an hour."

"Then I have just time, with your assistance, to get clear upon the subject. Turn over those papers and arrange the extracts in their order of time, while I take a glance as to who our client is." He picked a red-covered volume from a line of books of reference beside the mantelpiece. "Here he is," said he, sitting down and flattening it out upon his knee. "Lord Robert Walsingham de Vere St. Simon, second son of the Duke of Balmoral. Hum! Arms: Azure, three caltrops in chief over a fess sable. Born in 1846. He's forty-one years of age, which is mature for marriage. Was Under-Secretary for the colonies in a late administration. The Duke, his father, was at one time Secretary for Foreign Affairs. They inherit Plantagenet blood by direct descent, and Tudor on the distaff side. Ha! Well, there is nothing very instructive in all this. I think that I must turn to you Watson, for something more solid."

"I have very little difficulty in finding what I want," said I, "for the facts are quite recent, and the matter struck me as remarkable. I feared to refer them to you, however, as I knew that you had an inquiry on hand and that you disliked the intrusion of other matters."

"Oh, you mean the little problem of the Grosvenor Square furniture van. That is quite cleared up now — though, indeed, it was obvious from the first. Pray give me the results of your newspaper selections."

"Here is the first notice which I can find. It is in the personal column of *The Morning Post*, and dates, as you see, some weeks back: 'A marriage has been arranged' it says, 'and will, if rumour is correct, very shortly take place, between Lord Robert St. Simon, second son of the Duke of Balmoral, and Miss Hatty Doran, the only daughter of Aloysius Doran. Esq., of San Francisco, Cal., U. S. A.' That is all."

"Terse and to the point," remarked Holmes, stretching his long, thin legs towards the fire.

"There was a paragraph amplifying this in one of the society papers of the same week. Ah, here it is. 'There will soon be a call for protection in the marriage market, for the present free-trade principle appears to tell heavily against our home product. One by one the management of the noble houses of Great Britain is passing into the hands of our fair cousins from across the Atlantic. An important addition has been made during the last week to the list of the prizes which have been borne away by these charming invaders. Lord St. Simon, who has shown himself for over twenty years proof against the little god's arrows, has now definitely announced his approaching marriage with Miss Hatty Doran, the fascinating daughter of a California millionaire. Miss Doran, whose graceful figure and striking face attracted much attention at the Westbury House festivities , is an only child, and it is currently reported that her dowry will run to considerably over the six figures, with expectancies for the future. As it is an open secret that the Duke of Balmoral has been compelled to sell his pictures within the last few years, and as Lord St. Simon has no property of his own save the small estate of Birchmoor, it is obvious that the Californian heiress is not the only gainer by an alliance which will enable her to make the easy and common transition from a Republican lady to a British title.'

"Anything else?" asked Holmes, yawning.

"Oh, yes; plenty. Then there is another note in *The Morning Post* to say that the mariage would be an absolutely quiet one, that it would be at St. George's, Hanover Square, that only half a dozen intimate friends would be invited, and that the party would return to the furnished house at Lancaster Gate which has been taken by Mr. Aloysius Doran. Two days later — that is, on Wednesday last — there is a curt announcement that the wedding had taken place, and that the honeymoon would be passed at Lord Backwater's place, near Petersfield. Those are all the notices which appeared before the disappearance of the bride."

"Before the what?" asked Holmes with a start.

"The vanishing of the lady."

"When did she vanish, then?"

"At the wedding breakfast."

"Indeed. This is more interesting than it promised to be; quite dramatic, in fact."

"Yes; it struck me as being a little out of the common."

"They often vanish before the ceremony, and occasionally during the honeymoon; but I cannot call to mind anything quite so prompt as this. Pray let me have the details."

"I warn you that they are very incomplete."

"Perhaps we may make them less so."

"Such as they are, they are set forth in a single article of a morning paper of yesterday, which I will read to you. It is headed, 'Singular Occurrence at a Fashionable Wedding':

" 'The family of Lord Robert St. Simon has been thrown into the greatest consternation by the strange and painful episodes which have taken place in connection with his wedding. The ceremony, as shortly announced in the papers of yesterday, occurred on the previous morning; but it is only now that it has been possible to confirm the strange rumours which have been so persistently floating about. In spite of the attempts of the friends to hush the matter up, so much public attention has now been drawn to it that no good purpose can be served by affecting to disregard what is a common subject for conversation.

" 'The ceremony, which was performed at St. George's, Hanover Square, was a very quiet one, no one being present save the father of the bride, Mr. Aloysius Doran, the Duchess of Balmoral, Lord Backwater, Lord Eustace, and Lady Clara St. Simon (the younger brother and sister of the bridegroom), and Lady Alicia Whittington. The whole party proceeded afterwards to the house of Mr. Aloysius Doran, at Lancaster Gate, where breakfast had been prepared. It appears that some little trouble was caused by a woman, whose name has not been ascertained, who endeavoured to force her way into the house after the bridal party, alleging that she had some claim upon Lord St. Simon. It was only after a painful and prolonged scene that she was ejected by the butler and the footman. The bride, who had fortunately entered the house before this unpleasant interruption, had sat down to breakfast with the rest, when she complained of a sudden indisposition and retired to her room. Her prolonged absence having caused some comment, her father followed her, but learned from her maid that she had only come up to her chamber for an instant, caught up an ulster and bonnet, and hurried down to the passage. One of the footmen declared that he had seen a lady leave the house thus apparelled, but had refused to credit that it was his mistress, believing her to be with the company. On ascertaining that his daughter had disappeared, Mr. Aloysius Doran, in conjunction with the bridegroom, instantly put themselves in communication with the police, and very energetic inquiries are being made, which will probably result in a speedy clearing up of this very singular business. Up to a late hour last night, however, nothing had transpired as to the where-abouts of the missing lady. There are rumours of foul play in the matter, and it is said that the police have caused the arrest of the woman who had caused the original disturbance, in the belief that, from jealousy or some other motive, she may have been concerned in the strange disappearance of the bride.'"

"And is that all?"

"Only one little item in another of the morning papers, but it is a suggestive one."

"And it is —"

"That Miss Flora Millar, the lady who had caused the distur-bance, has actually been arrested. It appears that she was formerly a *danseuse* at the Allegro, and that she has known the bridegroom for some years. There are no further particulars, and the whole case is in your hands now — so far as it has been set forth in the public press."

"And an exceedingly interesting case it appears to be. I would not have missed it for worlds. But there is a ring at the bell, Wat-son, and as the clock makes it a few minutes after four, I have no doubt that this will prove to be our noble client. Do not dream of going, Watson, for I very much prefer having a witness, if only as a check to my own memory."

"Lord Robert St. Simon," announced our page-boy, throwing open the door. A gentleman entered, with a pleasant, cultured face, high-nosed and pale, with something perhaps of petulance about the mouth, and with the steady, well-opened eye of a man whose pleasant lot it had ever been to command and to be obeyed. His manner was brisk, and yet his general appearance gave an undue impression of age, for he had a slight forward stoop and a little bend of the knees as he walked. His hair, too, as he swept off his very curly-brimmed hat, was grizzled round the edges and thin upon the top. As to his dress, it was careful to the verge of foppishness, with high collar, black frock-coat, white waistcoat, yellow gloves, pat-ent-leather shoes, and light-coloured gaiters. He advanced slowly into the room, turning his head from left to right, and swinging in his right hand the cord which held his golden eyeglasses.

"Good day, Lord St. Simon," said Holmes, rising and bowing. "Pray take the basket-chair. This is my friend and colleague, Dr.

Watson. Draw up a little to the fire, and we will talk this matter over."

"A most painful matter to me, as you can most readily imagine, Mr. Holmes. I have been cut to the quick. I understand that you have already managed several delicate cases of this sort sir, though I presume that they were hardly from the same class of society."

"No, I am descending."

"I beg pardon."

"My last client of the sort was a king."

"Oh, really! I had no idea. And which king?"

"The King of Scandinavia."

"What! Had he lost his wife?"

"You can understand," said Holmes suavely, "that I extend to the affairs of my other clients the same secrecy which I promise to you in yours."

"Of course! Very right! very right! I'm sure I beg pardon. As to my own case, I am ready to give you any information which may assist you in forming an opinion."

"Thank you. I have already learned all that is in the public prints, nothing more. I presume that I may take it as correct — this article, for example, as to the disappearance of the bride."

Lord St. Simon glanced over it. "Yes, it is correct, as far as it goes."

"But it needs a great deal of supplementing before anyone could offer an opinion. I think that I may arrive at my facts most directly by questioning you."

"Pray do so."

"When did you first meet Miss Hatty Doran?"

"In San Francisco, a year ago."

"You were travelling in the States?"

"Yes."

"Did you become engaged then?"

"No."

"But you were on a friendly footing?"

"I was amused by her society, and she could see that I was amused."

"Her father is very rich?"

"He is said to be the richest man on the Pacific slope."

"And how did he make his money?"

"In mining. He had nothing a few years ago. Then he struck gold, invested it, and came up by leaps and bounds."

"Now, what is your own impression as to the young lady's — your wife's character?"

The nobleman swung his glasses a little faster and stared down into the fire. "You see, Mr. Holmes," said he, "my wife was twenty before her father became a rich man. During that time she ran free in a mining camp and wandered through woods or mountains, so that her education has come from Nature rather than from the schoolmaster. She is what we call in England a tomboy, with a strong nature, wild and free, unfettered by any sort of traditions. She is impetuous — volcanic, I was about to say. She is swift in making up her mind and fearless in cartying out her resolutions. On the other hand, I would not have given her the name which I have the honour to bear" — he gave a little stately cough — "had not I thought her to be at bottom a noble woman. I believe that she is capable of heroic self-sacrifice and that anything dishonourable would be repugnant to her."

"Have you her photograph?"

"I brought this with me." He opened a locket and showed us the full face of a very lovely woman. It was not a photograph but an ivory miniature, and the artist had brought out the full effect of the lustrous black hair, the large dark eyes, and the exquisite mouth. Holmes gazed long and earnestly at it. Then he closed the locket and handed it back to Lord St. Simon.

"The young lady came to London, then, and you renewed your acquaintance?"

"Yes, her father brought her over for this last London season. I met her several times, became engaged to her, and have now married her."

"She brought. I understand. a considerable dowry?"

"A fair dowry. Not more than is usual in my family."

"And this, of course, remains to you, since the marriage is a fait accompli?"

"I really have made no inquiries on the subject."

"Very naturally not. Did you see Miss Doran on the day before the wedding?"

"Yes."

"Was she in good spirits?"

"Never better. She kept talking of what we should do in our future lives."

"Indeed! That is very interesting. And on the morning of the wedding?"

"She was as bright as possible — at least until after the ceremony."

"And did you observe any change in her then?"

"Well, to tell the truth, I saw then the first signs that I had ever seen that her temper was just a little sharp. The incident however, was too trivial to relate and can have no possible bearing upon the case."

"Pray let us have it, for all that."

"Oh, it is childish. She dropped her bouquet as we went towards the vestry. She was passing the front pew at the time, and it fell over into the pew. There was a moment's delay, but the gentleman in the pew handed it up to her again, and it did not appear to be the worse for the fall. Yet when I spoke to her of the matter, she answered me abruptly; and in the carriage, on our way home, she seemed absurdly agitated over this trifling cause."

"Indeed! You say that there was a gentleman in the pew. Some of the general public were present, then?"

"Oh, yes. It is impossible to exclude them when the church is open."

"This gentleman was not one of your wife's friends?"

"No, no; I call him a gentleman by courtesy, but he was quite a common-looking person. I hardly noticed his appearance. But really I think that we are wandering rather far from the point."

"Lady St. Simon, then, returned from the wedding in a less cheerful frame of mind than she had gone to it. What did she do on reentering her father's house?"

"I saw her in conversation with her maid."

"And who is her maid?"

"Alice is her name. She is an American and came from California with her."

"A confidential servant?"

"A little too much so. It seemed to me that her mistress allowed her to take great liberties. Still, of course, in America they look upon these things in a different way."

"How long did she speak to this Alice?"

"Oh, a few minutes. I had something else to think of."

"You did not overhear what they said?"

"Lady St. Simon said something about 'jumping a claim.' She was accustomed to use slang of the kind. I have no idea what she meant."

"American slang is very expressive sometimes. And what did your wife do when she finished speaking to her maid?"

"She walked into the breakfast-room."

"On your arm?"

"No, alone. She was very independent in little matters like that. Then, after we had sat down for ten minutes or so, she rose hurriedly, muttered some words of apology, and left the room. She never came back."

"But this maid, Alice, as I understand, deposes that she went to her room, covered her bride's dress with a long ulster, put on a bonnet, and went out."

"Quite so. And she was afterwards seen walking into Hyde Park in company with Flora Millar, a woman who is now in custody, and who had already made a disturbance at Mr. Doran's house that morning."

"Ah, yes. I should like a few patticulars as to this young lady, and your relations to her."

Lord St. Simon shrugged his shoulders and raised his eyebrows. "We have been on a friendly footing for some years — I may say on a very friendly footing. She used to be at the Allegro. I have not treated her ungenerously, and she had no just cause of complaint against me, but you know what women are, Mr. Holmes. Flora was a dear little thing, but exceedingly hot-headed and devotedly attached to me. She wrote me dreadful letters when she heard that I was about to be married, and, to tell the truth, the reason why I had the marriage celebrated so quietly was that I feared lest there might be a scandal in the church. She came to Mr. Doran's door just after we returned, and she endeavoured to push her way in, uttering very abusive expressions towards my wife, and even threatening her, but I had foreseen the possibility of something of the sort, and I had two police fellows there in private clothes, who soon pushed her out again. She was quiet when she saw that there was no good in making a row."

"Did your wife hear all this?"

"No, thank goodness, she did not."

"And she was seen walking with this very woman afterwards?"

"Yes. That is what Mr. Lestrade, of Scotland Yard, looks upon as so serious. It is thought that Flora decoyed my wife out and laid some terrible trap for her."

"Well, it is a possible supposition."

"You think so, too?"

"I did not say a probable one. But you do not yourself look upon this as likely?"

"I do not think Flora would hurt a fly."

"Still, jealousy is a strange transformer of characters. Pray what is your own theory as to what took place?"

"Well, really, I came to seek a theory, not to propound one. I have given you all the facts. Since you ask me, however, I may say that it has occurred to me as possible that the excitement of this affair, the consciousness that she had made so immense a social stride, had the effect of causing some little nervous disturbance in my wife."

"In short, that she had become suddenly deranged?"

"Well, really, when I consider that she has turned her back — I will not say upon me, but upon so much that many have aspired to without success — I can hardly explain it in any other fashion."

"Well, certainly that is also a conceivable hypothesis," said Holmes, smiling. "And now, Lord St. Simon, I think that I have nearly all my data. May I ask whether you were seated at the breakfast-table so that you could see out of the window?"

"We could see the other side of the road and the Park."

"Quite so. Then I do not think that I need to detain you longer. I shall communicate with you."

"Should you be fortunate enough to solve this problem," said our client, rising.

"I have solved it."

"Eh? What was that?"

"I say that I have solved it."

"Where, then, is my wife?"

"That is a detail which I shall speedily supply."

Lord St. Simon shook his head. "I am afraid that it will take wiser heads than yours or mine," he remarked, and bowing in a stately, old-fashioned manner he departed.

"It is very good of Lord St. Simon to honour my head by putting it on a level with his own," said Sherlock Holmes, laughing. "I think that I shall have a whisky and soda and a cigar after all this cross-questioning. I had formed my conclusions as to the case before our client came into the room."

"My dear Holmes!"

"I have notes of several similar cases, though none, as I remarked before, which were quite as prompt. My whole examination served to turn my conjecture into a certainty. Circumstantial evidence is occasionally very convincing, as when you find a trout in the milk, to quote Thoreau's example."

"But I have heard all that you have heard."

"Without, however, the knowledge of preexisting cases which serves me so well. There was a parallel instance in Aberdeen some years back, and something on very much the same lines at Munich the year after the Franco-Prussian War. It is one of these cases — but, hello, here is Lestrade! Good-afternoon, Lestrade! You will find an extra tumbler upon the sideboard, and there are cigars in the box."

The official detective was attired in a peajacket and cravat, which gave him a decidedly nautical appearance, and he carried a black canvas bag in his hand. With a short greeting he seated himself and lit the cigar which had been offered to him.

"What's up, then?" asked Holmes with a twinkle in his eye. "You look dissatisfied."

"And I feel dissatisfied. It is this infernal St. Simon marriage case. I can make neither head nor tail of the business."

"Really! You surprise me."

"Who ever heard of such a mixed affair? Every clue seems to slip through my fingers. I have been at work upon it all day."

"And very wet it seems to have made you," said Holmes laying his hand upon the arm of the peajacket.

"Yes, I have been dragging the Serpentine."

"In heaven's name, what for?"

"In search of the body of Lady St. Simon."

Sherlock Holmes leaned back in his chair and laughed heartily.

"Have you dragged the basin of Trafalgar Square fountain?" he asked.

"Why? What do you mean?"

"Because you have just as good a chance of finding this lady in the one as in the other."

Lestrade shot an angry glance at my companion. "I suppose you know all about it," he snarled.

"Well, I have only just heard the facts, but my mind is made up."

"Oh, indeed! Then you think that the Serpentine plays no part in the maner?"

"I think it very unlikely."

"Then perhaps you will kindly explain how it is that we found this in it?" He opened his bag as he spoke, and tumbled onto the floor a wedding-dress of watered silk, a pair of white satin shoes and a bride's wreath and veil, all discoloured and soaked in water. "There," said he, putting a new wedding-ring upon the top of the pile. "There is a little nut for you to crack, Master Holmes."

"Oh, indeed!" said my friend, blowing blue rings into the air. "You dragged them from the Serpentine?"

"No. They were found floating near the margin by a park-keeper. They have been identified as her clothes, and it seemed to me that if the clothes were there the body would not be far off."

"By the same brilliant reasoning, every man's body is to be found in the neighbourhood of his wardrobe. And pray what did you hope to arrive at through this?"

"At some evidence implicating Flora Millar in the disappearance."

"I am afraid that you will find it difficult."

"Are you, indeed, now?" cried Lestrade with some bitterness. "I am afraid, Holmes, that you are not very practical with your deductions and your inferences. You have made two blunders in as many minutes. This dress does implicate Miss Flora Millar."

"And how?"

"In the dress is a pocket. In the pocket is a card-case. In the card-case is a note. And here is the very note." He slapped it down upon the table in front of him. "Listen to this. 'You will see me when all is ready. Come at once. F. H. M.' Now my theory all along has been that Lady St. Simon was decoyed away by Flora Millar, and that she, with confederates, no doubt, was responsible for her disappearance. Here, signed with her initials, is the very note which was no doubt quietly slipped into her hand at the door and which lured her within their reach."

"Very good, Lestrade," said Holmes, laughing. "You really are very fine indeed. Let me see it." He took up the paper in a listless way, but his attention instantly became riveted, and he gave a little cry of satisfaction. "This is indeed important," said he.

"Ha! you find it so?"

"Extremely so. I congratulate you warmly."

Lestrade rose in his triumph and bent his head to look. "Why," he shrieked, "you're looking at the wrong side!"

"On the contrary, this is the right side."

"The right side? You're mad! Here is the note written in pencil over here."

"And over here is what appears to be the fragment of a hotel bill, which interests me deeply."

"There's nothing in it. I looked at it before," said Lestrade. " 'Oct. 4th, rooms 8s., breakfast 2s. 6d., cocktail 1s., lunch 2s. 6d., glass sherry, 8d.' I see nothing in that."

"Very likely not. It is most important, all the same. As to the note, it is important also, or at least the initials are, so I congratulate you again."

"I've wasted time enough," said Lestrade, rising. "I believe in hard work and not in sitting by the fire spinning fine theories. Good-day, Mr. Holmes, and we shall see which gets to the bottom of the matter first." He gathered up the garments, thrust them into the bag, and made for the door.

"Just one hint to you, Lestrade," drawled Holmes before his rival vanished. "I will tell you the true solution of the matter. Lady St. Simon is a myth. There is not, and there never has been, any such person."

Lestrade looked sadly at my companion. Then he turned to me, tapped his forehead three times, shook his head solemnly, and hurried away.

He had hardly shut the door behind him when Holmes rose to put on his overcoat. "There is something in what the fellow says about outdoor work," he remarked, "so l think, Watson, that I must leave you to your papers for a little."

It was after five o'clock when Sherlock Holmes left me, but I had no time to be lonely, for within an hour there arrived a confectioner's man with a very large flat box. This he unpacked with the help of a youth whom he had brought with him, and presently, to my very great astonishment, a quite epicurean little cold supper began to be laid out upon our humble lodging-house mahogany. There were a couple of brace of cold woodcock, a pheasant, a pâté de foie gras pie with a group of ancient and cobwebby bottles. Having laid out all these luxuries, my two visitors vanished away, like the genii of the Arabian Nights, with no explanation save that the things had been paid for and were ordered to this address.

Just before nine o'clock Sherlock Holmes stepped briskly into the room. His features were gravely set, but there was a light in his eye which made me think that he had not been disappointed in his conclusions.

"They have laid the supper, then," he said, rubbing his hands.

"You seem to expect company. They have laid for five."

"Yes, I fancy we may have some company dropping in," said he. "I am surprised that Lord St. Simon has not already arrived. Ha! I fancy that I hear his step now upon the stairs."

It was indeed our visitor of the afternoon who came bustling in, dangling his glasses more vigorously than ever, and with a very perturbed expression upon his aristocratic features.

"My messenger reached you, then?" asked Holmes.

"Yes, and I confess that the contents startled me beyond measure. Have you good authority for what you say?"

"The best possible."

Lord St. Simon sank into a chair and passed his hand over his forehead.

"What will the Duke say," he murmured, "when he hears that one of the family has been subjected to such humiliation?"

"It is the purest accident. I cannot allow that there is any humiliation."

"Ah, you look on these things from another standpoint."

"I fail to see that anyone is to blame. I can hardly see how the lady could have acted otherwise, though her abrupt method of doing it was undoubtedly to be regretted. Having no mother, she had no one to advise her at such a crisis."

"It was a slight, sir, a public slight," said Lord St. Simon, tapping his fingers upon the table.

"You must make allowance for this poor girl, placed in so unprecedented a position."

"I will make no allowance. I am very angry indeed, and I have been shamefully used."

"I think that I heard a ring," said Holmes. "Yes, there are steps on the landing. If I cannot persuade you to take a lenient view of the matter, Lord St. Simon, I have brought an advocate here who may be more successful." He opened the door and ushered in a lady and gentleman. "Lord St. Simon," said he "allow me to introduce you to Mr. and Mrs. Francis Hay Moulton. The lady, I think, you have already met."

At the sight of these newcomers our client had sprung from his seat and stood very erect, with his eyes cast down and his hand thrust into the breast of his frock-coat, a picture of offended dignity. The lady had taken a quick step forward and had held out her hand to him, but he still refused to raise his eyes. It was as well for his resolution, perhaps, for her pleading face was one which it was hard to resist.

"You're angry, Robert," said she. "Well, I guess you have every cause to be."

"Pray make no apology to me," said Lord St. Simon bitterly.

"Oh, yes, I know that I have treated you real bad and that I should have spoken to you before I went; but I was kind of rattled, and from the time when I saw Frank here again I just didn't know what I was doing or saying. I only wonder I didn't fall down and do a faint right there before the altar."

"Perhaps, Mrs. Moulton, you would like my friend and me to leave the room while you explain this matter?"

"If I may give an opinion," remarked the strange gentleman, "we've had just a little too much secrecy over this business already. For my part, I should like all Europe and America to hear the rights of it." He was a small, wiry, sunburnt man, clean-shaven, with a sharp face and alert manner.

"Then I'll tell our story right away," said the lady. "Frank here and I met in '84, in McQuire's camp, near the Rockies, where pa was working a claim. We were engaged to each other, Frank and I; but then one day father struck a rich pocket and made a pile, while poor Frank here had a claim that petered out and came to nothing. The richer pa grew the poorer was Frank; so at last pa wouldn't hear of our engagement lasting any longer, and he took me away to 'Frisco. Frank wouldn't throw up his hand, though; so he followed me there, and he saw me without pa knowing anything about it. It would only have made him mad to know, so we just fixed it all up for ourselves. Frank said that he would go and make his pile, too, and never come back to claim me until he had as much as pa. So then I promised to wait for him to the end of time and pledged myself not to marry anyone else while he lived. 'Why shouldn't we be married right away, then,' said he, 'and then I will feel sure of you; and I won't claim to be your husband until I come back?' Well, we talked it over, and he had fixed it all up so nicely, with a clergyman all ready in waiting, that we just did it right there; and then Frank went off to seek his fortune, and I went back to pa.

"The next I heard of Frank was that he was in Montana, and then he went prospecting in Arizona, and then I heard of him from New Mexico. After that came a long newspaper story about how a miners' camp had been attacked by Apache Indians, and there was my Frank's name among the killed. I fainted dead away, and I was very sick for months after. Pa thought I had a decline and took me to half the doctors in 'Frisco. Not a word of news came for a year and more, so that I never doubted that Frank was really dead. Then Lord St. Simon came to 'Frisco, and we came to London, and a marriage was arranged, and pa was very pleased, but I felt all the time that no man on this earth would ever take the place in my heart that had been given to my poor Frank.

"Still, if I had married Lord St. Simon, of course I'd have done my duty by him. We can't command our love, but we can our actions. I went to the altar with him with the intention to make him just as good a wife as it was in me to be. But you may imagine what I felt when, just as I came to the altar rails, I glanced back and saw Frank standing and looking at me out of the first pew. I thought it was his ghost at first; but when I looked again there he was still, with a kind of question in his eyes, as if to ask me whether I were glad or sorry to see him. I wonder I didn't drop. I know that everything was turning round, and the words of the clergyman were just like the buzz of a bee in my ear. I didn't know what to do. Should I stop the service and make a scene in the church? I glanced at him again, and he seemed to know what I was thinking, for he raised his finger to his lips to tell me to be still. Then I saw him scribble on a piece of paper, and I knew that he was writing me a note. As I passed his pew on the way out I dropped my bouquet over to him, and he slipped the note into my hand when he returned me the flowers. It was only a line asking me to join him when he made the sign to me to do so. Of course I never doubted for a moment that my first duty was now to him, and I determined to do just whatever he might direct.

"When I got back I told my maid, who had known him in California, and had always been his friend. I ordered her to say nothing, but to get a few things packed and my ulster ready. I know I ought to have spoken to Lord St. Simon, but it was dreadful hard before his mother and all those great people. I just made up my mind to run away and explain afterwards. I hadn't been at the table ten minutes before I saw Frank out of the window at the other side of the road. He beckoned to me and then began walking into the Park. I slipped out, put on my things, and followed him. Some woman came talking something or other about Lord St. Simon to me — seemed to me from the little I heard as if he had a little secret of his own before marriage also — but I managed to get away from her and soon overtook Frank. We got into a cab together, and away we drove to some lodgings he had taken in Gordon Square, and that was my true wedding after all those years of waiting. Frank had been a prisoner among the Apaches, had escaped, came on to 'Frisco, found that I had given him up for dead and had gone to England, followed me there, and had come upon me at last on the very morning of my second wedding."

"I saw it in a paper," explained the American. "It gave the name and the church but not where the lady lived."

"Then we had a talk as to what we should do, and Frank was all for openness, but I was so ashamed of it all that I felt as if I should like to vanish away and never see any of them again — just sending a line to pa, perhaps, to show him that I was alive. It was awful to me to think of all those lords and ladies sitting round that breakfast-table and waiting for me to come back. So Frank took my wedding-clothes and things and made a bundle of them, so that I should not be traced, and dropped them away somewhere where no one could find them. It is likely that we should have gone on to Paris to-morrow, only that this good gentleman, Mr. Holmes, came round to us this evening, though how he found us is more than I can think, and he showed us very clearly and kindly that I was wrong and that Frank was right, and that we should be putting ourselves in the wrong if we were so secret. Then he offered to give us a chance of talking to Lord St. Simon alone, and so we came right away round to his rooms at once. Now, Robert, you have heard it all, and I am very sorry if I have given you pain, and I hope that you do not think very meanly of me."

Lord St. Simon had by no means relaxed his rigid attitude, but had listened with a frowning brow and a compressed lip to this long narrative.

"Excuse me," he said, "but it is not my custom to discuss my most intimate personal affairs in this public manner."

"Then you won't forgive me? You won't shake hands before I go?"

"Oh, certainly, if it would give you any pleasure." He put out his hand and coldly grasped that which she extended to him.

"I had hoped," suggested Holmes, "that you would have joined us in a friendly supper."

"I think that there you ask a little too much," responded his Lordship. "I may be forced to acquiesce in these recent developments, but I can hardly be expected to make merry over them. I think that with your permission I will now wish you all a very good-night." He included us all in a sweeping bow and stalked out of the room.

"Then I trust that you at least will honour me with your company," said Sherlock Holmes. "It is always a joy to meet an American, Mr. Moulton, for I am one of those who believe that the folly of a monarch and the blundering of a minister in far-gone years will not prevent our children from being some day citizens of the same world-wide country under a flag which shall be a quartering of the Union Jack with the Stars and Stripes."

"The case has been an interesting one," remarked Holmes when our visitors had left us, "because it serves to show very clearly how simple the explanation may be of an affair which at first sight seems to be almost inexplicable. Nothing could be more natural than the sequence of events as narrated by this lady, and nothing stranger than the result when viewed, for instance by Mr. Lestrade, of Scotland Yard."

"You were not yourself at fault at all, then?"

"From the first, two facts were very obvious to me, the one that the lady had been quite willing to undergo the wedding ceremony, the other that she had repented of it within a few minutes of returning home. Obviously something had occurred during the morning, then, to cause her to change her mind. What could that something be? She could not have spoken to anyone when she was out, for she had been in the company of the bridegroom. Had she seen someone, then? If she had, it must be someone from America because she had spent so short a time in this country that she could hardly have allowed anyone to acquire so deep an influence over her that the mere sight of him would induce her to change her plans so completely. You see we have already arrived, by a process of exclusion, at the idea that she might have seen an American. Then who could this American be, and why should he possess so much influence over her? It might be a lover; it might be a husband. Her young womanhood had, I knew, been spent in rough scenes and under strange conditions. So far I had got before I ever heard Lord St. Simon's narrative. When he told us of a man in a pew, of the change in the bride's manner, of so transparent a device for obtaining a note as the dropping of a bouquet, of her resort to her confidential maid, and of her very significant allusion to claim-jumping — which in miners' parlance means taking possession of that which another person has a prior claim to — the whole situation became absolutely clear. She had gone off with a man, and the man was either a lover or was a previous husband — the chances being in favour of the latter."

"And how in the world did you find them?"

"It might have been difficult, but friend Lestrade held information in his hands the value of which he did not himself know. The initials were, of course, of the highest importance, but more valuable still was it to know that within a week he had settled his bill at one of the most select London hotels."

"How did you deduce the select?"

"By the select prices. Eight shillings for a bed and eightpence for a glass of sherry pointed to one of the most expensive hotels. There are not many in London which charge at that rate. In the second one which I visited in Northumberland Avenue, I learned by an inspection of the book that Francis H. Moulton, an American gentleman, had left only the day before, and on looking over the entries against him, I came upon the very items which I had seen in the duplicate bill. His letters were to be forwarded to 226 Gordon Square; so thither I travelled, and being fortunate enough to find the loving couple at home, 1 ventured to give them some paternal advice and to point out to them that it would be better in every way that they should make their position a little clearer both to the general public and to Lord St. Simon in particular. I invited them to meet him here, and, as you see, I made him keep the appointment."

"But with no very good result," I remarked. "His conduct was certainly not very gracious."

"Ah, Watson," said Holmes, smiling, "perhaps you would not be very gracious either, if, after all the trouble of wooing and wedding, you found yourself deprived in an instant of wife and of fortune. I think that we may judge Lord St. Simon very mercifully and thank our stars that we are never likely to find ourselves in the same position. Draw your chair up and hand me my violin, for the only problem we have still to solve is how to while away these bleak autumnal evenings."

THE TATOOED ARM

by Marc Bilgrey

There are a number of cases that I've chronicled, involving my friend Sherlock Holmes that I have chosen not to publish. Some of these are of a very delicate political nature, and if they were released to the public, could seriously compromise the peace that exists between our nation and certain foreign powers. Other cases, I have also decided to keep in a locked box, in a bank vault, in Charing Cross, because, if the details of these were to come to light, they might potentially endanger the lives of a number of prominent public figures and their families.

There is one more class of case that I have kept private, due to the fact that they contain elements and/or events which I've deemed too sensational or fantastic to believe. The case which I'm about to recount, falls into this category. It is fair to note that in the years since these awful incidents occurred, the world has undergone many changes. While the passage of time has not dulled the impact of what transpired during those days, I believe that it has somewhat prepared the public to accept, or at least to approach this case with an open mind. It is with this philosophy that I have decided to chance its release. Having made these statements, I must admit that, had I not personally witnessed all that I am about to recount with my own eyes, there is no doubt that I would consider myself a skeptic.

The adventure began early one cold winter morning, while I was still residing in the rooms at 221b Baker Street. I was awakened by Sherlock Holmes, who urged me to dress immediately. When I asked him for an explanation, he merely said,

"Wear warm clothing, Watson, we are making a trip to the country."

With that, he left me to obey his orders. I knew my friend well enough to know that it was useless to attempt to elicit information from him. He would tell me more in his own time. I had no sooner finished shaving when the door was opened and Holmes stuck his head inside the room and said, "And do take your revolver."

My curiosity now thoroughly piqued, Holmes and I set off in a cab for Paddington station. Once there, Holmes purchased our tickets, and a moment later, we stepped into a train car and sat down.

"How would you feel about a day at the seashore?" asked Holmes.

Though I've occasionally made mention of Sherlock Holme's bizarre sense of humour, in previous accounts, I suppose I shall never entirely get used to it.

"It's February," I replied, feeling like the straight man in a music hall routine.

Holmes smiled, removed an envelope from his coat pocket and took out a letter. "Our friend, Inspector Lestrade, has been kind enough to invite us to a scenic little coastal village in Cornwall, called Harbourton. It seems there's been a murder there, one with some peculiar qualities."

"Peculiar?" I said, knowing well Holmes's interest in all things out of the ordinary.

It was then that Holmes began reading from the letter. "The victim was one Alvar Harris, a man of sixty-seven, who lived on a secluded farm, some five miles outside town. A week ago, a local woman, Millicent Stokes, who would periodically stop by Harris's house, from the village, to bring him groceries, found him missing. She had seen him alive only the previous afternoon, when he'd asked her to return the following day with the weekly newspaper, which she'd forgotten to bring him. After searching the property, Stokes discovered blood stains near the barn. Suspicion immediately fell upon Harris's neighbor, Edmund Collier, who lived a quarter mile away. Harris and Collier had been known to detest each other. It seems that the reason for that contention is that Harris would let his cows graze on Collier's land, despite Collier's numerous pleas to the contrary. Harris was, by all accounts, a taciturn man, with no living family, who seldom ventured into town. Collier, by contrast, is a retired Postal clerk, who lived with his own grown daughter, often socialized in the local village pub, and used his time, to pursue his avocation, which is sculpting."

I glanced out the window to see the buildings of London recede into the distance, as Holmes continued reading from the letter.

"Upon being questioned, Millicent Stokes, was ruled out as a suspect. An extensive search of Harris's house and grounds revealed no other evidence, nor did a search of Collier's house. Other than the circumstantial, there seemed to be nothing to tie Collier to the crime. This changed two days later, when a human arm washed up on the local beach and was found by a passing fisherman. An examination of the arm revealed two tattoos, which, a tearful Stokes, immediately recognized, as belonging to the deceased. Collier was promptly arrested, and another search of his house revealed a number of saws, which Collier claimed to use in his sculpting work. Due to the condition of the victim's arm, which was severed with razor-like precision, it soon became obvious that we had our culprit. When presented with this evidence, Collier maintained his innocence. The matter might have ended there, were it not for Collier's daughter, Katherine, who says that she and her father were home the entire night that the crime was committed. It is Katherine Collier who insisted that I contact you, Mr. Holmes, with the hope that you could perform a miracle, and save her father from the gallows." The letter ended there.

"It seems that Lestrade is satisfied that he has the guilty party, and that the case is solved," I said.

"When Lestrade feels satisfaction, the world trembles," said Holmes, with a half smile, then took a few photographs out of the same envelope that the letter had come from. "I must caution you, Watson, despite both your military and medical experience, you will find these photographs nothing short of gruesome."

Holmes handed me the pictures. Given his usual flair for the dramatic, I wasn't sure what to expect, but in this instance, he was not exaggerating. I stared at the photographs with revulsion. Each one was a picture of the severed arm, taken from different angles. I took note of the particularly strange manner with which the arm had been cut, then at the two tattoos on the upper bicep. The top one was of a nearly rectangular shape, and the one below it was an illustration of two intertwined vines. Further down, I noticed three dark circles, which were not tattoos, though exactly what they were, I wasn't sure, perhaps wounds of some kind. Then I saw an area of blackened puffy skin, which is common among drowning victims.

"What can you tell me about Mr. Harris from looking at his arm?" asked Holmes.

"It is the arm of a healthy man, if not somewhat overweight," I said, "The fingers have calluses, so it stands to reason that he worked with his hands."

"Excellent, Watson."

"The tattoos, are, of course, distinctive. Perhaps he was a lover of the art, or merely a follower of fashion. Since a number of royals created the vogue, the public has, as they always do, followed suit."

Holmes glanced at the photographs, then said, "The victim weighed twenty stone, stood six feet tall, had grey hair, spent much time outside, (no doubt tending to his animals). He was a widower who lost his beloved wife not more than five years ago, after which he sought seclusion. But, while many men who find themselves in similar circumstances turn to drink in an effort to quell their sorrows, Harris indulged himself with cakes, tarts, scones, pies, cookies, and eclairs. All of which came naturally to him, as his profession was that of a master baker. Since his wife's death, he has had no other romance in his life. He was a compulsive man, whose outward anger masked his inner emotional pain."

"How could you possibly know all that, Holmes?" I asked, stunned.

"The circumference of the arm indicated his girth, and from there one has only to gauge the proportions of the body and reconstruct it exponentially, much the way a naturalist, who specializes in paleontology does, when unearthing a new dinosaur bone. The hair color is evident by small follicles that are still intact. The dark complexion indicates someone who has spent much time in the sun. The second finger from the pinky has a lighter color around the third knuckle, obviously from the impression of a wedding band which was only removed within the last few days. If that wasn't enough to declare his eternal love, the tattoo of the intertwining vines, a popular image symbolizing such everlasting devotion, removes all doubt. As for his weight being a product of his own overindulgence, the illustration above the vines is that of a loaf of bread. A tattoo proclaiming one's profession is not uncommon, especially among certain classes. His anguish and compulsion is evident by the condition of his fingernails. They have been bitten, a nasty habit, which would suggest that he was alone, as few women would put up with such unhygienic and socially unacceptable behavior in their man."

"Astounding," I said.

"At the risk of repeating myself, Watson, it's really quite elementary. However, having said that, these photographs raise more questions than they answer. Would you care to speculate on what sort of instrument could have been used to sever this man's arm?"

"Other than perhaps having been caught in the gears of some large factory machine, of which I am unfamiliar, and even then, I'm frankly at a loss to explain the odd uneven nature of the cut. It appears unlikely that even a surgeon's knife could have achieved these results."

"My thoughts exactly."

"It's not often we agree on something."

"Don't sell yourself short, Watson, your observations are invaluable."

I looked out the window, as the countryside went by, and thought about poor Mr. Harris. A few hours later we arrived at Harbourton, and were met at the station by Lestrade and the local constable, a dour looking man called Dunbar. We were escorted to a carriage, driven through the sleepy little village, and into the hills beyond. A quarter hour later we turned onto a secluded road, and there we stopped at a cottage, which we were informed belonged to, Edmund Collier, the man in custody. The door to the cottage was opened by a beautiful woman of no more than twenty years, with pitch black hair.

"Mr. Sherlock Holmes, I presume," she said, curtsying, as if she were greeting a visiting noble, "I am Katherine Collins."

"Miss Collier," said Holmes, "this is my friend and associate, Dr. Watson. I take it that you are already acquainted with Inspector Lestrade, and Constable Dunbar."

"Yes," she said, looking none too happy about that fact.

We stepped into the living room, and Holmes went over to a painting that hung above a mantle. The portrait was of a gaunt man in his sixties, who was dressed in a plain white shirt and dark trousers.

"Your father," said Holmes.

"Yes," said Miss Collier, "he traded a local painter for a sculpture he'd made of the man. A portait for a portrait."

"You contend that on the night of the murder you were here?" said Holmes.

"Yes," said Miss Collier, "I was with my father the entire night. When we heard the news the next day, from the constable, it came as a complete shock to us as it had to everyone else."

"Is it possible that your father could have gone outside that night without you hearing him?" asked Holmes.

"No, Mr. Holmes, even if I had not seen him, I certainly would have heard him leave, since I have the room next to his and am a very light sleeper. In addition, the floorboards groan, and the doors and windows squeak when opened. Though, as I understand it, whoever did perpetrate this heinous act would have needed more than a few minutes's time to do it."

"Quite so," said Holmes, "may we look around?"

"Of course," replied the girl.

I accompanied Holmes through the house's few rooms, each of which contained wooden sculptures. Most of them were busts, or small figurines. In a shed behind the house, we found a workroom, with a table on which rested a number of saws of various sizes, as well as hammers, axes, and other craftsman's tools. From there, we went outside, and saw a horse and cart. Here, Holmes knelt down, and examined the cart's wheels. After a moment or two, he stood up, and met the gazes of Lestrade and Dunbar, who were standing a few feet away, watching us. Katherine Collins went over to Holmes and said, "Is there any hope for my father?"

"If you're asking me if I believe that he murdered Mr. Harris, the answer is no."

"That's preposterous," said Lestrade.

"We have the right man," said Dunbar, "of that you can be certain."

"When it comes to crime, nothing is certain," said Holmes, "except uncertainty. Keep your spirits up, young lady. I expect to bring you good news soon."

On the trip up the road, in Dunbar's carriage, I wondered if Holmes should have been so optimistic. I'd seen nothing that cast doubt on the official version of the case, let alone that would point to Edmund Collier's innocence. But once Holmes had an idea in his mind, there was no talking him out of it. My concern was for Miss Collier. I didn't want her to have unrealistic expectations, and as a result, subsequently be disappointed.

In five minutes time we stopped in front of another cottage. This one was bigger than the previous one, and the grass in front of it, a bit overgrown.

"We've preserved the scene," said Lestrade, as we walked up the path to the front door, "for what it's worth."

Holmes turned to Lestrade, seemingly unamused, then Dunbar unlocked the door, and we went inside. The living room was simply furnished with a wooden table and a few chairs. On a cabinet were some framed photographs of a fat man, whom I assumed was Harris, with a plump woman, presumably his late wife. A search of the pantry turned up tins of dried fruit, chocolate, and some jars of jam. On a counter were a stale loaf of bread and a few traditional Cornish pies, which, judging by the smell, had gone bad.

Then we went outside and walked to the barn, which was empty. On the ground, in front of it, were the blood stains that Lestrade had mentioned in his letter. Holmes examined them, then drew his attention to a horseless cart that stood nearby. As he had done at the previous cottage, he inspected the cart's wheels and after that, seemed to take notice of a small wren that had landed on a nearby log. The bird was eating a worm. Holmes then walked to some shrubs not far from the barn and examined them. I turned to Lestrade and Dunbar, who were watching the proceedings, with what I took to be expressions of extreme boredom.

"And the prisoner," said Holmes, returning from his foray into the bushes, and directing his attention to the two lawmen, "may I speak with him?"

"By all means, Mr. Holmes," said Dunbar, smugly, "if it'll hasten your departure from our midst, you're welcome to have a brief chat with him."

It was now obvious that Lestrade and his new found friend were enjoying themselves immensely at our expense. While this annoyed me no end, Holmes seemed to be oblivious to their attitude. When we arrived back in town, the lot of us descended upon the local jail. Edmund Collier greeted us in his cell with the enthusiasm of a condemned man resigned to his fate. He looked even more gaunt and frail than in his portrait. Holmes's interview was short and seemed to add nothing of substance to the case. Afterward, Holmes asked Dunbar if he could recommend lodgings for the night. The Constable gave us the name of the town's only inn and public house, The Harborview, which, it turned out, was a short walk away.

Once there, and finally free from Lestrade and his shadow, Holmes seemed to relax a bit. In the public house we ordered poached cod for dinner and after it arrived, Holmes said, "We seem to have a most singular case, Watson, one filled with many twists and turns."

"Despite Lestrade and Dunbar's claims to the contrary," I intoned.

"Neither of our friends seems to have the slightest concern with the fact that Collier, a man of no more than seven stone, is supposed to have taken on Harris, who was twenty stone, in a fight, using what was undoubtedly a blunt instrument, based upon my examination of the blood stains, and single handedly, overpowered him, removed the body, presumably for burial in some secluded spot, of which, incidentally, there are certainly are no shortage of in that region. And yet, all this was done clandestinely, without his daughter's knowledge, consent, or cooperation."

"She could have been lying," I said, reluctantly.

"You don't believe that any more than I do."

"And that does not explain the arm."

"No," said Holmes, finishing his dinner. "If we are to believe Lestrade and Dunbar, a simple murder, which was committed for no other purpose than to quell an annoying neighbor, resulted in a piece of the victim being found five miles away from the scene of the crime at a beach."

"It does beg certain questions," I said.

"Indeed, at the risk of repetition, such as how would a frail, slight fellow overpower a man over three times his size, lift the body onto a cart, and, rather than bury it privately and conveniently in a secluded area, instead, choose to, at enormous risk of discovery and capture, cut the body into pieces, and drive five miles to dispose of it in the ocean."

"Quite a conundrum, indeed."

"To say the least," said Holmes, "but then I have neglected to mention one trifle. What do you make of this, Watson?" Holmes produced a small glass vial from his pocket and handed it to me.

"Where did you get this?" I asked, examining the ampoule.

"From the bushes near Harris's barn, right from under the noses of Lestrade and his friend."

There were bits of a brown residue on the glass, which could have indicated a number of substances, but the odor, though faint, was unmistakable. "It's chloral hydrate."

"As you know, it is a powerful, quick acting tranquilizer."

"Could Alvar Harris have been drugged, then beaten to death?"

"The idea does seem to complicate matters."

"It also suggests a careful premeditation of the crime, which would appear to further rule out Mr. Colliers as the perpetrator."

"We may be approaching a record, Watson, for drawing the greatest number of similar conclusions on a single case," said Holmes, smiling.

As we were paying the bill, Holmes asked the barkeep if he knew of any land in the nearby hills that was available for purchase.

"Now and again," responded the ruddy faced man, "are you considering moving here, sir?"

"Yes," said Holmes, "I have an idea to become a dairy farmer."

"Oh?" said the barkeep, wiping his hands on his dirty apron, as he looked at Holmes incredulously.

"How is the farming here?" asked Holmes.

"The farming is fine," said the barkeep, "but if you'll be owning cows, my advice is to keep a good watch on them, as lately there's been a rash of theft."

"Cattle rustling?"

"From all accounts, done at night. Yet, no one's reported a local farmer with any more cows than their own."

When we had exited the public house, I turned to Holmes and exclaimed, "What was that all about?"

"Just a theory I'm pursuing," he replied, smiling, "no need for concern, I have no immediate plans to move from our lodgings at Baker Street any time in the near future. Now come, Watson, it's imperative that we get some salt air immediately."

It was late afternoon, as Sherlock Holmes, and I walked through the cobble stoned village streets, and in a short time found ourselves on the town's rocky beach. Other than a few fishermen, sitting near beached boats, repairing their netting, the place was deserted. The sky was overcast, and a cold north wind blew across the ocean before us. Holmes wandered off, looking in all directions. I glanced at the village behind us, then to the right, and, in the distance, saw a rather imposing manor house high atop a cliff, overlooking the water. When I noticed Holmes staring at it as well, I went over to one of the fishermen and said, "Pardon me, but would you happen to know who lives there?"

The craggy faced man, barely looking up from his mending, responded, "It belongs to Dr. Phillip Paxton, my biggest customer."

"He eats a lot of fish?" I asked.

"Not 'im, 'is pets." When the man noticed my perplexed look, he added, "He's a scientist. Keeps aquariums of fish, big ones too, and even seals. Bloody hungry, they are. In the last two months, he's doubled his orders. I provide 'im with at least a hundred pounds a week lately, as does my friend over there, and so do some of the other men, too."

I thanked him for answering my question, then rejoined Holmes, and we returned to the inn. When we were back in our room, I recounted my brief exchange with the fisherman, as Holmes lit his pipe, and to my surprise, replied,

"Dr. Phillip Paxton, is the scion of the tea importing family of the same name. Though at one time a prominent naturalist and marine biologist with the public aquarium at Regent Park Zoological Gardens, he was expelled by the Marine Biology Society and forced to resign from his position at the aquarium, due to his unorthodox theories on ocean life.Keep in mind that many a scientist whose ideas were scorned in their own lifetime, were then accepted by later generations."

"How is it that you are aware of such a man?" I asked.

"Watson, I make it my business to read the newspapers and when I received Lestrade's letter I remembered, Paxton had left London to live in his ancestral home in this part of Cornwall. As I've told you, upon occasion, when I explain my methods, they seem much less dazzling, not unlike a stage magician revealing his illusions."

I took a sip of brandy from my flask and reflected upon what we'd learned in the last few hours. Holmes went to the window, took a puff from his pipe, and looked out at the now darkened sky. On the table, I noticed a copy of the local newspaper that had probably been left by the maid when she'd turned down our sheets. The headline read, Local Man Held On Murder Charges.

Holmes turned to me, and said, "I suggest that we get some rest. We have a most busy day ahead of us, and we will need to get an early start."

"But," I said, "haven't we already questioned everyone connected with the case and looked at the scene of the crime?"

"There is much that remains to be done," said Holmes, in his usual cryptic way.

I knew better than to ask him what would be on tomorrow's itinerary. Instead, I had another sip of my drink and readied myself for bed.

When I awoke in the morning, Holmes was gone. The moment I finished dressing, he burst into the room.

"There you are, Watson, put on your coat and hat, and we'll be on our way."

Outside the inn was a waiting trap and driver, and we got inside.

"I thought of someone whom we haven't spoken to," I said, "Millicent Stokes, the woman who reported Harris missing, and found the blood in front of the barn."

"I questioned her before you arose," answered Holmes, while the driver guided his horse through the cobblestone streets. "As I had thought, she had no relevant facts to add to our investigation, but I would have been remiss if I hadn't consulted with her."

"Oh," I replied, crestfallen. For an instant I felt as if I might have actually stumbled upon an idea that Holmes had somehow overlooked.

"You've no doubt visited the aquarium at Regent Park," said Holmes, abruptly changing the subject.

"Certainly," I replied, "As a school boy I went quite often. I was fascinated by watching the fish, as are most children."

"Today we will be visiting, what I surmise, will be a miniature version of that great "fish house", as it's called by the public. We'll be paying a call on Dr. Phillip Paxton."

"Presumably, this is in connection with the case."

Holmes laughed. "Surely you don't think all this salt air has made me balmy, do you, Watson? I believe that Dr. Paxton's scientific expertise may be able to shed some light on this case."

Then Holmes fell silent, as the carriage went up an incline. A few minutes later, we came to a stop in front of Phillip Paxton's manor house. Judging by its fine stone work, it looked to be at least three hundred years old. Holmes instructed the driver to wait for us, even though it might be some time till we returned. The driver nodded, and Holmes and I walked toward the house. As we did, I couldn't help admiring the breathtaking view of the ocean below. The house's huge door was answered by a gruff looking butler, who looked more in build as if he belonged in a pugilist's ring than in a gentleman's residence. When Holmes mentioned that we were acting in an official capacity on behalf of the local constable, the man's expression softened, and we were invited into the great hall and seated on chairs that looked as old as the house itself. The servant asked us if we'd like some tea. When we politely declined, he bowed and left.

The great hall had high stone walls, on which were hung medieval tapestries, crossed swords, and a family coat of arms. Ancient ornately carved wooden tables stood against a number of the walls, as did oversized vases, which held dried plants. The only anomaly was, where one might traditionally have expected to see framed oil portraits of ancestors, there were, instead, elaborate paintings of fish. I saw tuna, herring, sole, bluefish and cod. Before I had time to fully contemplate their significance, a man in his sixties, wearing a white surgeon's coat, walked into the hall.

"I am Dr. Phillip Paxton," he said, "and you must be Sherlock Holmes. Of course, I have read a number of your cases. And this must be your chronicler, Dr. Watson."

"We've come to discuss a matter with you, with which you may be of some assistance," said Holmes.

"Indeed," said Dr. Paxton, "I'd be most pleased to help in any way I can. But first, would you please indulge me? I insist upon showing you my little laboratory."

We went down a wide corridor. On the walls hung more paintings of fish. Within a moment we were in a vast gallery which contained massive glass aquariums, and, as Holmes had predicted, easily rivaled the ones at Regent Gardens, and those at the Surrey Zoological Gardens as well.

"Here are my friends," said Dr. Paxton, gesturing at the first aquarium, "these are some of the local species, mackerel, cod, and bluefish."

We passed one tank after another, each one larger than the last, till we came to a stop in front of an aquarium that was the size of a house. Inside it, grey seals swam about as if they had not a care in the world. A muscle bound man appeared, with a ladder, placed it on the side of the tank, then took a bucket, climbed up, and dumped fish into the water.

Dr. Paxton watched the seals for a moment, then turned to Holmes and myself and said. "I'm researching every aspect of these beautiful creature's lives. I'm sure, Mr. Holmes, if your reputation is accurate, that you may have heard about my, uh, differences with the institute."

"Small-minded thinkers, no doubt," said Holmes.

"Ah," said Paxton, "I see that you grasp the situation fully. But here I have no one to answer to, no need to please would-be benefactors. Those relics back in London scoffed at any idea that didn't fit into their narrow views of the world. Science should not have to bow before the feet of bankers in order to march forward."

"Well put," said Holmes. "I need not remind you, it was only a short time ago that Mr. Fulton's steam engine was the subject of similar derision by the same sort of self-appointed experts."

Dr. Paxton seemed very pleased by Holmes'ss comments, as he took us to one more aquarium. This was double the size of the previous one. In it were dolphins.

"Bottle nosed dolphins," said Holmes, "magnificent animals. There are those that contend that they possess a certain innate intelligence."

With this, Dr. Paxton's eyes lit up. "You surprise me, Mr. Holmes."

"I have found that many worthy ideas start at the fringes of society, and are initially rejected by the mainstream," said Holmes, "only to be eventually accepted by the very same naysayers and disbelievers, who then attempt to claim credit for them."

"I suspect that law enforcement's gain is science's loss," said Paxton, as he led us back through the glass gallery.

"This is the entirety of your sea menagerie?" asked Holmes.

"Yes, excluding those organisms on the slides under my microscope."

It was an amazing collection, I thought. I couldn't imagine that there could be another one like it, in private hands, in all of England. We returned to the great hall, again and sat down. Then Holmes produced the photographs he'd shown me on the train.

"Before you view these, Dr. Paxton, I must warn you of their graphic nature."

"I'm a man of science, sir," said Paxton, blinking.

"Very well," said Holmes, "if you've read the local newspaper in the last few days, you'll have heard of the human arm that was found on the beach, not far from here."

"I'm afraid I'm much too involved in my work to keep up with the news."

"I'd like you to look at these photographs and give me your professional opinion. Is there any sea creature you know of that could have done this to a man?"

Holmes gave Paxton the photographs. Paxton studied them carefully, then said, "There are no teeth marks that would indicate a shark, rare as such an attack is on humans. Even so, it would not be so smooth a cut, as this."

"Could a whale have been responsible?"

"I dare say not, once again, in the few documented cases I know of, there would be signs of biting, and the skin and bone would be jagged. Even piranhas, which are native to South America, and are never found in these cold waters, would leave traces of their tiny razor-like teeth. I see no evidence of anything of the sort here. I know of no fish or ocean mammal capable of inflicting such damage in precisely this way."

Paxton returned the photographs to Holmes, who stood up promptly, and said, "Thank you, Dr. Paxton, you've been of invaluable assistance. Come, Watson, our driver awaits."

We returned to the village and stopped in front of the Inn, whereupon Holmes told me to go up to our room and wait for him, as he had "some errands to attend to." I stepped out of the carriage, and it pulled away quickly. As I walked through the simply furnished lobby, and up the stairs, I wondered what my friend was going to do. Once in our room, I passed the time by reading a book

I found on a shelf about tin mining in Cornwall. Though I found the style somewhat dry, to say the least, the subject was surprisingly engaging. It was past dusk, when Sherlock Holmes returned, and in a very excited state.

"Come Watson," he said, "and bring your revolver. We are rapidly approaching the dénouement of our case."

"But how — ?"

"There's no time to explain, every moment we delay may cost lives."

We rushed out of the inn, into the same trap that had taken us to the manor in the morning. It was now night, and a full moon hung above us.

"We're off to the manor," whispered Holmes, presumably, so the driver would not hear him.

"At this hour?" I replied.

What was Holmes getting us into? I thought. By his tone, I suspected we would hardly be attending a formal dinner party. Though the reason for our nocturnal visit eluded me, my confidence in Holmes's ability to prevail was unwavering.

When we were halfway to the manor, Holmes instructed the driver to take another route, to the left, bringing us back inland. I was completely perplexed, as we were now heading away from the manor. The road turned again and we entered a thick grove of trees. Luckily, the moon provided us with some light, or we'd have surely been lost. Suddenly, Holmes commanded the driver to come to an abrupt halt. Then Holmes struck a match, lit a lantern, and instructed me to step out of the carriage. When I had done so, he exited as well, and dismissed the driver. The carriage sped off, leaving Holmes and me alone in a dense forest.

"Follow me," whispered Holmes, holding the lantern.

I couldn't help asking myself the obvious questions. Where were we? Why were we here? And what in blazes were we doing? We walked for a few minutes. In the subdued light, I stumbled in some ruts in the hard dirt. Soon after, we reached a boulder that resembled an apple. Then Holmes reached into his coat, removed a rolled up paper, and held the lantern up to it. After a cursory glance, he pocketed the paper, walked a few paces, and turned around. "Here, Watson, follow me, and stay very close behind."

At this I could take no more. Patience is a virtue, only up to a point. "Now, Holmes, I think it's about time —"

"You're quite right, Watson. When this manor was built, over four hundred years ago, there was much concern over the then, very real possibility of sieges, and the masons who built it were instructed by their lord and master, to provide an escape tunnel into this forest."

"Ingenious, but how did you know about its existence?"

"There'll be plenty of opportunity to go into that later, but right now time is of the essence."

He held up the lantern, which revealed a set of stone steps that were all but covered by thick foliage. "Keep your revolver handy, Watson," he said, as we descended the stairs and came to a rusty iron door. It was padlocked. Holmes pulled out a set of keys, selected one, slid it into the lock, and it snapped open. Then the door followed suit with a soft creaking sound.

Holmes held up the lantern and I saw a tunnel directly ahead of us. I removed the gun from my pocket and held it tightly, as we stepped into the cavern. It was dark and smelled of mold. The lantern lit the way, as we trod through the seemingly endless tunnel. It's been said that man's most primal fear is darkness, and at that moment I had no doubt of it. Eventually, the passageway became narrower, and then, at last, we came to an opening. Here Holmes turned to me and whispered,

"Do not speak, Watson. Now we must wait."

Holmes doused the lantern and through the entrance in front of us, we saw a vast cave unfold that was illuminated by an eerie, flickering light. There was a narrow ridge immediately outside the opening where we stood. We walked a few paces, stole a quick glance over the edge and there, some twenty-five feet below, was an immense grotto, filled with water. We returned to the tunnel and then, all at once I heard voices. They were muffled at first, but I recognized Dr. Paxton's above the others. "That's it," he said, "come on now, let's not keep her waiting."

"Yes sir," said another voice. This one had a tinge of North Country in his inflection.

"Careful, with that," said Paxton, "let's not spill any."

"It's heavy, sir," said another voice, this one distinctly cockney.

"No back talk," said Paxton, sternly.

Then Holmes and I saw the three men emerge from another tunnel, and stand on the ledge, not more than a few feet away from us. We pulled back to avoid being seen. Besides Paxton, I recognized the other man as his servant,(though he was now wearing a workman's shirt and a pair of soiled trousers), and along with them was the man we'd seen on the ladder, feeding the fish. What followed next will haunt me till the end of my life. One of the men pulled up a bucket of fish and emptied its contents over the ledge into the water below. The other man took a second bucket and did the same. For a moment there was silence, and then I heard splashing in the water. Then something rose out of the water the likes of which I've never seen before. It was a massive tentacle, of the sort one might see on an octopus, except that this was at least fifty feet high, and had the circumference of a large Roman column. It was covered with suction cups of various sizes.

A second tentacle of equal size appeared along its side, thrashed around in the water for a few minutes, and then they both vanished into the depths from which they had come. Before I could catch my breath from beholding such a sight, Paxton turned to his men and said, "Bring me the main course." At this, one of his henchmen disappeared from view, and then returned immediately, with a portly man, whose arms were bound behind him with rope, and gagged across the mouth with a handkerchief. Holmes took out his revolver, then gestured to me that we were going to step forward and reveal ourselves. We moved quickly into the open, with our revolvers aimed at the trio. "Good evening, Dr. Paxton," said Holmes.

Paxton and his men turned abruptly, as did their prisoner.

"You're trespassing, Mr. Holmes," said Paxton.

"A small transgression compared to what you are engaged in," replied Holmes.

"What do you know?" asked Paxton.

"I'm afraid I know everything, Paxton. Dr. Watson and I just now witnessed your little pet."

"I'm sorry to hear that," said Paxton.

"And now," said Holmes, "I must ask you to unhand that man and step aside."

"On the contrary, Mr. Holmes, "said Paxton, holding on to the bound man, "if you or Dr. Watson, advance even one step, I shall push this man over the precipice to his reward."

"Then we are at a stalemate," replied Holmes.

"Not quite," said Paxton, "if you do not drop your weapons, I will make good on my threat regardless."

"And if we obey, you will send this man to his doom nonetheless."

"It's a sad day, when a man of science like myself is not trusted."

"If you throw this man to your creature, I will subsequently shoot you, and then you shall join him."

"I'm disappointed in you, Holmes," said Paxton, "your reputation is that of a man of intellect, not violence."

"And yours is of a genius gone wrong."

"Your barb stings me," said Paxton, "it sounds like something I'd expect from those narrow pinheads at the Zoological Gardens, or the Marine Biology Society."

"To be fair, Paxton, "said Holmes, "I actually admire your theories."

"Your insincere flattery is pathetic. You don't even know my work."

"I refer to your monograph on the mating calls of blue whales, your monograph on interspecies communication of sea mammals, your monograph on instinctual memory in dolphins, your monograph detailing —"

"I am most impressed, Mr. Holmes, I see I have misjudged you."

"It's not your theories I quarrel with, doctor, it's your methods."

"Sadly, they are necessary to further my work."

"The animal …" said Holmes.

"The animal, as you call her," said Paxton, "is my affair, and one I choose not to discuss with outsiders."

"Then allow me," said Holmes, "this creature, whom Watson and I just witnessed, is a giant squid. It was long thought to be a legend, one that dates back to antiquity, and was, for millennia, routinely dismissed as being the disturbed visions of intoxicated sailors. All that changed seven years ago, in 1888. when the carcass of just such a giant squid, washed up on a beach in New Zealand. Needless to say, it was quite celebrated news, not only in the scientific world, but internationally. However, a live one has never even been photographed, let alone been captured. It is nothing less than a discovery of monumental and historic proportions."

"You are correct," said Paxton.

"You've had him for only two months," said Holmes.

"How on earth did you know that?" asked Paxton.

"The local fishermen," replied Holmes, "where you only recently increased your demand for their services. The amounts of fish you've been purchasing is not commensurate with the seals, dolphins, and others in your sea menagerie."

"Yes," said Paxton, "by my estimation, she eats at least five hundred pounds of fish a day."

"Perhaps you should amend that statement. As of late, the creature has been dining on a more varied diet of beef, by way of the livestock you've been clandestinely abducting from the local farmers. And then there's the matter of the occasional human being, as well, such as Mr. Harris, and now this man, a recluse from the nearby hills, no doubt."

"You claim to know my work," said Paxton, "yet you fail to understand what a true pioneer and visionary must endure. What I have done will alter the course of modern marine biology. But before I reveal her to the world, she must be studied, tested —"

"And fed human sacrifices." said Holmes.

"What is the loss of a few peasants in the name of science? Future generations will revere my name as the man who brought the feared leviathan of the bible to humanity. Now then, Holmes, I suggest that you and your friend relinquish your firearms."

Before Holmes could respond, a voice behind us said, "I have a gun trained at your backs. Do not turn around. Obey the doctor."

Holmes let the revolver fall from his hand, as I did the same with mine.

"Gentlemen," said Paxton, "may I introduce my man, Gregory. When running an operation of this size and complexity, I cannot stress the importance of having enough good help. Now then, Mr. Holmes, Doctor Watson, will there be any further questions?"

"I have one," I said, "How did you, in fact, capture this creature?"

"Sarah, for that is her name," said Paxton, with an expression on his face I've seen on men extolling the virtues of their wives or mistresses, "came to me entirely by chance. This grotto has an opening that leads to the ocean."

"Originally used to escape from invading Norsemen, then later used by smugglers," said Holmes.

"Is there anything that you *don't* know?" asked Paxton.

"Now it is *you* who flatter *me*, Doctor," said Holmes.

"To continue," said Paxton, "I have modified the cave opening with a door that opens and closes, remarkably quickly, I might add, using a mechanism of springs, and pulleys. I open it slightly, once a day, to allow seawater to cleanse the grotto. In any case, I had baited a trap with fish, hoping to ensnare dolphins, which I eventually did, and seals, which also followed, but then I had the idea to set my sites on a whale. Instead, one night, to my extreme surprise and elation, I found this marvelous behemoth instead." Paxton looked at Holmes and myself, and smiled. "Story time is over, gentlemen, and dinner time commences."

I saw Holmes turn, duck, and pounce upon the assailant behind us. He subdued the man with a roundhouse punch to the jaw, knocking him cold. I grabbed our revolvers. Then Holmes and I faced our opponents once more.

"It seems that we're at that impasse again," said Paxton, "rather like a tedious game of badminton."

Just then I heard footsteps. Paxton and his two men turned as I leapt and pulled the bound man toward us. Then Lestrade and Dunbar appeared, with pistols drawn.

"It's about time, Lestrade," said Holmes, "how much did you hear?"

"Enough to be satisfied that Edmund Collier is innocent of the murder of Alvar Harris," replied Lestrade. Then he turned to Paxton and his men. "Hands up, please. You will be so kind as to accompany us."

"But what will become of Sarah?" asked Paxton.

"The monster will be turned over to the Regent Aquarium, no doubt," said Lestrade.

"No, I cannot allow that," said Paxton, "that pack of imbeciles will not get my Sarah." With that he took a step.

"Don't move," said Lestrade, brandishing his gun.

Paxton looked away, then abruptly ran past Lestrade. As he did, Lestrade discharged his revolver, hitting Paxton in the leg. Paxton stopped, clutched his wound, then reached out to the cave wall, on which were a series of levers. He pulled one down and we heard loud echoing noises throughout the cavern.

"He's opened the door!" exclaimed Holmes.

"No one shall have my Sarah," declared Paxton, looking as if he were in a trance.

"Come along now," said Lestrade, "the hangman's noose awaits you."

"I shall not be punished for my genius," said Paxton, who then ran to the precipice and leapt off it.

I watched in horror as he plunged into the water, then saw a gargantuan yellow eye, twice the size of an archer's target, peer out from the muck, and a mouth from a nightmare opened and issued a roar like thunder, as a tentacle wrapped itself around Paxton, and dragged him under the churning depths. More tentacles appeared and flailed about, splashing and crashing, then slid under the water, and all was quiet. Holmes, Lestrade, Dunbar and Paxton's men stood silently, transfixed. After a few moments, we turned, went into the tunnel, and quietly made our way through it. When we emerged in the forest, there was a police wagon waiting, accompanied by a few sturdy looking men.

"What will you tell the Yard, Lestrade?" asked Holmes.

"Oh," said Lestrade, still apparently quite shaken, "I…I'll tell them about the gang of cattle thieves, of course. But what I don't understand, Holmes, is how you knew that Paxton — ?"

"You supplied the photographs, Lestrade, of the tattooed arm. Between the dark circles, which I immediately surmised were the marks of the creature's suction cups, and the odd angle of the cut . . ."

"The cut?"

"How the arm had been severed. There were no signs indicating that a saw or similar instrument had been used, nor were there any teeth marks that would suggest an animal, either a land or an aquatic one. That ruled out all the obvious possibilities, however, it occurred to me that the damage to the arm resembled nothing so much as the effect of the plates in a bird's beak, its rhamphotheca. Birds tear or crush their food. Yet, or course, no bird of that size is known to exist. But a squid processes a beak, which has been duly compared to that of a bird. Then I thought of the find in New

Zealand, seven years ago. When Paxton looked at the photographs of the severed arm and denied any knowledge of it, I knew we had our man. The impressions of the creature's suction cups alone should have elicited comment. The arm itself was released unknowingly, through the grotto's door, upon one of Paxton's admitted daily cleansings."

"Amazing," said Lestrade.

Lestrade and Dunbar got into the wagon, as did Holmes and I, and we started off, back to the village.

The next morning, we checked out of the inn, and were met at the train station by Katherine Collier. She thanked us profusely for clearing her father of the murder charges. Then Holmes and I climbed aboard the train, and it pulled out of the Harbourton station. We were well on our way back to London, when I turned to Holmes and said, "So, Paxton's men had been ordered to find cows to feed the creature?"

"Yes, and poor Mr. Harris happened to stumble upon them one night, as they were engaged in the act of stealing a couple of his Guernseys and paid the ultimate price. Since he had been their first human casualty, they weren't sure what to do with him, and decided to bring him back to their master, who then, it seems, had the idea that fat men might, shall we say, round out the creature's diet. My examination of the suspect's wagon wheels proved that his vehicle hadn't been employed in the crime. The tyre tracks were not deep enough to account for the additional weight of Harris, Paxton's men, and the cows."

"The cows?"

"That's correct. Paxton had his men inject them with the tranquilizer, in order to take them clandestinely. That's why none of the local farmers or anyone else ever saw or heard any of them being abducted. They were unconscious and lying flat in a wagon. For the same reasons, I knew that the suspect, Edmund Collier couldn't have done it either. His wagon was too small, and the ground showed no signs of it being employed in such a venture. However, on the way to the siege tunnel, Watson, you lost your footing in the deep impressions of Paxton's wagon tracks. And we've previously discussed the absurdity of Collier lifting Harris."

"What a vile and horrible evil lived within Paxton," I said.

"Odd how evil can sometimes cohabit very amiably with genius."

"And Paxton's house?" I asked, "You knew it as if you'd lived there."

"You can thank my brother Mycroft for that. After I left you yesterday morning, I sent him a telegram with instructions to contact one of his highly placed masonic associates. The house dates back five hundred years, and as a result, I suspected it would have a siege tunnel. Mycroft received the architectural plans immediately, then dispatched them by courier, whom I met at the train station."

"This was quite a singular adventure, to say the least."

"Perhaps, you'd do well not to relay this one to the public, Watson. I wouldn't want your readers to think that you'd taken to flights of fancy like those of the French novelist, Jules Verne."

"You have a good point," I said, as I watched Holmes light his pipe and then stare out the window, at the passing countryside. I looked through the opposite window while I pondered the fate of Dr. Paxton. With his death, what great discoveries would the world be deprived of? Then I thought of the creature and its return to the primordial waters from which it had come. Would humanity ever see its like again? Or was it destined to remain an elusive phantom for all eternity? I was reminded of something that Sherlock Holmes had once said to me upon the completion of another case. "With even the most satisfying answers, there are always more questions."

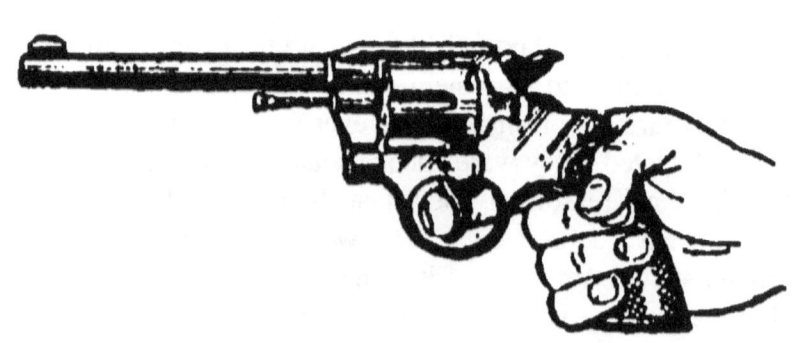

BE GOOD OR BEGONE

by Stan Trybulski

Having retired to a small villa on the Riviera where I have been living comfortably for the past dozen years, I found myself bored to tears. After endless days of morning gardening, followed by large noon-time repasts and long afternoon naps under the Mediterranean sun, I longed for the days when I assisted my good friend Sherlock Holmes. Sifting through a carton of notes of old Holmes cases, my hands came to rest on that most tragic of all adventures; the time Holmes inveigled me to travel to New York City with him on what he called a long get-away trip.

It was in the middle of February and we were staying at the Waldorf-Astoria where Holmes had rented a suite for a fortnight. Lounging on a sofa, drinking my third cup of morning tea and reading the local papers, I was surprised to suddenly see a cream-coloured envelope slide under the door. Setting down my tea cup in its saucer, I walked over and picked up the envelope. Inscribed in beautiful handwriting on the front was the name Mr. Sherlock Holmes. I set it on a side table and went back to my now lukewarm tea and my reading. About ten minutes later, the door to one of the inner rooms opened and Holmes appeared, freshly shaved and clad in his favourite smoking jacket.

"Tea still warm, Watson?" he asked, briskly rubbing his hands in anticipation.

"Don't get too excited, Holmes, it's not exactly our English breakfast tea."

He tapped the teapot, then tipped it and poured some of the liquid into a cup and sipped it. He didn't bother with sugar, no longer needing as much as when he still used heroin on a daily basis.

"Hot, and it'll do, I dare say, on a morning like this."

"There's an envelope for you on the table," I said, gesturing with the newspaper.

Holmes walked over to the table and picked up the envelope. I went back to my reading, trying to find the sports section and the cricket scores. There had been a test match the day before between England and the West Indies and the two teams were very competitive, their records against each other just about even. I was keen on finding a story, any story on the action. But there was none, not even an AP wire blurb. I was about to throw the newspaper down in disgust when Holmes's voice broke in.

"It seems we've been invited out tonight, Watson."

"By whom?"

"The Honorable John McSorley Pickle, Beefsteak, Baseball Nine, and Chowder Club."

"It doesn't sound like a very reputable organization."

Holmes fingered the invitation. "It will be held at McSorley's Old Ale House," he said.

"Holmes, you've brought me all the way to New York to take me to an ale house?"

"Not just any ale house, Watson. McSorley's is the most famous ale house in New York City, quite possibly the Western Hemisphere, old boy. Good ale, raw onions and no ladies. What more could a man ask for?"

"It doesn't seem that appetizing, I think I'm going to pass."

"How about steaks and ale, then?"

"Steaks and ale? Seems rather mundane."

"This is a beefeater, Watson."

"A Beefeater, you mean …"

"No, Watson, not one of your Tower of London hearties. This is a McSorley's beefeater. A veritable feast, a meat eater's paradise. Think of t-bone steaks, prime ribs, broiled pork chops and sausages, washed down with all the ale you can drink."

"I've never heard of such a thing. Let me see the invitation." I took the card from his hand and turned it over. "Your presence is requested for an evening of steaks and ale. 6 p.m." and with the address 15 East Seventh Street, New York City, all inscribed in a fancy scroll.

"I thought you were vegetarian now, Holmes." I raised an eyebrow at him.

"We simply cannot refuse an invitation like this," he said.

"Who on earth knows that we are here in New York?"

"That is exactly what we are going to find out, dear fellow."

The yellow cab dropped us off in front of a run-down brick tenement building. Wet snow was falling and the streets and sidewalks were slushy.

"Are you sure this is the right place?" I asked Holmes.

He pointed upward with his walking stick to where a sign hung over a pair of battered wooden doors. It read McSorley's Old Ale House. A sign in the window announced "No back room for women."

We opened the door and went inside and pushed through a second set of swinging doors that served to keep out the cold. A bar was set on one side and scarred wooden tables were scattered on the other, a cast-iron pot-bellied coal stove set smack in the middle of the room. The floor was covered with sawdust and the walls were adorned with all manner of memorabilia: photos, newspaper articles, drawings. The bar was crowded with ale drinkers being served by a sour-faced man with a grizzled, worn face. Spread along the bar were plates of cheese and crackers and mugs filled with mustard to add piquancy to the snacks. Two grey-jacketed waiters hustled back and forth from the bar, carrying multiples of mugs of light and dark ale to the tables. Each table held a mustard-filled mug similar to the ones on the bar.

"The beefeater must be in there," said Holmes, pointing to another room in the back.

We walked over and peered inside. Only more scarred tables occupied by ale drinkers. A waiter started to pass by with a tray of empty mugs destined for a quick washing and refill.

I tapped him on the shoulder. "Excuse me, young man; we are here for the beefeater."

"If you find it, let me know," he said with a quick laugh, then dashed over to the bar and dropped off the used mugs and scooped up a half-dozen full mugs in each hand and hurried off again.

"There's an empty table over by the stove, Watson," Holmes said. "I suggest we sit and warm ourselves."

Holmes was tapping his fingers on the cast iron side of the stove when the waiter came over.

"What can I can get you gents?"

"Two of your best," I said.

"Light or dark?" he asked.

"Both," Holmes said.

The waiter went off and returned a few moments later with four mugs, two with light ale and two with dark.

Holmes took out the invitation. "Does this mean anything to you?" he asked the young man.

The waiter took the card and looked at it, then handed it back. "Someone's having you on," he said. "We don't have a beefeater until the summertime and that'll be at Coney Island."

I looked around the room; all the men at the bar were workingmen, carpenters, masons and the like. The tables seemed to be occupied by more working men with a few down and out professional types mixed in. The Great Depression was as ugly here as in England. I sipped my ale, the light mugs first. Holmes occupied himself with the dusty and faded memorabilia that covered the wall behind us. The waiter came back and shoveled some coal into the stove, the added fuel renewing the heat. The warmth was relaxing and the ale was smooth and strong, as a good as Yorkshire stout, and I told the waiter to keep it coming.

"Would you gents like anything to eat?" he asked.

"Some cheddar, if you have it."

"A large or small plate?" the man asked.

I looked over at Holmes. "What about you?" I said.

He had taken out his favourite magnifying glass, a sterling-plated Sheffield with a bone handle and was peering at some faded, tiny script in an ancient news story. "Are you hungry?" I asked him again. He waved me away with a quick motion of his free hand.

"We'll have a large plate," I told the waiter, "and four more mugs of ale."

Lost in concentration, Holmes had not touched his ales, so I reached over and took one of them and drank deeply. Holmes ignored me, so after I finished the first, I appropriated the second. The waiter returned with four more. "Your cheese plate will be right out," he said.

Finally, Holmes put away his Sheffield magnifying glass and turned back toward me.

"What was on the wall that attracted your attention?" I asked him.

"Amazing, Watson," he said. "It was a contemporary account of the Battle of Waterloo." He picked up one of the mugs of ale the waiter had just brought and sipped. "Glad you came, old boy?"

I was about to answer when the waiter returned with our cheddar cheese plate. Bending over to set the food down, he stumbled and fell against a chair, dropping the plate. Appalled by his clumsiness I was about to berate him when he collapsed to the floor. Several men at the bar turned at the commotion and stared at the stricken lad. Holmes bent over and knelt beside the fellow who was lying chest down on the sawdust planking, his face turned aside.

"Watson," Holmes said sharply, "see what you can do for him."

I eased around the table and knelt next to the man. The floor underneath him was turning red. I felt his pulse and looked at the widening stain, the sweet smell of death in my nostrils replacing the bitter taste of the ale in my mouth.

"Can you save him?" Holmes said.

I shook my head. "I'm afraid the wound has reached his heart."

The waiter's lips moved silently, words trying to form. Then finally, a rasp emitted from his mouth, soft sounds mingling with a bubbling froth. I heard the word but didn't believe it. "Moran," the man said. "Moran." A voice soft with impending death … and something else.

Holmes started at the voice as if he knew it. He ran a hand along the nape of the man's neck and a thick tousle of hair dropped suddenly around his shoulders. The front of the man's jacket had turned red, bits of sawdust clung to the sogginess. Holmes turned the man gently over and pressed his right hand under the man's left collar bone, trying to staunch the spurting of blood. The stab wound was too deep for any but the most sophisticated medical procedures, but the forlorn look on Holmes's face told me to say nothing. He already knew. With his other hand, he touched the man's moustache, and then with a pinch of his finger he suddenly peeled it off. There was no mistaking the lips that had once capti-vated him.

"Irene," he said. "Irene. My God, it's you."

"It's a woman," someone at the bar muttered.

"*The* woman," Holmes said, his words a furious assault at the man who had just spoken. Irene Adler, whom he always called "*the* woman," and here she was dying on the floor of a New York ale house.

Her eyes fluttered open and tried to focus on him. "Sherlock," she said, "Thank God." Her eyes closed and her head listed to one side, like a ship making its final bow before it sinks beneath the waves. Holmes held her in his arms.

"She's gone, Holmes," I said, my back to him, as I looked around the tavern, trying to both fathom who had killed Irene Adler, and who might now try to assassinate Holmes. From the minute I had heard Irene whisper the name "Moran," I knew my companion was in mortal danger. Moran was Colonel Sebastian Moran, the right-hand man of that Beelzebub of crime, Professor Moriarty, who had sworn to kill Holmes before he left this mortal earth. "Lock the door and call the police," I shouted to the barkeep. I turned back to Holmes. He had placed his overcoat over Irene's lifeless body and was looking at the sawdust on the floor.

"I thought Irene had been dead these many years, captured with Sidney Reilly in Russia. I don't know how or why, but she came here to warn you, Holmes, she may have saved your life."

Holmes stood. Taking out his handkerchief, he placed a few bits of sawdust into it and wrapping it up, stuffed it back into his breast pocket. His face was ashen, filled with a deadly combination of anguish and fury. For only the second time in his career had he been this emotional. The first time was when I stood in the way of a bullet during that business of the three Garridebs.

Holmes took several deep breaths, exhaling slowly each time. "She wasn't sent here to warn me, Watson," he said. "She was sent here to die."

I reached into my pocket for my service revolver, suddenly realizing that I had left it in the hotel suite, not wanting to run afoul of New York's strict gun laws. "You still are in danger," I said. "Whoever killed Irene could still be here."

"Undoubtedly so," Holmes said. "But killing me was not the purpose of the assassin's visit."

I looked at the crowd sitting at the tables and standing at the bar. "Well, the New York police will be here soon, hopefully they find him."

"I will find him first."

"How?" I asked. "Among this mob of ale-swillers? Not unless someone points him out to you."

"Watson, once again, you denigrate the power of deductive reasoning." He looked at the bar. "There were twenty-three drinkers, ale-swillers as you call them, at the bar only a few moments before Irene was struck down. Now, there are twenty-four. So that is where I will start my search."

"But still, Holmes, it is surely an impossible task. Let the police handle it."

"Impossible? Was it impossible in *A Study in Scarlet*, "The Five Orange Pips," "A Case of Identity," or the several dozen other of my solutions you wrote about and were so handsomely rewarded? At least in this moment of grief, do not disparage my abilities and do not stop me from bringing Irene's killer to swift justice." His right hand was in his jacket pocket, where I knew he carried the gold-plated derringer he always took with him when he was out for the evening.

"You won't have much time before the police arrive," I said.

"Whoever killed Irene stabbed her from behind and did it quickly, just as she was at our table. It was intended that we see her die."

"By who and why?"

"Professor Moriarty, of course. He has vowed to kill me, but his diabolical mind would take more intellectual pleasure in having me suffer by seeing the woman struck down before my eyes. But right now, that is a distraction, we must concentrate on the stabbing itself. For there lies the solution to the problem."

"What was Irene doing in New York?"

"I'll explain later, Watson, it's inconsequential to the problem at hand."

A chill ran through me as I listened to Holmes describe the brutal killing of the only woman he had ever totally respected as "the problem." I suddenly seized up the unfinished mug of ale and swallowed it, then drank another.

Holmes ignored me, staring down at the floor. "When the killer withdrew the blade, blood would have immediately started to spurt out. Look at the side of the pot-bellied stove." He pointed out a trail of tiny red spots on the black metal surface.

"And the sawdust, too, I take it."

"Very good, Watson, but unimportant. Not to worry, however, good fellow, for look at the sawdust on the floor just to right of the corpse."

I shuddered again at the cold steel emotion of this man. Yet, I knew the total sublimation of his feelings to scientific examination had a purpose. I looked down and saw that there was a circular scuffing in the sawdust. "But what does it mean, Holmes?" I said.

"Aha, Watson, it could mean everything. Or it could mean nothing. You see, when the killer reached around to stab Irene, he set his right foot forward. And he would have had to keep it forward as he withdrew the blade from her bosom." His voice quavered as he said those words but suddenly once again, he was only steel.

"So Irene's blood spattered onto the killer's right shoe." I was able to follow his reasoning so far. "Holmes, please sit back down for a minute."

"I'm all right, Watson."

"You may be the detective, but I am the surgeon. So sit down."

Holmes took the chair next to the stove and I sat across the table from him.

"Holmes, you have told me many times that detection is an exact method, an exercise in logic and science, that there is no room for emotion. Only analytical reasoning."

He sipped some of the ale. "Yes, but to what purpose, Watson? The law can never provide the justice that the fiend behind this deserves." He reached into the watch-pocket of his vest and withdrew a small sack of tobacco and some papers. I watched as he deftly rolled a thick cigarette.

"Reminds me of the time we were in Jamaica," I said. "The Problem of the Rum Keg."

"Those were the days, Watson. Heroin, cocaine, all still legal."

"The police are outside," the barkeep announced, walking towards the front door. He unlocked it and went back to his station by the ale pumps.

"Let the police do their job," I said.

"Much of this is elementary, as you know, but I cannot let the hired hand get away."

Again, Holmes fumbled with the derringer in his pocket.

I grabbed Holmes by the wrist. "Just don't doing anything foolish. The killer might provide something useful against Moriarty."

"Good old Watson. Don't you see, the woman's death was a mere taunt to let me know how helpless I am to stop what devilish machinations the fiend is conjuring up? Nevertheless, I intend to bring him to justice. But I'll need help. Lestrade always acts as a spur to my deductive reasoning as he always seems to get it wrong. But since he's not here, you'll have to do."

"Me, Holmes? Once again, you're asking me to assist you in solving a crime?"

He nodded slowly, a wan smile on his face.

A rush of cold air caressed my neck as the inner doors flew open and were held by two uniformed police officers. They stood at attention as a short stout man in a long grey coat and bowler hat strode in behind them. An unlit cigar was jammed into a pair of grim lips that were as red as his face. Wisps of snow drifted to the floor as he shook his coat.

Holmes looked at the New York detective. "Yes, Watson, let's see if you're up to the task."

The detective took the cigar out of his mouth and looked around the tavern room, his eyes stopping when they saw the body of Irene Adler on the floor. He moved towards the bar, the crowd in front of him parting like the Red Sea before Moses. The barkeep had already pumped two mugs of cold dark ale for the detective and slid them down the damp wooden surface. Without blinking, the detective seized the mugs of ale and lifting one to his lips, drained it without taking it away from his mouth, then set it down and polished off the second one, again in one long swig.

The detective leaned back against the bar and nodded slightly towards the barkeep, who immediately drew two more ales from the tap. Stretching his right arm out, he caught the two fresh mugs as they slid towards him. This time, he sipped the ale more slowly. Looking at Holmes, his face broke into a mischievous grin.

"So you're the famous Sherlock Holmes," he said,

The crowd in the room all turned towards us, gawking to see the British consulting detective they had read about in the barbershops while waiting to get their hair cut.

Holmes lifted his fedora. "Aloysius G. Murphy, I presume. Vicious Aloysius, to be more precise."

Murphy's grin widened. "You Englishmen and your preciseness. Yes, Vicious Aloysius is a name I've picked up over the years." The grin was still on his face.

"My gawd, Holmes, he looks like a common street hoodlum," I said.

"This is New York, Watson. Societal distinctions such as we have in that blessed little plot called England don't matter very much here."

Suddenly, the detective's voice bellowed out. "My name is Aloysius G. Murphy. Police Captain Aloysius G. Murphy."

He grinned at the assemblage. "That's right. Vicious Aloysius. But only my enemies call me that. Is anyone here my enemy?" His bellow was higher pitched now, just below a scream.

The tavern room was silent.

"My worst enemies just call me Vicious. Is anyone here my worst enemy?"

The room stayed silent.

I leaned towards Holmes's ear. "Still," I said, "can we trust him? A policeman who goes by the moniker of Vicious Aloysius?"

"A well-earned moniker, no doubt," Holmes whispered back. "But the only thing we have to fear is that he will find and kill Moriarty before I do. And that is something I cannot allow."

Murphy suddenly slammed one of the ale mugs on the bar top, the sharp sound bringing my attention back to him. "This is a homicide investigation. That's murder to you louts. No one can leave. Everyone is a suspect and everyone will be searched. And then we will all have a little talk." His grin turned to a leer with that last pronouncement. "Barkeep, close down the kitchen, I'm going to need it. But leave the stove on." He made a circular motion with his hand, walked over to our table and sat down.

"So, Holmes," he said, "do you think your vaunted deductive reasoning can solve this case before I can?"

"Undoubtedly," said Holmes. "Are you turning the investigation over to me?"

Murphy reached into a back pocket of his trousers and pulled out a leather covered, lead weighted sapper and set it on the table. Then he reached into the outer pocket of his overcoat and pulled out a pair of brass knuckles, their inside surfaces covered with a pink padding. He set the knuckle dusters down next to the sapper.

One of the waiters came over and set a half-dozen mugs of ale on the table. "These are on the house, Captain," he said to Murphy.

Murphy ignored the man and kept his eyes locked on Holmes. "Since the barkeep locked the door right away, the killer is still in this tavern. When I leave here, I'll have him in cuffs and a written confession in my pocket."

"You mean you'll beat a suspect in front of all the witnesses?" I said.

The evident shock on my face made Murphy's grin even wider. "Anybody here wanna be a witness?" he yelled out. The uniformed officers guarding the front door laughed. Everyone else was silent. Murphy stood up and placed his fists on his hips. He stared at the crowd and pointed to a large wooden sign above the ice cooler.

"*Be Good or Begone*," he read the sign out loud. "This is me precinct and that's me motto."

He sat back down and nodded towards Holmes. "Okay, let's see what you can come up with."

Holmes nodded back and then stood. Now Murphy, the hoodlum detective, would be receiving a lesson in how a fine mind would triumph over his crude police methods. Holmes looked at the men drinking at the bar and then slowly sauntered along the row until he reached the end, then started walking back. Midway, he stopped and seized the collar of a rough-looking fellow who tried to twist loose. Holmes held the collar tighter. "He's all yours, Vicious," he said.

Murphy picked up his sapper and knuckle duster and walked over to the bar. "Come along you," he said to the man as he shoved him towards the kitchen. The door closed behind them. I sat there stunned. What had Holmes done? Or rather not done. What kind of detecting had that been? Where were the connected principles of deductive reasoning, where were the repeated applications of *modus ponens*? Had Holmes's mind gone soft over the murder of Irene Adler?

My worrisome fugue was interrupted by a fearful slamming and banging from the kitchen, followed by sharp screams of anguish. Everyone in the tavern turned towards the closed door. More slamming and banging caused some of the patrons to turn back to their ales. This was followed by more screaming, muted and mixed with long sobs. The kitchen door flew open and Murphy stood there, wiping sweat off his face with an apron. Kneeling on the floor, moaning in pain was the suspect, his face bruised and bloodied. Murphy latched onto his collar and dragged him across the sawdust floor to the front door. "Let him go, boys," he said to the pair of uniforms.

The hoodlum-detective came back to our table and sat down. "You were wrong, Holmes. The great Sherlock Holmes was wrong. That man is innocent."

"Holmes is never wrong," I said.

"No, Watson, this time I'm afraid Captain Murphy is right. I seem to have made a terrible mistake."

"Don't you worry, old-fashioned police methods will get the right man." A smirk crept over Murphy's face. He drank another mug of ale.

"Holmes will solve this murder," I said. "He always has."

"You are as stubborn as your scientific friend, aren't you, Dr. Watson?" The smirk was still on Murphy's face. "Do you think I should let Holmes continue his 'investigation' or spare him further embarrassment?"

"It's you that'll be embarrassed."

Murphy finished his ale and made another circular motion with his hand. "We shall see, Dr. Watson, we shall just see." He turned back to Holmes. "Although I'm in charge here, I could be induced to allow you to continue your floundering. A friendly wager as to which of us nabs the miscreant? I'll even let you proceed first."

Holmes stared at him. "Justice is not something that follows the turn of a roulette wheel; to be dispensed in return for pecuniary rewards."

"I was thinking of something more to your liking," the policeman said.

Holmes slowly sipped his ale. "Pray continue," he said.

Murphy reached inside his suit jacket and took out a small wooden box. He casually set the object on the table in front of Holmes. "Go ahead, open it."

Holmes ran his fingers over the top of the box, then fiddled with a small brass clasp. Yet he still waited, not undoing the clasp, only watching Murphy's face.

"Afraid, Holmes? Afraid of what's inside? Or perhaps you are afraid your so-called powers of deductive reasoning have abandoned you?"

"Holmes is afraid of nothing," I said, reaching for the box.

My good friend clamped his hand over it. "Watson, I am truly touched by your support, but I think I can do this myself." Flicking the brass clasp, he lifted up the top of the box. His face paled as he saw the contents: a small hypodermic needle, a length of rubber tubing, and a half-dozen glassine envelopes (the kind stamp collectors use) that contained a white powder. I remembered the many nights when Holmes had nodded off in our rooms at 221B Baker Street after injecting heroin, and I felt sick, for I knew the desire that must be coursing through his mind and body at that very moment.

"Holmes is not interested in your silly wager," I said, anger filling my voice.

"Why don't you let Holmes speak for himself, Dr. Watson?"

Holmes slowly closed the box. "And if I should fail to find the killer this time?" he asked.

The hoodlum-detective leaned back in his chair and made a sweeping gesture with his ale mug. "Then you shall announce to this motley group that Aloysius G. Murphy is the greatest detective of all time, not you. Then you will salute me." He laughed at the thought. "And you, Dr. Watson, will write one of your stories, describing it exactly."

"That's a story that never will be written!" I declared.

Holmes tapped his fingers on the top of the box. "The wager is on," he finally said.

Murphy made another sweeping gesture with the ale mug. "The stage is all yours."

Holmes stood and bowed. "And I shall perform an act far greater than you have dreamt of." He took his walking stick and strode the length of the bar, his hand running lightly over the backs of the drinkers. When he reached the end, he nodded at the barkeep and turned, walking slowly back towards the other end. When he reached the middle of the bar, he stopped and rapped his walking stick on the bar top. The man to the right of the stick swiveled his head and smiled. "You'll never pin this me on me, Mr. Sherlock Holmes." He took a saltine cracker and daubed it with mustard from a mug on the bar. He popped it into his mouth and chewed and swallowed. Saluting Holmes with his right hand, he collapsed to the floor.

Dead.

"I don't know how you did it, Holmes," the hoodlum-detective said.

"The clues were all elementary, my dear Captain. Anyone with half a brain could have followed them to the conclusion that the happily-departed imbiber was the man who stabbed the woman to death."

Murphy stared at Holmes. "What clues? I don't see any clues."

"You wouldn't. Your kind of detective never does." Holmes took out his tobacco pouch and rolled another cigarette. Lighting it, he puffed casually and sat back. Exhaling the smoke through his nostrils, he smiled grimly. "I'll explain it to you, although I doubt it will make a difference in how you conduct your future investigations. First, just before the woman was stabbed there were twenty-three men drinking at the bar. As I knelt beside her on the floor, I counted twenty-four. The original twenty-three imbibers I had only glanced at, as any study of their faces would have been banal compared to the first-hand account of the Battle of Waterloo." He gestured at the ancient newspaper on the wall. "That was certainly more worthy of my intellectual attention."

A waiter approached the table but Holmes waved him away. He puffed on the cigarette again and flicked a bit of ash on the floor. "In any event, a physiognomic study was totally unnecessary to the solution of the murder."

"How so?" I asked. My note pad was out. Murphy still leaned back in his chair.

"It was snowing when we arrived and it was still snowing when the good captain arrived. So when I walked along the bar I was on the lookout for a damp coat."

"But the men wore different materials," Murphy said. "More than one coat may have remained damp."

"Quite so. But as you can feel, the coal stove keeps the room rather warm. The men all had their caps pushed back, all, that is, except our now dead suspect, who kept his pulled down in an effort to hide his face." Holmes puffed again on the cigarette. "Then there were the hands of the barflies, all rough. Hands built for labour, not hands made to strike down beautiful women in a crowded room. These men were, still are, shaken by the woman's murder. I observed their hands trembling as I passed by. All except the killer, whose hands were calm, fingers unmoving, the singular mark of the professional assassin."

He dropped the cigarette to the floor and ground it with his heel. "Unfortunately, my dear Captain Murphy, he has escaped your brutal clutches." Holmes gestured to the mug of mustard Murphy was holding in his hands.

"But he saved the State of New York the cost of a trial and execution," Murphy said. He walked over to the man's body and prodded it with the toe of his boot.

I leaned forward across the table. "Holmes, you promised that you would explain to me how you knew Irene Adler was still alive and what she was doing here."

"That I shall, dear friend. I am afraid that all these years I haven't been quite truthful with you."

"You mean you've been keeping secrets from me?"

"A secret, Watson. The greatest secret of my career."

"Whatever do you mean, Holmes?"

"The woman and I have been together over the past two decades. We have met many times, during many cases, to renew our love for each other. Caracas, Saigon, Tangiers were only a few of the places where our love was reconsecrated during nights of heated bliss."

"Caracas? You mean when we solved the mystery of "The Giant Roach of Caracas" you were romancing Irene? And Saigon, the "Case of the Mutilated Agent?" Well, strike me up a gum tree, as Lestrade would say. Your deductive reasoning was a little slow on that one. Now I know why. I had to find a new literary agent after that."

"Slow on purpose, my dear Watson. He wasn't getting you the contracts your recitations of my cases deserve. So he had to go. I did you a favour, old boy."

"Good old Holmes," I laughed. "Always looking out for me. Well, I have to admit my new agent does work a bit harder." I sat back in my chair. "But why was Irene in New York?"

"We were to meet again; she had also reserved a suite at the Waldorf. Moriarty must have been on to her, had her followed and planted a false story that Moran was out to kill me. She thought she was warning me."

"Holmes, you knew right away that this dead fellow was the real killer, didn't you?"

He nodded. "Of course, Watson, did you expect anything different? Remember the possibility that there were blood spots on his right shoe, they were a dead giveaway."

"But that man you first pointed out was innocent and he took a terrific beating."

Holmes shrugged. "I knew he was innocent, but I didn't like his face. Besides, his assistance with the investigation was invaluable."

"How so?"

"The dead man was known to me as Edgar, a highly trusted assassin used by Colonel Moran. There was no way I could let Vicious Aloysius take Edgar into custody. His brutal methods would have been effective and Edgar would have spilled the beans about

Moran and Moriarty. I told you that I will bring them to the justice they deserve. So I had to show Edgar just how brutal Murphy was and convince him that he would talk before leaving here. I was sure Edgar had the means to prevent his being taken alive, I only had to prompt him into using it before he talked."

"But what about the sawdust you collected, what clue was that?"

Holmes clenched his jaw. "Not a clue, dear fellow, a *memento mori*."

Murphy approached the table, still holding the mug of poisoned mustard. "Our police lab will determine what poison the dead man used. Do you have any suggestions?"

Holmes shook his head, no longer interested in helping the hoodlum-detective.

"By the way, for the record, what was the dead woman's name?"

"Irene …" I started to answer before Holmes cut me off.

"Mrs. Sherlock Holmes," he said, pocketing the box with the syringe and the heroin. "Watson, since I don't intend to be good, let us begone."

✗

NEW ADDRESS?

DON'T FORGET TO TAKE
SHERLOCK HOLMES WITH YOU!

Changes of address should be mailed to:

> Wildside Press, LLC
> Attn: Subscription Dept.
> 9710 Traville Gateway Dr. #234
> Rockville MD 20850

Or via email: wildside@wildsidepress.com

NOT A SUBSCRIBER YET?

Visit wildsidemagazines.com *to subscribe online!*

Or if you're in the U.S., mail a check or money order (payable to Wildside Press) for $39.95 for the next 4 issues to:

> Wildside Press LLC
> 9710 Traville Gateway Dr. #234
> Rockville MD 20850

THE ADVENTURE OF THE HAUNTED BAGPIPES

by Carla Coupe

"**A**h, Watson, there you are!"

Sherlock Holmes stood at the table that held chemical apparatus. His shirtsleeves were rolled to his elbows, baring muscular forearms, his fingers stained and sooty. He tipped a small amount of a vile green liquid into a retort and quickly capped it. As he held the retort over a gas flame, the solution turned brown and filled the glass with curling smoke.

"You look pleased, Holmes," I said. "What are you working on?"

"Oh, nothing much." He gently tilted the vessel, coating the sides with the brown liquid. "Merely a method to preserve burnt paper so that it may be subject to further analysis without disintegrating."

"Very useful, I am sure."

I consulted my pocket watch. It was almost four o'clock, the hour at which Holmes had requested my presence. I had quit my surgery in response to his note, although in truth it was no hardship to abandon my quiet rooms.

"What is this about?" I settled into a chair by the fire. The day was chill and grey, one of a long procession during the cold, wet weeks late in 1889. The warmth of the coals eased the ache from my old war wound.

Holmes carefully placed the retort on the table and turned toward the door, his eyes bright. "Let us await explanations, for I believe our visitor has arrived."

Only then did I hear the front door close and Mrs Hudson's gentle murmur. Holmes snuffed out the flame of the burner and wiped his smudged hands upon his equally filthy handkerchief. He rolled down his sleeves and donned his jacket before moving to stand beside the fire.

After a soft knock, Mrs Hudson entered, ushering in a tall, broad-shouldered young man. The young man paused inside the door and thrust the fingers of his left hand through his black hair. It had been pomaded and now erupted into a halo of curls. His gaze moved between Holmes and me for a moment, then settled on my friend.

"Mr Holmes?" His voice was a light baritone.

"I am Sherlock Holmes, and this is my colleague, Dr John Watson."

"Gentlemen." The young man sketched a bow before taking the chair Holmes indicated. "My name is Albert McMahon, and I have a most curious problem."

Holmes settled on the settee, crossed his legs, and drew out his pipe. "You intimated as much in your letter, Mr McMahon. Before you explain your difficulty, however, please tell us how a man who worked in the timber industry in Canada came to reside in Edinburgh for the past six months?"

Although familiar with Holmes's deductive powers, I was still surprised at the quickness of his observations. McMahon's brows rose comically, and his mouth hung open for a moment before he let loose a piercing whistle.

"I must admit I had my doubts about you, Mr Holmes." He smiled. "But if this is an example of your abilities, I know I am consulting the right man for the job."

"This is hardly a taxing matter." Holmes waved a negligent hand. "When a man retains his distinctive Canadian accent and sports a Canadian penny on his watch fob, the location of his origin is clear. Your hands show the callusing peculiar to those who wield axe and saw on a daily basis, and you are missing the very tip of your left forefinger, another injury common to the trade. Your clothing, although recently purchased, is not unworn, and the cut of your coat is popular among the Scots these days. In addition, the slight burr and intonation atop your native accent are those of Edinburgh … Old Town, I believe?"

"You are correct on all counts," McMahon said, his smile broadening. "My father and mother emigrated to Canada before I was born. My great-uncle Fergus McMahon was a man of considerable wealth, and unfortunately he could not forgive my father for leaving Scotland. He informed my father that neither my father nor his heirs would ever benefit from his fortune."

"Not an uncommon attitude," Holmes said, puffing slowly on his pipe. "Although regrettable for the innocent heirs."

McMahon nodded. "Imagine my surprise, therefore, when, eight months ago, I was in receipt of a communication from my great-uncle's solicitors, informing me I was to receive half his fortune, including a town house in Edinburgh. My cousin, James Knox, benefitted from the remainder. Following the solicitors's instructions, I wound up my affairs in Vancouver and arrived in Edinburgh a little over six months ago."

"All this is very interesting," said Holmes. "But what of your problem?"

"I'm working my way up to that, sir." McMahon rubbed his hands together — a nervous gesture — and I could see the calluses that Holmes had remarked upon, as well as the missing tip of his finger. An old injury, by the colouration.

"I took up residence in my great-uncle's home, which is situated in Hangman's
Lane, behind St. Giles, in the shadow of the Castle. It is a tall, narrow stone building, several centuries old. I now own the tenements in the lane, as well."

McMahon assayed a smile, but it more resembled a grimace.

"I must be honest, Mr Holmes. From the first night I spent there, I have never rested easily. The chimneys howl and the floors creak, and if I were the type of man who believed in ghosts … well, it would be all too easy to do so after living in that house."

"If it is so uncomfortable, why do you stay?" I asked.

"A provision in my great-uncle's will requires me to reside in the house for one full year before claiming the rest of my inheritance. He was a leading light in the campaign to provide decent accommodations for the deserving poor, and he insisted that I continue his work by not becoming an absentee landlord. As a consequence, if I fail to sleep there for more than two nights in a row, I will forfeit the money." McMahon sighed. "Believe me, gentlemen, I could use that fortune."

Holmes leaned forward, eyes sharp and attentive. "And what would you use that fortune for, Mr McMahon?"

McMahon coloured and repeated his nervous hand-wringing. "Miss Caroline Fraser and I have loved each other for many years. Although we did not make any promises when I left Vancouver, we would have married before if I could have afforded to maintain a wife. Sadly, she has a brother who is simple, and who also needs support. This money would provide amply for our happiness, as well as for the care of her brother."

"Most commendable," I murmured.

"I see." Holmes leaned back, his voice cool, as always when the subject of matrimony arose. "And if you do not fulfill the terms of the will, who then benefits? Your cousin?"

"No. My portion will be given to a charity my great-uncle supported: the Society for the Betterment of the Working Poor."

"I see. Do similar restrictions apply to your cousin's inheritance?"

"I do not believe so. He received my great-uncle's cottage in Kirkcudbright as well as half his fortune, but he resides in Edinburgh."

"Are you acquainted with this cousin?"

"We have dined together a number of times," McMahon said with a shrug. "He seems a pleasant enough fellow, although rather absent-minded. At least half of the times he was engaged to dine with me he became so engrossed in his medical research that he completely forgot our appointment."

I nodded. I knew several such types, for whom the intellectual challenge of research proved far more engrossing than the allure of society, and even of family ties. Edinburgh, as a seat of medical learning, was undoubtedly filled with hosts and hostesses confronted with empty places at dinner parties while their expected guests laboured in their laboratories far into the night.

"Medical research?" I asked, my professional curiosity piqued.

"Yes. Something to do with improving the vigour of the indigent population."

"Your situation appears straightforward," said Holmes, clearly impatient with my digression. "And now, please explain your problem."

McMahon hesitated, a frown forming. "It began about a fortnight ago, and it would not be too strong to say that the events of that night will haunt me forever."

Holmes spared me a glance before turning back to our guest. "Describe that night, if you will."

"I doubt I can, Mr Holmes. It was … horrible." He took a deep breath, as if to steady his nerves. "My housekeeper fled from the house that night, and now she refuses to stay after dark. I, myself, find it difficult to remain inside after the sun sets. My tenants have fled, leaving those once-bustling buildings empty." McMahon gripped the arms of his chair so tightly that his fingers paled. "Tell me, Mr Holmes, have you ever heard the legend of the Old Town's haunted bagpipes?"

"I have," said Holmes, his expression one of tolerant amusement. "Residents have regaled visitors with the story for many years."

"Apparently I inhabit the wrong social circles," I said. "Although I have visited Edinburgh, I have never heard the tale."

McMahon opened his mouth as if to speak, but Holmes anticipated him.

"It concerns a secret underground passage that supposedly existed in the time of Mary, Queen of Scots. The passage is said to link Edinburgh Castle and Holyrood Palace, all the way at the far end of town." Holmes drew on his pipe. "According to the tale, about a century and a half ago, a bagpiper made a bet that he could walk the length of it. He started at the Castle, piping merrily. The crowds were able to follow him through the streets above by the sound of the skirling."

I was amused to note the slight burr that had crept into Holmes's speech. My friend was a consummate actor, and as I have said before, he would have been considered a brilliant artist if he had decided to tread the boards.

"They followed his tune down from the Castle," Holmes continued, "along the top of the hill. In the vicinity of St. Giles, the piping stopped suddenly, in the middle of a note. And that was the last ever heard of the piper."

McMahon shuddered. "That is precisely the story my great-uncle wrote in a letter he included for me, Mr Holmes. He added that, according to legend, the piping stopped exactly beneath his house."

"Poor fellow was overcome by some noxious gas, most probably," I said, not bothering to hide my impatience with such fancied horrors. "The atmosphere in old passages and cellars can be fœtid and unwholesome."

Holmes lifted an eyebrow. "Some say the Devil was so captivated by the man's playing that he carried the piper off to Hell."

"Well, what of it?" I laughed. "As long as he and his bagpipes stay there, and he does not go about waking the neighbours."

Obviously affronted by my levity, McMahon glared. "That is exactly what he has been doing for the last month, Doctor."

I glanced at Holmes, expecting to find him as dubious about McMahon's pronouncement as I. Instead, his expression was grave.

"You have heard the piping yourself?" Holmes asked.

"Everyone in the lane has heard it and is terrified. That is why they have all left."

"Nonsense," I said, disturbed by Holmes's apparent acceptance of such a patently ridiculous tale. "There must be another explanation. You said the house's chimneys are noisy. Or perhaps it is some peculiar trick of the wind carrying the sound of bagpipers playing at the Castle. Why should a ghost who has kept quiet for over a hundred years suddenly decide to return and frighten people?"

Holmes smiled. "That, my dear Watson, is what I am anxious to discover."

"As am I," McMahon said. "But the piping has done more than merely frighten, gentlemen. Two of my elderly tenants succumbed to terror after hearing the bagpipes, and a young woman recently miscarried."

"Tragic," murmured Holmes, his eyes hooded, smoke wreathing his head as he puffed on his pipe.

"It is not unknown for a shock to carry off the elderly," I asserted, ignoring Holmes's sarcastic tone and hoping McMahon did not notice it. "Nor to bring on miscarriages, if indeed these events are connected to the piping." Although Holmes and I had encountered the occasional inexplicable incident, most of what credulous individuals deemed otherworldly could be explained by science and logic. I was certain that was the case here, as well.

"What would you have us do, Mr McMahon?" Holmes asked.

"I must return to Edinburgh on the morning train," he replied. "I would be very grateful if you, at least, would accompany me and investigate the cause of this. In order to claim the money, I must continue to live there for six additional months, and I admit that the prospect of even one more evening alone in that house fills me with dread."

"There you have it, Watson." Holmes emptied his pipe into the coal scuttle. "Will you join us? Or do the delights of hearth and home prove too alluring?"

His tone stung, but I set aside my annoyance. "Of course I will come. Tonight I shall arrange to have my practice covered for a few days." I nodded to McMahon. "I will meet you both at King's Cross in the morning."

"Mr Holmes, thank you. And you as well, Doctor." McMahon rose and shook our hands. "I am exceedingly grateful to you."

Once we had seen him out the door and into Mrs Hudson's capable ministrations, Holmes turned to me.

"Sit down, my dear fellow. We shall have an early supper together and then you shall return home to make your arrangements and pack for the morrow, while I carry on a few inquiries regarding the McMahon family." He rubbed his hands together, perhaps in unconscious emulation of his client. "I have the feeling this is a more complex affair than a howling chimney, Watson."

The following morning at 10.00, we prepared to depart King's Cross on the Special Scotch Express to travel the four hundred miles to Edinburgh.

McMahon and I had already settled into our compartment when Holmes arrived on the platform. There were only moments to spare before the train departed.

"Mr Holmes!" McMahon called from the window. "Hurry!"

Steam and shouting filled the station as the train pulled from the station and Holmes joined us, flinging his valise onto the overhead rack and collapsing onto his seat.

"You cut that rather fine," I said.

"My investigations took rather longer than I anticipated." Holmes refused to say more, and when he proved disinclined toward conversation, staring out the window deep in abstraction, I endeavoured to make up for his lack of sociability.

McMahon and I discussed the timber trade in Vancouver, military life in the far-flung reaches of the Empire, and the race to the north between the trains of the Great Northern Railway and the London and North Western Railway. We passed Abbots Ripton and the topic of the rail disaster that had occurred there occupied us until we reached York.

After a hurried luncheon, Holmes returned to staring out the window. McMahon settled back in his seat and appeared to doze, and I followed suit.

Night and heavy clouds had descended by the time the train pulled into Waverley Station. We collected our bags and stepped out onto the streets of Edinburgh, the great granite sphinx of the North, crouching high on her towering rock, looking across the intervening plains to the waters of the Firth of Forth and the North Sea. Fascinating, regal, splendid, and cruel.

As we left the station, we caught our first glimpse of Edinburgh Castle, bleak and menacing, through a cloud of fog and rain.

McMahon paused beneath a street lamp, his gaze following mine.

"A grim sight," he said. "I must admit, gentlemen, the view strikes me with fear, even on the sunniest of days."

"Grim indeed." As Holmes spoke, the lamp-light emphasized the curve of his nose, the firm set of his lips and jaw. "Part castle, part fortress, part prison. Wars have been plotted there; dancing has lasted deep into the night; murder has been done in its chambers."

I shuddered and looked about for a cab. "This is no time to stand here chatting. Let us find shelter from this confounded rain."

Holmes laughed. "Rain, Watson? You are growing soft. This is not rain, it is just a good Scottish mist."

"Mist?" I tucked my muffler closer around my throat. "Hardly. I am soaked to the skin and my teeth are chattering."

We were fortunate to quickly engage a cab, and McMahon instructed the cabbie to let us out in front of St. Giles.

"Why St. Giles?" I asked. "Are we not bound for Hangman's Lane?"

McMahon smiled apologetically. "The lane is too narrow for cabs. We must go from St. Giles by foot."

"Of course we must," I grumbled, staring out at the gutters, which were fairly running with muddy water. My wound ached, and I longed for a fire and dry clothing.

We left the shelter of the cab outside the Kirk. Rain dripped from the eaves and darkened the sooty stone. A pungent mixture of mildew, smouldering coal, and rotting refuse caught in my throat. We followed McMahon as he crossed the yard, splashing through puddles on the pavement.

With a grim smile, McMahon paused before a narrow opening between two buildings. "Welcome to Hangman's Lane." He turned and disappeared into the mist.

I paused for a moment. Although I was accustomed to London's old neighbourhoods, with their winding streets and ramshackle buildings, they paled in comparison with the dank path that fell away before us.

"A narrow, steep little byway, eh, Watson?" Holmes clapped me on the shoulder. The brim of his hat dipped as he bent his head, sending a stream of water onto my coat.

"What a miserable place."

Shoulder to shoulder we made our way down the slippery pavement.

"I do not like it, Holmes. No lights in any of the windows. Every building looks positively deserted."

McMahon appeared before us. "As I explained in London, they *are* deserted,

Doctor. One house in particular has not been opened for over one hundred years, but since the piping began, the rest of the inhabitants have fled. Due to my great-uncle's charity, the rents have always been reasonable, but now I have lowered them to the vanishing point, and still there are no takers."

We stopped before the only house that appeared inhabited. One window was illuminated, and a lamp burned beside the heavy oak door. McMahon took a large key from his greatcoat pocket and, with some difficulty, opened the door.

"Mrs Rennie?" he called as we stepped inside, our coats and hats dripping. "I hope she has not left yet, or at least — Ah! There you are."

An old woman hurried into the hall, the candle she carried casting a glow over her old-fashioned lace cap and starched apron. "Och, ye have returned, Mr McMahon. The Lord be thanked."

"Yes, and I have brought Mr Sherlock Holmes and Dr Watson with me."

She fussed over our wet things, the flickering candlelight casting sinister shapes across the age-blackened paneling.

"Good Lord, it is dark in here," I murmured as I brushed the dampness from my jacket collar.

Once she was satisfied with the disposition of our garments, Mrs Rennie lifted the candle. "If you will kindly step this way, there is a brae blaze aburnin' and candles lit in the back parlour."

As I turned my foot caught, and I stumbled. Holmes grabbed my arm, steadying me.

Mrs Rennie shook her head. "Go canny, gentlemen. This corridor is nae so smooth as once it was."

"I apologise, Doctor," McMahon said. "The house has settled, sending the boards out of true. I forgot to warn you."

We carefully made our way down the dim corridor. The room at the far end blazed with light, and it took a moment or two for my eyes to adjust. I glanced around at the comfortable, well-used furniture and the heavily carved mantelpiece.

"What a magnificent old room. Just look at that fireplace."

"Aye," said Mrs Rennie with a frown. "Once there was life in this old house. Full of lords and their ladies, they say. But here, will you be standing on the hearth and dryin' your breeks." At her insistence, we arranged ourselves in front of the fire.

"Brandy will help chase away the cold, as well." McMahon filled the glasses with a generous hand. I took a grateful sip, welcoming the heat that spread through my chilled limbs.

Between the brandy and the warmth of the fire, we were soon comfortable, although the room smelt strongly of damp wool. A gust of wind rattled the windows, and a low moan sounded from the chimney. I glanced at Holmes. He raised an eyebrow and nodded once; he had heard it as well. I did not doubt that we would have McMahon's mystery solved that evening.

Mrs Rennie pulled a heavy shawl around her shoulders.

"I have left a tasty cock-a-leekie pie in the oven for your supper, Mr McMahon. An' now, if you'll forgive me, I'll unshunk mesel' away."

"Thank you for staying so late, Mrs Rennie." McMahon set down his brandy. "I appreciate everything you have done."

She smiled up at him. "You're a good man, Mr McMahon. And you have your two friends to keep you company. Dinna fash yersel'. I'll return in the morn, early."

He walked her to the door, then disappeared into the kitchen, returning with a heavy, earthenware dish, his hands protected by a folded dish-towel.

"Mrs Rennie is not a fancy cook, but her cock-a-leekie pie is delicious," he said, removing the lid and releasing the heavenly scent of chicken and leeks.

After supper — and McMahon was right, the pie was very tasty — Holmes settled beside the fire and lit a cigarette.

"Now, please describe where you have heard the sound of bagpipes."

McMahon indicated the far wall. "There. From inside the old Hurley house."

"What do the Hurleys have to say about it?" I asked, cradling another glass of brandy.

McMahon frowned and shook his head. "No one has lived in that house for many years, Doctor. It is one of the fatal houses."

"Fatal houses?" I glanced at Holmes. His expression was somber.

"Houses marked generations ago by the great plague," he explained. "Buildings harbouring those with the disease were marked by a large cross. No one dared enter or leave. Furniture was destroyed and doors and windows sealed. If the bodies of victims still remain inside, the plague is supposed to lie captive, ready to escape and spread sickness and death through the city if the doors are opened."

"A tale fit to frighten the credulous, Holmes. Germs cannot sustain themselves for such a length of time." I shrugged. "At least, we have no medical evidence that they can."

The wind picked up again, rattling the windows and sending another low moan from the chimney. It sounded like the cry of the damned. I suppressed a shudder.

"There!" I said. "That must be what you heard. Just a peculiarity in the construction of the chimney."

"No." McMahon suddenly lifted his head, his eyes glittering in the firelight, and raised his hand. "Dear God, it has begun again!"

I shall never be able to describe the sound that crept into the room, a sound that grew more and more intolerable with every passing moment. The chimney's howl was sweet as a cathedral choir in comparison to the infernal clamour that echoed in our brains and shredded our nerves.

McMahon and I clapped our hands over our ears, while Holmes leapt to his feet and dashed to the wall shared with the Hurley house, pressing his hands flat against the vibrating plaster. His high brow furrowing, he swept his palms across the wall in broad arcs, gradually concentrating his movements toward the door leading to the corridor.

"It is shaking the very foundations!" Holmes cried over the din.

As he moved down the corridor, the noise lessened, resolving itself slowly into the recognizable sounds of a bagpipe's drone.

"The Devil's Piper." McMahon's hands shook as he clasped them together. "Doctor, you must admit that this is more than a superstition, or the sounds made by a noisy chimney."

My own hands were none too steady as I nodded. "I beg pardon for doubting you." I reached for the brandy, poured McMahon a tot, and handed him the glass.

"What shall we do, Mr Holmes?" McMahon swallowed the brandy. "Shall I send for the authorities?"

Holmes appeared in the doorway and settled his cuffs, his eyes bright. "And have them put the Devil in gaol? No, I have a better plan. I suggest we call on the old gentleman himself."

I regarded Holmes with concern. Had the excessively loud noise addled his wits?

"What in Heaven's name do you mean?" I asked.

"Exactly what I said." Holmes turned and dashed toward the front of the house. "Come along, Watson!" he called. "And bring a lantern!"

I turned, and McMahon caught my sleeve.

"Doctor, what does he intend to do?"

I glanced at McMahon. His colour had returned.

"I will leave the explanations to Holmes."

McMahon retrieved a lantern from a shelf, and we hurried after my friend.

Holmes had retrieved our damp coats and hats from the cupboard. I quickly donned mine, and at a look from Holmes, bent to retrieve my service revolver from my valise, still sitting in the hall.

McMahon waited beside the door, muffled in coat and hat, confusion writ over his features. "Mr Holmes, will you please — "

"How do you feel about a spot of breaking and entering?" Holmes said, throwing open the bolts and flinging the door wide. Sleet coated the pavement with a frosty rime, but Holmes did not falter as he descended the steps.

I slipped my revolver into my coat pocket and lit the lantern before following him out the door, McMahon close on my heels. By the time we made our way to the neighbouring house, Holmes was waiting impatiently by the entrance.

"Light, Watson!"

A shallow stone portico provided a modicum of shelter from the worst of the sleet. I held the lantern up, illuminating the massive oak door, and glanced around. We need not worry about attracting the attention of passersby, for every building along the lane appeared dark and deserted. The sound of the piping was muffled, barely audible over the patter of sleet. Holmes studied the door intently, then shook his head.

"There is no use in trying to break down the door. It is as solid as Gibraltar."

"A good deal more solid than the house itself," I replied, pointing to the stained, shadow-shrouded stones overhead. A wide crack split the huge stone that acted as the lintel, the massive stone beam supporting the opening for the door, and bearing the weight of the wall. "Look."

Holmes glanced up. "The building is settling."

"What about the windows?" I asked.

McMahon shook his head. "They are all boarded over or tightly shuttered."

"Then there is nothing for it," Holmes said with a shrug. He removed an iron ring from his pocket. From the ring depended a collection of thin pieces of metal, and he held them up to the light. Selecting one, he knelt and inserted it into the keyhole. Metal scraped against metal.

McMahon's fingers plucked at my sleeve. "Doctor, are those — "

"Picklocks," I replied, lifting the lantern high so Holmes could see. Shadows danced over the stones, turning the already gloomy scene macabre. I could not blame McMahon for feeling trepidation. "If you would prefer to return to your house …"

"No." He drew in a deep breath and released it slowly. "I asked for your help. The least I can do is share the danger."

After a few moments, Holmes straightened with a smile. "Success, gentlemen."

The door, although unlocked, did not yield easily. Our feet slipped on the icy stoop as Holmes, McMahon, and I set our shoulders to the wood. For several minutes the rusted hinges remained adamantly immovable, despite our efforts and breathless exclamations of encouragement.

"We cannot succeed," I panted. "It will not budge. We must find another way inside."

"I refuse to be foiled!" Holmes settled himself more firmly against the door. "Watson, I beg your help."

"Please, Doctor." Despite the chill, perspiration beaded McMahon's brow.

I felt ashamed. How could I refuse their entreaties? I resumed my position.

"Put your back into it, man!" cried Holmes.

Perhaps it was Holmes's encouragement, perhaps simply a fortuitous application of pressure. I pushed against the weathered oak as the hinges groaned. "It is moving, Holmes!"

Holmes glanced up. "So is that crack in the lintel."

I raised my gaze. The great granite lintel, which had supported the enormous weight of the old stone walls for many hundreds of years, shifted. The crack that split it in twain visibly widened. "Good Lord, Holmes! Hurry inside! We must close the door before the wall collapses."

Mindful of the danger, McMahon and Holmes squeezed through the opening, and I collected the lantern before following. We pushed against the door and it closed with the finality of a coffin lid.

We leaned against the weathered oak, panting with exertion. Our laboured breaths and the hiss of the lantern were the only sounds in that dank, still place.

"The piping has stopped." McMahon whispered, as if loath to disturb the silence. A small cloud formed before his lips in the frigid air.

"Indeed," replied Holmes with a single nod.

The only sound apart from our quiet footsteps was the occasional creak of the house. In many ways, I would have preferred the din of the piping to that unnatural stillness.

Holmes relieved me of the lantern and stepped farther into the hall. He turned in a slow circle, the lantern illuminating mouldering panels draped with cobwebs and stained with mildew. A decaying stair disappeared into the blackness above.

"We very well could be the first to set foot inside since the house was closed," I said.

Holmes gave an enigmatic smile, but did not speak.

McMahon coughed. "It smells like a tomb."

I inhaled cautiously. The atmosphere was so cold it was difficult to discern any scent other than stale air, but I breathed deep again. "There is also something … unhealthy. It reminds me of a smell I have encountered before.…" I hesitated, then shook my head. "I cannot quite place it."

We crossed the hall, Holmes at the fore. He peered into a chamber on our left, lantern-light illuminating walls hung with ancient tapestries, the fabric now torn and drooping from the weight and the ravages of damp and beetle. A heavy oak table, coated with dust, was set for a meal never finished. The silver was blackened, the pewter dull. A goblet lay on its side, as if overturned during a frantic flight to safety.

I shuddered, touched by the reminders of long-past tragedy.

Holmes finished his calm perusal of the room and turned away.

"Nothing of interest here," he said, moving down the corridor.

We followed close behind, our footsteps echoing hollowly on the wide planks. The smell of decay grew as we moved deeper into the house.

Holmes stopped before a half-closed door and cautiously pushed it open. The hinges creaked horribly.

Three large wing chairs faced the cold, empty fireplace. Woolen batting sprang from rents along the edges, where the upholstery had rotted and parted. My breath caught at the stench of corruption.

"A drawing room," I said, holding my handkerchief over my nose and mouth. McMahon followed suit.

Holmes moved slowly into the room, swinging the lantern about to light each of the far corners before proceeding. He approached the chairs, their seats hidden by deep shadows.

"Watson."

He dropped my name into the silence like a stone into a still pond.

I stepped to Holmes's side.

"This chair is occupied," he said, and lifted the lantern.

Light spilled over the back and arm of the chair, picking out a hairy thigh, a wiry forearm, an unmoving chest bound by thick ropes. The poor wretch in the chair was as naked as the day he was born.

"Good Lord." I took an involuntary step back.

"What is it?" McMahon walked around us, his coat brushing close to the chair.

"Have a care, man!" I cried. "For the love of Heaven, do not touch it!" I leapt forward and dragged him from the dreadful thing.

Holmes frowned. "Watson?"

"Look!" I said, taking the lantern from Holmes and holding it high.

McMahon gasped, and even Holmes's vaunted self-control wavered. The man's milky, sightless eyes were red and swollen, his cracked lips stretched in a parody of a smile. Large, black swellings clustered at throat, beneath his arms, around his groin. The remainder of the cadaver's skin was waxy and tinged with green.

"The black death," I whispered. "Impossible."

Holmes took the lantern from my nerveless fingers and moved to the other chairs.

"He is not the only victim, Watson. Look here."

An old man sat in the next chair. He was also naked and bound, and displayed the hideous symptoms of the plague. Another corpse occupied the last chair, a woman, as unclad and marked with corruption as the others.

"This house has been vacant for over a hundred years." Disgust and pity warred in McMahon's expression. "Have they been here all this time?"

"They cannot be the original plague victims," I replied. "Even in this cold, decay could not be postponed for long."

Holmes nodded. "Less than a week?"

"Three or four days at the outside, but I would have to examine the corpses to make certain."

"There is no need for that." Holmes spoke with conviction. "Although intellectually satisfying, I doubt that identifying a definitive time of death is important for these poor devils."

A sudden tremor shook the building as the huge, groaning cacophony began again. The furniture rattled, and we stumbled over the vibrating floorboards as we dashed to the corridor. A crack across the ceiling lengthened and widened, sending plaster dust drifting down.

"This way," Holmes cried over the din, heading toward the back of the house. More plaster fell from the walls and ceiling, as the house fairly quivered from the noise. As had happened before, shrieks and moans eventually resolved into the sound of bagpipes played by some monstrous hand.

Holmes gestured toward a small door at the far end of the hall. McMahon and I followed close behind. I am not a coward, but the circumstances so unnerved me that I slipped my hand into my coat pocket and grasped my revolver. Stopping before the door, Holmes closed the shutters on the lantern until only a sliver of light was visible. The noise increased as he opened the heavy oak, until I thought I should go mad from the clamour in my head. The lantern light was barely adequate to see the narrow stone steps leading down, the centre of each tread worn into a deep curve. We steadied ourselves by resting our hands on the cold, smooth stone walls, and as we descended, a rosy glow grew in the depths.

Holmes stepped into the cellar and the noise stopped, the sudden cessation almost as painful as the din itself. My ears rang.

"'Ands in the air," commanded a deep voice. Even those few words marked him from Whitechapel, not Scotland.

McMahon gasped. Holmes slowly raised his hands, still holding the lantern. I remained on the stair and could not see the man who threatened us. I hesitated, hoping to gain the advantage for long enough to venture a shot, but Holmes spoke before I could move.

"Why, it is Bully Joe Perkins," said Holmes, sounding unruffled. "Watson, surely you remember him from the incident with the false fishmonger at Lambeth."

"Well, Mr 'Olmes." Bully Joe laughed hoarsely. "I never reckoned on meeting you 'ere. And Dr Watson. Come down where I can sees you."

I released my revolver, removed my hand from my pocket, and joined McMahon and Holmes in the cellar. Bully Joe held a heavy revolver in one hand, and a truncheon, no doubt leaded, in the other.

"'Oo's your other friend?" he asked, gesturing toward McMahon.

McMahon gave his name, and Bully Joe laughed again. He jerked his head toward a doorway in the far wall.

"Go on."

He stayed well back. Holmes tread warily as he stepped to the door, glancing around the room before him.

"We 'as company," called Bully Joe. "Mr Sherlock 'Olmes, his friend, Doctor Watson, and another gentleman you'll recognize."

The chamber we entered was filled with machinery, none of which I could immediately identify. Iron pipes, drive belts, and gears co-existed side-by-side with a haphazard collection of glass boxes of varying sizes. To one side, a glass partition walled off a section of the room, which appeared to be partially composed of the granite bedrock upon which the Old City was built. Next to that, an open door in the stone wall led into darkness, probably into the maze of tunnels that burrowed beneath the Old City.

A pale young man wearing spectacles stood at the far side of the chamber, behind a scarred table upon which rested an extensive collection of chemical apparatus. He looked like a faded water-colour version of our client, and the remarkable resemblance enabled Holmes to hazard a name before any introduction.

"Mr James Knox," said Holmes, unruffled.

The young man's chin snapped up, and his lip curled. "*Doctor* James Knox."

"I beg your pardon." Holmes sketched an ironic bow.

"Cousin James!" McMahon stepped forward. "What is the meaning of this?"

Dr Knox hesitated for a moment, his features shadowed. "Good evening, cousin. I cannot say I am pleased to see you. You would have been well advised to heed my warning and leave with the others."

"Warning?" McMahon stared at the machinery surrounding us. "This is the source of those horrible sounds?"

Knox nodded brusquely. "It is the result of a necessary part of my research. However, it does have the added advantage of frightening off the curious and meddlesome." He glared at Holmes. "Well, perhaps not all of them."

"You are the reason my tenants have been frightened into leaving?" McMahon appeared stunned. "But why?"

"So he could work in peace, no doubt." Holmes studied a complex assortment of gears that connected to a lever on one side of the chamber. He raised his gaze, following a long crack that rose up the wall to the roughly plastered ceiling. "One would not wish to be interrupted by the rabble during one's researches."

"I wished them gone because of the danger!" Knox's spectacles flashed in the gaslight. "If you remain, you are all flirting with death."

"Death?" Holmes coolly looked at Bully Joe, still brandishing his revolver. "Do you mean from our pugilistic friend here, or more in the manner experienced by the cadavers we happened upon in the parlour?"

Knox frowned. "Do not mock that which you do not understand."

"Perhaps I understand more than you realize."

"I doubt that very much," said Knox. He crossed his arms over his chest and met Holmes's gaze steadily. "However, you have a certain reputation for a superficial type of cleverness, Mr Holmes. I am curious about what you believe you understand."

Holmes laughed. "Even the most cursory investigation reveals that you are one of the leading proponents of the Campaign for Eugenics in Great Britain, and author of *Characteristics of Inferior Races: A Study of the Dilution of Celtic Physiology by Lesser Populations*."

I glanced at Holmes. His researches the previous evening had certainly borne ripe fruit. I had read Galton's *Hereditary Genius*, and *English Men of Science: Their Nature and Nurture*, but had no idea Holmes was aware of the subject of eugenics.

"I don't fink the Professor — " began Bully Joe.

"You are not being paid to think." Knox returned his attention to Holmes. "You have read my work?"

"Yes. A most impassioned plea for selective breeding, with more emotion and less scientific rigour than the works of your leader."

Holmes shrugged and ran a finger carelessly across the laboratory table. "Personally, despite the fact that he obviously read my own contribution but failed to cite it, I found Galton's treatise on the individuality of fingerprints more interesting than his papers on eugenics."

As Holmes spoke, Knox's complexion darkened and his hands clenched. He drew a deep breath and appeared to calm himself before replying.

"An understandable reaction in one who champions the inferior. Still, it is no matter."

"I do not understand!" cried McMahon. "Why should we concern ourselves with talk of fingerprints and breeding? It is far more important to discover whether or not those poor souls upstairs really died of the plague and to grant them a Christian burial."

Knox laughed. "You are a true son of the soil, Albert. Healthy and unpretentious, good Celtic stock." His lip curled. "And like your parents, with all the imaginative power of a plough horse."

His fists raised, McMahon took a step toward his cousin.

"I wouldn't try it," said Bully Joe, raising his weapon.

I caught hold of one of McMahon's arms, and Holmes the other. "Insults are the recourse of the weak," remarked Holmes, as the two of us pulled a recalcitrant McMahon away from Bully Joe and toward the glass wall. He fixed McMahon with a glittering gaze and spoke softly. "They do not deserve a response."

After a long pause, McMahon nodded. Holmes and I released him.

I turned to Knox, my professional curiosity and concern unabated.

"Did they die of the plague? Mock me if you will, but I ask as a fellow medical man."

"Then you will surely appreciate the importance of my researches," said Knox with a satisfied smile. "To answer your question, yes, they did succumb to the black death. A particularly virulent strain I discovered here, in this very house."

"Here?" I was appalled. We had walked through the house, innocent of the knowledge that an agonizing death lurked just inside. Were Holmes, McMahon, and I somehow infected?

"Indeed." Knox's expression grew animated. "When I was a young medical student, I was intrigued by the idea of a plague house, where contagion filled the air before the house and its oc- cupants were sealed off from the outside world. When I discovered that Great Uncle lived beside one, I increased the frequency of my visits. One day I noticed a loose shutter on a rear window and made my way inside. As I explored the deserted chambers, I discovered a jar of calves-foot jelly that contained a culture of plague bacteria."

"Good God," I breathed. "Surely you did not keep it?"

"But of course." Knox gestured to the machinery surrounding us. "With the financial assistance of … well, that is neither here nor there. Suffice it to say I created this laboratory to avoid outside inter- ference with my work. Over time I cultivated the bacteria, increas- ing its virulence a hundredfold. You saw the results in the parlour."

"*You* infected those poor wretches upstairs?"

He lifted one shoulder, then let it drop. "They were from the dregs of society. A thief. A beggar. A prostitute. I used them as I would use cattle, for the advancement of the human race."

Bully Joe laughed. "They died squirming an' screamin', their last breaths bubblin' in their throats. I left 'em there to scare off nosy-parkers."

"But what of your Hippocratic oath?" I asked.

"What of it?" He spat the words. "The slums of Britain are teeming with the degenerate, barely intelligent enough to exist, fit for only the most menial of employment. I propose to rid the country of that burden. I have recently developed a pneumonic strain of the bacterium — "

"Dear Lord, no!" I could not believe my ears. "Such a strain could kill millions!"

"Transmission via the air," Holmes said, unable to conceal his horror at the thought. "What we originally assumed were bagpipes playing is in fact part of a pneumatic air pumping system. The joints of the glass chamber are sealed with rubber gaskets, as is the door." He gestured at the belts and gears covering the walls. "Through your machinery, you can lower the air pressure within your experimental chamber, thereby protecting you from contami- nation by the air-borne bacteria."

My gaze met Holmes's, and he slowly patted his coat pocket. I grasped his meaning instantly — deep within the corresponding pocket of my own coat lay my revolver. I slipped my hand into my pocket and curled my fingers around the cold metal.

"Very clever, Mr Holmes." Knox selected a vial from a rack on the table. "You are quite correct: the machinery controls the air pressure within the glass chamber, allowing me a place to safely expose an experimental subject to the plague. It is powered by rushing water deep beneath us. The apparatus is particularly noisy, but very effective at preventing contamination. After all, I do not wish to die, nor does my associate." He held the vial up to the light, studying it intently. "The resemblance to the sound of a bagpipe drone was particularly fortuitous, and with the judicious spread of rumours of the Devil's Piper, I was able to frighten off the inhabitants of the neighbouring tenements." His gaze shifted from the vial to McMahon. "Save for my interfering cousin and his two companions, who will now pay for their temerity by becoming my first human experimental subjects for the pneumonic plague."

He gestured to Bully Joe, who grinned unpleasantly.

"Right. Through there," Bully Joe said, pointing to the iron door, propped open and ringed with a rubber gasket, which led into the glass chamber. On the floor of the chamber, the bloated bodies of a dog and several cats provided evidence of the deadliness of Knox's bacteria.

"Forgive me if I decline to participate in your experiment," said Holmes and leapt toward a lever nearby. "Now, Watson!"

Holmes grasped the lever and depressed it. I now understood the reason for his careful study of the mechanism. He had chosen correctly, for gears turned and belts groaned as they began to move.

"No!" cried Knox. He stepped back from the table, still clutching the vial of death.

The unexpected movement and noise provided the distraction Holmes had no doubt intended. Holmes snatched the lantern from the floor and flung it onto the table. The lantern glass shattered, releasing burning oil to spread across the table top and drip onto the stone floor.

Around us, the mechanism continued unchecked as more gears engaged. The house shook and our heads throbbed as we were assailed by that appalling noise.

Sharp, stabbing pain radiated from my ears. The door to the glass chamber was open, and the air pressure in the entire room was being reduced by the pneumatic pump. I gulped air and winced as the air pressure within my ears and without became equal.

Apparently stunned by the rapidity of Holmes's actions, Bully Joe only roused himself when Holmes moved toward the stair. He raised his revolver and aimed at Holmes. Without hesitation, I drew my weapon and fired. My bullet struck Bully Joe in the forearm, and he dropped his gun with an oath. He was not completely unarmed, however, for he still wielded the truncheon.

McMahon, quickly comprehending our purpose, rushed Bully Joe before he could bring the truncheon to bear on Holmes.

Leaving McMahon to take on Bully Joe, I turned to Knox, who was frozen in place as if petrified, the vial still held high above the stone floor. The fire from the lantern was spreading rapidly, reaching greedy fingers toward the ceiling.

Somewhere in that infernal clockwork mechanism a gear slipped, jerking the belts, and with a terrible grinding sound the entire building shuddered. The crack in the wall widened and other cracks appeared in the ceiling as plaster dust rained down upon us. Suddenly a large piece of plaster fell, striking Knox on the shoulder, sending the vial flying.

"No!" he screamed, frantically reaching for the container.

"Watson!" Holmes cried.

I turned. Bully Joe was sprawled on the floor, his neck twisted at an unnatural angle. McMahon stared down at him, his hands clenched tightly at his side.

Holmes caught McMahon's sleeve and propelled him through the door in the stone wall. Holmes held out his hand, gesturing anxiously.

"Quickly, man!"

I dashed to his side through the smoke and falling plaster. We passed through the portal together, then turned and closed the door after us. It was then I witnessed a sight that will forever be imprinted upon my memory: James Knox, surrounded by hellish flames, staring down at the broken vial before him.

We were indeed in the dank and foetid labyrinth of underground passages beneath the city. We stumbled through those dark tunnels for what seemed hours, until at last we emerged from the stone warren into the confines of the Castle itself, nearly sending the guards into an apoplectic fit. After exhausting explanations, we were permitted to leave, and in the early morning's watery light, made our way back to Hangman's Lane.

There we were greeted by the fire brigade, who were preparing to depart after battling a blaze that, in the words of one participant, "Looked as if ol' Horney hissel' decided to destroy the house."

Of the Hurley house, only a smouldering pile of stones remained. The structural deficiencies we had noted contributed to the cataclysmic collapse, and the fire that followed completed the work.

Fortunately, McMahon's house was relatively undamaged. The adjoining wall would require some repair, but the foundation of the house remained sound. After receiving McMahon's heartfelt thanks, Holmes and I retrieved our valises and retired to the Royal, where we breakfasted lavishly in a private parlour.

"What an appalling night," I said, tucking into my kippers with relish.

"Indeed, my dear fellow." Holmes leaned back in his chair and drew upon his cigarette. Smoke curled toward the ceiling. "Dr Knox's proposal was quite Draconian. If he had released the pneumonic plague upon the population, there was no guarantee it would only infect those he deemed worthless."

"Exactly!" I waved a bit of buttered toast. "He might have released a contagion that would wipe humanity from the face of the earth."

We sat quickly for a moment, contemplating the horrific possibility.

"Still," I ventured, "he is dead, and that should be an end to the entire matter."

Holmes paused. "Is it?"

Unsettled, I looked at him. "What on earth do you mean?"

"There were one or two moments," he replied slowly, "when I glimpsed a malevolent force behind Knox's actions. A presence I thought was checked."

"I do not understand, Holmes."

He gave me a smile, almost kindly, and poured another cup of tea. "Do not 'fash yerself,' as the Scots say. No doubt I am fretting over spectres."

I buttered another slice of toast. "If you say so."

"I suppose I do." Holmes flicked his cigarette into the flames. "After all, fire is a great purifier."

DR. WATSON'S BLUES

(TUNE: BLUE PRELUDE)

by Len Moffatt

Let me sigh, let me cry 'cause I'm blue ...
Holmes has gone from this London town!
Won't be long 'til my stories are through ...
That fight at the Falls put him down!

All the plots I could steal, beg or borrow
Would not sell without Holmes in his role.
Without Sherlock to peddle tomorrow
Agent Doyle may have to go ... on the dole!

Here I go, now you know why I'm grieving:
I have the blues, money to lose ... Good Bye ...

www.ingramcontent.com/pod-product-compliance
Lightning Source LLC
Chambersburg PA
CBHW020958180626
46814CB00003B/1152